THE SPANISH GARDEN

ALSO BY CHERRY RADFORD

THE SPANISH GARDEN

Cherry Radford

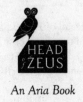

An Aria Book

This paperback edition first published in the UK in 2022 by Head of Zeus Ltd,
part of Bloomsbury Publishing Plc.

9 7 5 3 1 2 4 6 8

A catalogue record for this book is available from the British Library.

ISBN (PB): 9781801103916
ISBN (E): 9781801103909

Cover design: Leah Jacobs-Gordon
Typeset by Siliconchips Services Ltd UK

Printed and bound in Great Britain by
CPI Group (UK) Ltd, Croydon CR0 4YY

Head of Zeus Ltd
First Floor East
5–8 Hardwick Street
London EC1R 4RG

WWW.HEADOFZEUS.COM

MUSIC PLAYLIST

Create a free Spotify account and listen to some of the music in *The Spanish Garden*.

Chapter 3
'Acaba De Nacer' – Ketama (Antonio Carmona, José Miguel Carmona, Juan Carmona)

Chapter 13
'Can't Fight This Feeling' – REO Speedwagon (Kevin Cronin)
'Pray' – Take That (Gary Barlow)
'U Don't Have To Call' – Erykah Badu (Chad Hugo, Pharrell Williams)

Chapter 15
'Contigo Me Equivoqué' – Chiquetete (Manuel Pareja Obregón)

Chapter 16
'El Ciclo de la Vida' (The Circle of Life) – Lebo M., Maria Ayo, Nick Glennie-Smith (Elton John, Hans Zimmer, Lebo M., Tim Rice)

Chapter 18
'Seabird' – Alessi Brothers (Billy Alessi, Bobby Alessi)
'Oh Lori' – Alessi Brothers (Billy Alessi, Bobby Alessi)
'Make Me Smile' (Come Up and See Me) – Steve Harley &
Cockney Rebel (Steve Harley)

Chapter 19
'Angels' – Robbie Williams (Guy Chambers, Robbie
Williams)

Chapter 21
'Contigo en la Distancia' – Antonio Serrano, Leonardo
Amuedo (César Portillo de la Luz)

Chapter 24
'A Whole New World' (Aladdin's Theme) – Peabo Bryson,
Regina Belle (Alan Menken, Tim Rice)

Chapter 27
'Voces' – Chambao (María del Mar Rodríguez)
'Lo Bueno y Lo Malo' – Chambao, Estrella Morente
(Ray Heredia)
'La Estrella' – Estrella Morente, Vicente Amigo (Vicente
Amigo)
'Volver' – Estrella Morente (Carlos Gardel, Alfredo Le Pera)

Epilogue
'De Alguna Manera' – Soleá, José Enrique Morente, Pitingo,
(Crescencio Ramos Prada, Luis Eduardo Aute)

I

The day of the accident was also the last day of shooting *Challenging Gardens*. The last that *year*, that was; it would be back on the telly, as ever, with a new series in the spring. But Andie – newest and youngest member of the presenting team – had an overwhelming sense she wouldn't be in it.

While the camera was off her, she stopped clipping at the dead limbs of a camellia and sat down on the garden wall in the hazy sun. The other three were all on top form today, chuffed with the viewer ratings, looking forward to taking a well-earned break. What was the matter with her? Okay, there'd been the typically enthusiastic filming of little top-knotted Accident Andie pouring compost down herself when the bag split; an unresolved argument about whether the camellia could be incorporated into the design rather than 'replanted in the local park' (heartlessly chucked in the skip); and the elephant-in-the-garden question as to why this particular plot had been selected, given that its owner was just too lacking in soul, rather than funds, to sort it out himself. But none of this was new. As Johnny would say, one shouldn't take the show – or oneself – too seriously.

Johnny. She watched him looking over his shoulder at the camera with a twinkly-eyed grin as his arm muscles tightened on the spade. All soft curly hair the colour of earth, all sing-song Oirish from the Emerald Isle. Understandably, adored by every female gardener in the country. Unbelievably, *hers.* For five months now. Well, unofficially anyway; the public still thought there was a chance he'd get back with his ex-wife, the equally adored TV interior designer Caroline O'Connor. This was a fantasy that, for some reason Andie couldn't fathom, Johnny and Caroline liked to maintain.

She breathed out heavily, reminding herself that she probably shouldn't be taking Johnny seriously either. Even though he'd twice mentioned having a son with her, to add to his two daughters. But then, that was really another reason to keep her distance; she hadn't yet told him that, despite her famous skill at propagation, there was a possibility she was infertile.

'Well, that's this week's mishap over and done with,' Steve said, flumping down next to her and patting her on the back with his huge hand. Builder-gardener Steve, even more staggered to have been plucked from obscurity onto the show than she was, and possibly the only presenter completely presenting his true self on it.

'Uh. D'you think somebody deliberately cut that bag open?'

'Probably.' He gave her half his KitKat.

'Ah, thanks.'

They sat and watched Paul – the channel's answer to

Alan Titchmarsh, but off camera, an easily irritated wasp of a man – doing his well-qualified bit about the wonders of having a pleasant seating area for a glass of wine.

Then it was time for Andie to introduce her Mediterranean corner, homage to the owner's childhood as an expat in Malta. A slim cypress led to an area with an urn, a fan palm, a bit of lavender and rosemary, and a soft yellow phlomis she'd managed to get slouching over the edges of Steve's gravel path – but that was all the space she'd been allowed. A shame, because the soil lent itself to making the whole garden Mediterranean – but of course that would be too much of an egg-basket popularity risk for the programme. The camera lingered on her longer than she wanted – hungover Paul had been a bit of a minimalist today – so she found herself adding that these were the shapes and scents that had first inspired her love of gardening, in a little paradise created by her expat grandmother in Southern Spain.

They wanted to film the four presenters on their break, when they'd all rather be discussing their holiday plans, so the director suggested a follow-on from what Andie had said about the garden that first inspired her. Paul's inspiration had been Kew Gardens; Johnny couldn't decide between his parents' nursery or the National Trust place near his family home in County Down; and Steve's had been his father's prize-winning allotment. It made for an untypically heartfelt bit of footage. Then the spell was broken by the usual ludicrous nick-of-time finishing of the garden and champagne celebration with the owner.

It was over. There were hugs and back slaps all round. Andie smiled and fought off inexplicable tears.

Johnny's arms came around her. Everybody on set knew about them; it was staggering their relationship hadn't yet reached a newspaper. 'Andie, Andie... no *way* will they not have you back in the spring,' he whispered, kissing her cheek. 'And meanwhile, we have so much to look forward to. I'll see you later, my gorgeous, got to dash to pick up the girls.'

She smiled, but did she *want* to be back in the spring, playing garden clown? Being interviewed about nothing very much for women's magazines and radio programmes? Trying not to look at the curdling stream of adoration and hatred coming at her from Twitter? Johnny and finances aside, maybe she'd been happier when she was working full-time for Gerard at Summerby Garden Designs. But her agent said she needed at least two seasons there to become more established professionally – and, the cheeky cow had reminded her, *romantically*.

Romantically, she was looking forward to the little holiday she and Johnny had talked about. She sometimes spent a weekend at his rambling place in a quiet street in Richmond, sleeping in what he promised had always been *his* room, not *theirs*. But the rooms that bothered her were those of Lilac and Jasmine – his two little girls, eight and four, whom she and Caroline's lover weren't allowed to meet. *Yet*, Johnny would always add, without being clear as to what exactly would change this rule. Meanwhile, there were photos everywhere of these two little blondies she felt she already knew, and she'd admired the Grade One Piano with Merit certificate in Lilac's Harry Potter bedroom, stood up some knocked-over plastic animals on the shelf next to Jazzy's little pink bed. What harm could possibly come from her meeting them?

Andie pondered this as she crawled along the A316, past the turning that would later take her to Johnny's, and onwards to her garden flat in Teddington – where, by the time she'd found somewhere to park, had a bath and changed clothes, it would be time to crawl back along the A316 to get to his place *no earlier than six*. All to avoid the girls before Caroline picked them up for the weekend. She wasn't even allowed *two hours* in their presence, it seemed, even though she could surely just be introduced as one of Daddy's work friends dropping by for a cup of tea.

Once finally home, she was in no mood to rush out again. Strung out by her mixed feelings about the show and the thought of a second helping of the manic traffic, she started running the bath and considered messaging Johnny that she would be arriving *no earlier than eight*. Once up to her neck in Radox bubbles, hair happily released from the topknot and floating around her, she considered telling him she'd be there *no earlier than tomorrow*. She could call her friend Shefali back about when they were going to try the new ballet and flamenco classes, so they could decide which they were going to book for September. Curl up on the sofa with some porridge and a film. Relax, re-ravel. But the family of plastic ducks Johnny had given her had joined her in the bath, and his maidenhair fern on the windowsill looked at her forlornly – as would the bedroom's soft toy robin who sang authentically if you pressed his tummy. Then there was the holiday to decide on...

'Where're you all *going*?' she asked the traffic, as it honked and rushed around her. Shouldn't they be coming *out* of

London for the weekend, rather than into it? Her phone had pealed two WhatsApps, but there wasn't a prayer of pulling over and answering it. She battled on – and had a near-miss with the side of a turning lorry that left her palpitating. Finally, she pulled into Johnny's drive and breathed a sigh of relief. She was here now, in one piece, and was going to have a lovely chilled-out weekend with Johnny.

Although… weren't there two little faces peering at her from an upstairs window?

Her heart thudded. Had she made a mistake? She checked her phone on the seat next to her and saw a missed call and two panicky messages from Johnny: Caroline had got the alternate weekends mixed up, insisting he'd agreed to swap, and would be picking the girls up… oh God, in about forty minutes. As she got out – what else was she supposed to do, drive off like a crazy fan? – the girls waved enthusiastically. They must have shouted down to Johnny, because he soon appeared at the front door, smiling anxiously and beckoning her in. 'Didn't you get my message?'

'Not 'til now. What shall I do?'

Before he could answer, the girls had bounded down the stairs.

'Hello, Andie!' Lilac said. 'D'you *really* not mind worms?'

'Well, it took a few years!'

Jazzy pulled her thumb out. 'I *love* worms. I've got a cuddly one.'

'He's a *snake*, silly,' Lilac said, raising her eyes to the heavens.

'No, it's—'

'Girls! Let's make Andie some tea, shall we?' Johnny said.

'And she can meet Tallulah,' Jazzy suggested.

'Oh, I *love* that cat's name,' Andie said, forgetting she wasn't supposed to have met the cat. 'Or is she a dog?'

'She's a *cat*!' the girls cried out, as if somehow Andie should have known that.

'D'you like cats?' Jazzy asked, looking up at her with her father's pale blue eyes and putting a little hand with a turtle bracelet on Andie's arm.

'Yes! I haven't got one at the moment, but I spent much of my childhood following one around wherever she went.' Maybe that sounded weird; only-children do funny things.

Andie was just closing the front door when Tallulah jumped through the cat flap and started purring as she wound round everyone's legs. 'Oh, she's *lovely*,' she said, stroking her black-and-white fur.

In the kitchen that smelled of baked beans, Johnny made Andie an Earl Grey tea while Jazzy brought the biscuit tin over.

Lilac tutted at the supper plates by the sink and started stacking them in the dishwasher.

'Wow – impressive,' Andie couldn't help remarking to Johnny.

'I only do it here,' Lilac said, turning around. 'Mummy's too fussy about how I put the things in. It's im*poss*ible.'

Johnny stifled a laugh and then glanced at the kitchen clock and the two little rucksacks by the table and asked if they'd got everything they needed. Lilac ran upstairs to find her latest *Harry Potter*. Jazzy just asked if she could take Tallulah with her to Mummy's, and hearing for what sounded like the umpteenth time that she couldn't, said she was going to follow her around until Mummy came.

They were alone. 'Oh my God they're *so* sweet...' she

whispered. 'But what d'you want me to do? Shall I pop out to Waitrose or something, so I'm not here when Caroline turns up?'

Johnny put a hand on her arm. 'No, no... well, unless you *want* to.'

She shook her head. There was nothing for her to be ashamed of; Caroline and Johnny had started divorce proceedings long before she'd even met him. If anything, Caroline should be grateful to her for keeping him happy while she had an affair with her own co-presenter.

Johnny stood up. 'Let's take our teas into my study and look at the dates for that villa in Provence I was telling you about. It's a miracle they've got a week free, and just when the girls will be in Minorca with Caroline! We need to act fast.'

'Okay.'

His laptop was already open at the page. She hadn't been keen on the idea of France, but it was a quaint little farm, had a prettily planted pool area, and was completely surrounded by lavender fields and woodland. 'Oh!'

'But didn't you have something on that week?' he asked.

'Don't think so, but...' She fetched her bag from the kitchen and came back. 'Oh, I've left my phone in the car. Back in a sec.'

The front door wouldn't open. 'Where's the key to...?' she called out.

He came through to the hall. 'Ah. Didn't show you the door guardian.'

'The what?'

He reached up to a clicky thing you had to fold back to let

the door open – presumably to stop little people wandering onto the drive. 'I'll start checking the flights…'

Outside, it had started to drizzle. She moved her car further up the drive so Caroline would have more room for her probably large one, and went back inside with her mobile.

In the hall, Jazzy was following a harassed Tallulah around.

'The other thing I used to do was pull a long bit of wool around with me. She might prefer that.'

Tallulah stalked purposefully towards the cat flap.

'Oh *no*,' Jazzy said, folding her arms crossly. 'She's going out again.'

'Well, maybe she's got business to attend to do.'

'*Business?*'

'Yes, you know… her outside loo.'

'Poo and pee business!' She laughed, her mouth turning up at the corners just the way her father's did.

'Yes! I'm sure she'll be back soon – it's raining.'

'Andie?' Johnny was calling out from the study. 'Come on, we need to… Your tea's getting cold.'

She went back to him and sat down, looked at the calendar in her phone. 'Let's see, week of the sixth… nothing I can't move!' she said quietly, not wanting Jazzy to hear what they were talking about.

Johnny clicked on the booking and gave her a quick, wordless squeeze. 'We'll do the flights later,' he whispered. 'I better get these girls ready; Caroline'll be here soon.'

'Gawd.'

'I told her you might be here, don't worry.'

There was a screech of brakes and some shouting outside.

Andie stood up in alarm. 'Oh no, the cat!'

'No, no, she's very—'

Then a scream. From Lilac, above. Who then thundered down the stairs, shouting 'Daddy! Quick! *Help*!'

The three of them rushed out through the open door towards a commotion: a wild-eyed man shouting into a phone, a woman collapsing as she was helped from her car, three people crouching on the pavement around a child... blonde, a turtle bracelet on her wrist as she waved her arm, wailing for Daddy. Jasmine.

2

Andie sat on her garden bench with the phone to her ear, barely listening.

'...and letting the papers run with *I'll never forgive myself*,' her agent was saying, 'when they've already done their *Four-year-old daughter run over while Accident Andie distracts Johnny O'Connor with holiday plans*. I know you're upset, but... I mean, it's not as if the child *died*, she's going to be f—'

'She's called *Jasmine*,' Andie said. 'Did you know the femur is one of the most painful bones to break? She's *not* fine. Another month in hospital, missing her holiday and the first few weeks of starting school.'

'Poor little—'

'And I *will* never forgive myself for forgetting that door safety thing; it's a miracle she's alive.'

Hilary started the don't-blame-yourself arguments that Andie had heard all week. Watching the neighbour's black cat drop down from the fence into her garden, she was once

13

again flung back to the moment when Caroline arrived and pulled Lilac from her arms, Johnny got into the ambulance with Jazzy, and she was suddenly alone, picking up Tallulah and burying her face in her fur...

'Andie? I said, you need some help. I can recommend a good counsellor who can—'

'*No.*'

Hilary sighed. 'Well take a holiday then, somewhere qui—'

'I won't get offered the next series now, will I.'

There was a pause. 'I don't know. I think you should... keep your options open. This *will* blow over, I assure you. Especially now Caroline's not looking quite so much the perfect mum, frequently going off for the weekend and leaving the girls with the nanny.'

'What?'

'I *knew* you weren't listening.'

'Uh... that doesn't help anybody. Johnny's never complained about her parenting, so I don't know where that's come from. Hilary, I've got to go... things to do.' Although heaven knew what, other than rerunning the wash load she'd left in the machine for days.

'Well hang on, I've got some news. The publisher. They aren't fazed; they'd still like to see a proposal for the little Mediterranean gardening book. And didn't Gerard Summerby want your input on his Mediterranean show garden for the Hampton Court Palace Garden Festival?'

Andie looked over at the neglected rockery and felt underqualified to even *talk* about Mediterranean gardens, let alone write about or design them. There was no denying it; gardening had become a bit of drag. *Gardening*, that she'd once so loved. The show had somehow sucked all the joy and meaning out of it.

'Andie? Take yourself off to the Med, and hopefully you'll come back refreshed and inspired, able to put this behind you.'

'I'll think about it.'

'Okay. Speak soon.'

She put down the phone. Johnny had said she should take a friend to the farm in Provence that they'd booked, now that he had to stay home for Jazzy, but that didn't seem right and she'd told him to cancel it. Shefali had invited her to join her family in the villa they were renting on Zakynthos, but she wasn't convinced Shefali's husband would be happy about that, and of course there'd be little Zara, reminding her of Lilac and Jasmine... Gerard had told her to book a holiday any time in August, saying he could manage – his new boyfriend would be helping him out. Maybe she should go somewhere on her own, like she used to in the boyfriend-less years between Fabian and Johnny... but she hadn't even started googling anything. In fact, she couldn't seem to do anything but stay up half the night watching *Escape to the Château DIY* – despite no previous particular interest in France or renovations – and spend most of the day napping or looking at her phone.

A WhatsApp pealed. Johnny. This was probably why she couldn't seem to make any plans; she kept wondering if there'd be a chance to meet up with him, even if only briefly. So far, however, he'd only once managed to call, and his WhatsApps seemed to be on a dutifully once-daily schedule.

'*How are you doing?*' he'd written. '*I forgot to mention: Jazzy got out before, when I forgot the door guardian.*

Couple of months ago. You were new to it, I should have checked – it's just as much my fault as yours.'

She couldn't think how to answer. Shefali had told her stories of forgotten stair gate closures, a trapped finger, a swallowed button. Even Gerard had a hair-raising tale about an escapologist nephew. How did parents live with the risks and the guilt? Especially somebody as easily distracted as her? She wasn't cut out to be a mother; her possible infertility was probably for the best.

'*Did Jazzy like Tessie the Turtle?*' she asked. Super-soft, perfect four-year-old arm size, adorable floppy legs – sent with a black-and-white cat card.

A minute passed. '*Intercepted, I'm afraid. But I have them. And one day you will give them to her yourself.*'

One day.

'*Or maybe Caroline will come to her senses.*'

Andie boiled with anger and hurt; it was the only thing she could do for Jazzy, and it had been denied her. '*How's Jazzy? Have they got the pain under better control?*'

'*Yes, thank God. Sorry, I have to go. Take care sweetheart xxxx*'

So that was it for another day. Why did he have to go? He never said. He'd never been a one for long messages or calls, but now it was as if they'd been reduced to the kind of length she might expect as a prison inmate. Despite his assurances, something had changed between them. They seemed to have spent five months together – or as 'together' as Johnny's childcare arrangements and starry work schedule allowed – being enthralled with each other but not actually communicating. Now the spell was broken, what was left? She had to face it: she'd probably not only lost the series and her passion for gardening, but Johnny too.

She bent over double. It was back again, that ball of pain in her stomach. It would go, The Ball, if she went to bed for an hour, reminded herself that it was just nerves, concentrated on her breathing and remembered her blessings – even though she seemed to be losing them at an alarming rate. But she didn't want to go to bed again; the sun had peeped out for a bit for the first time all week. Damn The Ball, she'd somehow deal with it here. *Breathe*. What were the good things again? She was very healthy and strong – apart from her susceptibility to The Ball – and loved gar… *dancing*. Dancing classes with Shefali. Like they'd been doing since they were eleven. What else? *Breathe*. Thanks to the money her parents had left her, she had a cute garden flat in a quiet road in Teddington, with not too monstrous a mortgage, and since the show, some savings. *Breathe*. She had a wonderful garden design boss, Gerard – although he didn't yet know she'd started to hate gardening… Ah, this was a good one: *her parents were no longer around to see what a mess she'd made of her television success* – although her mother wouldn't have been the least surprised. The Ball pushed harder, making her lean forward more… and half fall off the bench, Accident bloody Andie again, grabbing the armrest as her head almost plunged into the dual terror of the yucca blades and the bee-buzzing lavender next to her.

'God's *sake*!' She slumped back onto the bench, head in her hands. Wiped a bit of lavender from her nose… which was maybe what did it: she was back in Grandie's Spanish garden, just turned eleven, sitting on the shady stone bench under the olive tree – with The Ball.

Grandie had just sworn, having scratched herself yet again on one of the long thorns from the crimson-red bougainvillea she was wrestling. 'Oops, you didn't hear that, okay?' Andie just carried on glaring at the gravel beneath her feet, mesmerised by the dappled shade dancing in the hot breeze.

'Andie?' Grandie came and sat down next to her, patting her leg; it was too hot for a hug. 'Mum and Dad just want time to themselves, that's all. Didn't think you'd like all the sitting for ages in the car.'

'But they didn't tell me, or even say *goodbye*.' She'd woken up that morning to find them not only gone but so absent, their room so tidied, that it looked like they'd rubbed out the week they *had* been there. As well they might; they hadn't seemed to enjoy a single moment of it, their heads still in England, their anger about her failed school entrance exams as bristly as when the letters landed on the bristly doormat.

Grandie swiped a fly away from her mouth, pushed the strands of escaped grey-blonde hair from her damp forehead. She smelt of plants and earth. Around them, birds twittered, sighed and whooped. 'Look, darling, don't quote me on what I'm going to say, but I think you're old enough to understood something about Mum and Dad. Your mother's disappointment – about everything, let's face it – is mostly about *herself*. She wanted to be a doctor but ended up a science teacher in a third-rate private school; she wanted a wealthy, successful husband, but ended up with my dear Linden, who never really had the fight to take his swimming to the top level, and has been happier being an NHS physiotherapist – except for the disappointment this has caused Gillian. It hasn't helped that they only managed to have one child; if you'd had siblings, at least the pressure would have been distributed.'

'You're right. Nothing's good enough for Mum. She moans about living in Hersham rather than Weybridge, and always coming here for August holidays rather than...' She put a hand to her mouth. 'Oh God sorry, that sounds awful.'

Grandie laughed. 'You think I hadn't noticed? That's why, now you're a bit older, I told them to leave you with me while they go off to Malaga and Marbella.'

Andie looked up. 'It was *your* idea?'

'Could you have stood another three weeks of them being so damn miserable?'

Andie shook her head.

'Nor me. Honestly, you'd think you were off to Borstal in September, not a well thought-of secondary school. You said you loved the open day?'

'I did, and there was a girl who's going to be in the same class, who also loves dancing and drawing, and this teacher let us watch some of the rehearsal for the dance show.'

Grandie gently elbowed her. 'Sounds perfect. I don't think you would've thrived at either of those pushy private schools, doing far too much homework every night instead of dancing, or playing rounders with your friends in the garden. You're a bright girl in your own way, and if you're happy and work hard, you're going to do very well, you'll see. Ha – and Mum and Dad will have more money for trips together, while you and I can have our own adventures.'

'Oh?' Andie said, smiling.

'Well… I'm thinking of exploring new beaches, a flamenco show that would have bored them to tears, the cowboy filming place they think sounds tacky – and making new "rooms" in the garden, of course. I'm going to try and take those crazy acacias in hand to make a little round shady space for the swingball game we're going to buy! Come and see what you think.'

'Okay!' Leaving The Ball on the bench, Andie followed Grandie along the path, past the winding steps up to the Lookout Post that gave you a fabulous view over the whole bay, past the wooden swing in the giant fig tree, and the bricks surrounding the tangle of needle-covered branches of a giant cactus. 'Uh, this ugly awful thing!' Andie said, stopping to look at it in horror.

Grandie turned around. 'What? Now don't you go upsetting my beautiful Eve!'

'*Eve?*'

'Yes. She's an Eve's pin cactus. And she's a masterpiece of self-sufficiency who deserves your respect. She stores water like a camel, and she makes "needles" to stop herself being eaten, control her temperature, and stop herself losing water.'

Andie considered Eve for a moment. 'She's not in my little book of cacti.'

'More fool that book. And more fool those two private schools. They are all three seriously missing out. Some are destined to be different! And before you say again that she's ugly, look at the beautiful candelabra branching of her strong arms! And… look there.'

'Where?'

'*There.*'

'Oh!' Eve had managed to produce a single, lusciously pink flower.

Andie sat up, opened her eyes. Picked up her phone... and put it in her pocket. She needed the laptop for this.

In the kitchen, she set the wash off again – she might be needing some of those clothes sitting in the washing machine. She fired up the laptop.

'Come on, let's *go*. It won't be anything like the same, but I'll be *there.*'

Not a hotel; she needed quiet and privacy. An apartment – hopefully near where Grandie's house was, and that lovely beach... although she couldn't remember what it was called. They hadn't *needed* to call it anything, because it was right below the house. She found a San José agency with good pictures and plenty of description of the properties.

Her heart stopped.

She scrolled back... too far... then down again... No. It couldn't be... but it *was*. Almost unrecognisable from the road, the garden a jungle now, after twenty years, but the kitchen, that inner courtyard, the view from the living room... She winced at the 'from' price, but then looked at the available dates. There was something about it being new – recently put on the website, they must have meant, and yes – available from the first of August, for a minimum of a month. She could spend August there, like she'd done every year until she was fifteen! Until Grandie had died and her parents had heartlessly sold it. Now it could be hers – if only for a month – like she was sure Grandie meant it to be. That crazy little house over the sea, with its wild paradise of a garden.

3

San José. She gasped and pulled over to where it looked like many a car had stopped to admire the view of the village – or perhaps take a walk over to the rounded, tawny hills with their mountainous backdrop. Hills of fuzzy scrub and the odd stubby fan palm. The semi-desert landscape that didn't appeal to everyone – and certainly not to her horticultural friends. This, along with the feeling that it wouldn't be the same without Grandie, was why it had taken her twenty years to return. Far too long.

She got out of the rented, red Panda. Even after just a half-hour drive from the airport, the heat pressing down on her felt twice as intense – and it was only ten o'clock. Smiling to herself, she remembered Grandie saying, *What you don't get done by ten o'clock, won't get done that day*, and could well believe it.

She took out her phone and snapped the white village and its ribbon of cobalt sea sitting between two mountains. On the left, the houses and apartments climbing up the rocky hill above the little marina looked unchanged but were now mirrored by smart new homes on the opposite slope – that she hoped didn't stretch as far as Grandie's house, which used to be the last but one on the coastal road coming up out of the village before looping back into it.

She got back into the car and drove down the main street, noticing a lot more shops and restaurants, and some smart, new, low-rise apartment hotels. There were also more people around than she remembered, but they were still nearly all Spaniards, by the look of them. The village had certainly gone up in the world, but seemed to be keeping its modest and very Spanish charm.

She spotted the estate agent's place and parked outside. The tatty exterior and faded photos in the window didn't match up to the turquoise website, but it didn't matter; she just needed the key and in ten minutes she'd be in Grandie's old house!

Inside, there was a frowning, middle-aged man sat in front of a computer and a squeaky desk fan, rather than the friendly woman with a smattering of English that she'd been emailing.

'Is Mónica here? I've been writing with her,' she managed in Spanish.

The man shook his head. 'Not here today.'

'Oh. I'm Andrea Butts. For Casa Higuera?'

He turned to his computer. *Of course* or *welcome* might have been nice, but after less time than he could possibly have needed to check, he shook his head again. '*No disponible*,' he said to the screen.

Not available. Well of course it wasn't! She'd booked it.

He hadn't understood her. 'I have it for all of August,' she said in Spanish.

'No.'

'I reserved it, with Mónica,' Andie said, a cold sensation coming over her. 'I've paid a...' She couldn't remember the word for 'deposit' in Spanish.

He made a couple of clicks with the mouse and shook his head.

'I *have*!' she said in English, forgetting herself, and pulled out her phone to go into her banking app... but there was no record of a deposit going out. Had she used a credit card? 'Wait...' She went to Emails, but reading the last one from Mónica, she noticed how, if she looked at the Spanish tenses more carefully, it said she was *going to* confirm, not that she *was* confirming. 'Oh God...' There was a prick of tears; how could she have been so bloody stupid? 'When *will* it be available?'

He shrugged. Maybe the middle of September, maybe not, he seemed to be saying, and started talking about how it was high season, everything was rented, but there was a small house in a nearby village.

'No! I have to be *here*!'

A woman about her own age walked in, and she noticed a wide-eyed exchange between her and the man.

'Mónica?' Andie asked.

The woman looked over to the man, as if waiting for permission to answer.

'There's no reservation for you here, Señorita Butts,' the man said. *Ignacio Méndez*, according to the plastic box of business cards. There'd been a nasty fascist bullfighter called Ignacio in a novel she'd read, and Méndez sounded very like the Spanish word for to tell a lie.

'I'll just have to find a hotel,' Andie said, concentrating on not bursting into tears in front of this horrid man.

There was further shaking of the head from Ignacio.

The woman, Mónica or not, had been biting her lip – but suddenly talked quickly and quietly to him, getting raised eyebrows and a nod in return.

'I have a friend that has nice apartment hotel, in this road, a little more up,' she said in English. 'She has apartment for her family that she keep free, maybe she can rent you. I can ask?'

'Oh, yes please!'

Ten minutes later, she was standing in front of the little balconied Hotel Apartamento Valentina, just where the road starts to curve round and up the hill towards Grandie's house.

'Andrea?' A pretty, forty-something, Spanish lady came out to greet her, introducing herself as Valentina.

'Andie, yes.'

'Welcome, *Andita*!'

'Ha – that's what my grandmother's gardener used to call me.'

'Good! Come, I show you the room,' Valentina said in English. 'There is maybe a week where you move to a studio if arrive my sister and her two boys, but you can have until September.'

It was a compact, two-bedroomed apartment, cosy with its colourful paintings and rugs hanging on the walls, a wrought-iron balcony in the kitchen-living room giving a view over the village and a glimpse of the beach.

'It's lovely. So kind of you to let me rent this; I understand it's not usually available.'

'Well, when I hear they…' She cleared her throat. 'There was some… problem?'

'Yes. I came here to rent the house where my grandmother lived and created a wonderful garden. Now I'll just have to look at it from the road. At least I can probably walk to it from here.'

'Casa Higuera?' Valentina asked, hesitantly.

'Yes! D'you know it?'

'Of course, everybody knows it! But don' walk there in this heat; wait for the morning.' She put up a finger. 'I have idea… I know a gardener – an English man! – who has gone there. Maybe he can talk with the owner and you can visit.'

'Oh, that would be great!'

'Okay, come down when you're ready. I'll try call to Ben.'

'Thanks.'

She opened her suitcase and saw the clothes she'd imagined hanging up in either the garden-view little bedroom she used to use, or Grandie's old room with its balcony looking out to sea… The clothes turned into a stinging blur, so she kicked off her Crocs and flopped back on to the bed, letting the tears track down her face and onto the pillow. She'd been an idiot not to follow up about the deposit, but there was something odd going on here. Her rental *had* been agreed, she was sure of it… and now she had a whole month here, which, without the comforting memories of Grandie's house and garden around her, sounded like rather an excessive amount of Billie-no-mates beach holidaying.

Andie! Not like you to be such a grump, Grandie had

said to her once – probably after a call from Mother. She got up and washed her face, changed into a cornflower blue sundress, and went out onto the balcony with the cold, bubbly water Valentina had given her. She looked over between the white buildings at the sparkling calm sea, and then along the road of little shops that would eventually curve and go up the hill towards Grandie's house. At least it sounded like she'd be able to *visit* the garden, and she could drive around and enjoy returning to all those wild beaches she went to with Grandie, maybe go to some concerts and flamenco shows...

She went down to see how Valentina had got on with the phone call.

'He not answer. But you know, you can visit him; he works in the garden *botánico* in San Rafael, open until two o'clock. Fifteen minutes in the car, very easy. Look.' She shook open a little treasure-hunt-style map. 'Leave the village, turn to the right when you see "San Rafael", and follow the road.'

Valentina was right. Driving here, on these small but well-made roads, reminded her of pushing cars along the roads on Shefali's daughter Zara's playmat a few years ago; you couldn't really get lost. You just had to be careful not to be too distracted by the beauty of the rounded hills with their herds of white goats, and the isolated white farms hiding behind a few eucalyptus trees. And the coast – she was soon driving along it, exclaiming 'Wow!' as the road wound along the side of the rocky mountains, the sparkling, dark-blue sea further and further beneath her. Then a short, steep slope inland took her to a blind summit... and the huge valley where, on the opposite side, stood the old gold-mining village of San Rafael. She wouldn't need a map to find the botanical garden; in the sparse vegetation of the orange-and-ochre landscape, the concentration of palm trees and an intensity of green stood out like an oasis.

She crawled down the road towards it, then passed through derelict mining cottages before entering the main village of loved-looking old and newer houses sporting posters for the local art group. She parked outside the entrance to the gardens, an elegant old terracotta-coloured building that had probably been something important in the village's mining days but now served as a flora and fauna information centre for the Cabo de Gata-Níjar Natural Park. Entrance was free, but she stuffed a ten-euro note into the collection box; after all, the place – or one of its employees, anyway – was hopefully about to make it possible for her to visit Grandie's garden.

She wandered along the network of smooth-stone paths, looking for an English-looking gardener. Or *any* gardener, in fact. Apart from an elderly French couple and a young Spanish family with a buggy, there was nobody around. She enjoyed the scents of thyme, rosemary and scorched earth, but was irritated by the habit of feeling she had to name everything before looking at the labels. Couldn't she just stop being a gardener for once? It wasn't easy anyway, given the surprising variety of vegetation in this peculiar semi-desert climate and volcanic terrain – and the fact that everything was in Spanish.

'How's your Spanish?'

She turned around. Good God, Valentina had said he was young, but she hadn't mentioned sun-kissed, smiley and frankly gorgeous. But she wasn't here to fall for the earthy charms of yet another gardener.

'Rusty GCSE, and devoid of plant names. But actually, it's *you* I'm looking for.'

'Ah.' A lopsided smile suggested he was used to being sought out.

She blushed – hopefully not noticeably, in the face-reddening heat. 'You're Ben?'

'I am. And I just got a message from Valentina telling me to look out for a weary-looking, newly-arrived, blonde English girl. What can I do for you?'

Quite a lot, if she weren't thirty-five to his early twenties, and still possibly in a relationship with another twinkly-eyed gardener.

'Valentina tells me you know the people in Casa Higuera at the top of the hill. I was wondering if you could ask them if I could have a look round the garden, because my grandmother created it, and I haven't seen it since, well... and I was going to rent it but—'

'Whoa! Start again?' he said with a laugh.

'I'm sorry, I'm probably not making sense; I've been up since four this morning.'

'Okay! Let's sit down with a Coke,' he said, beckoning her to follow him over to the machine.

They took their drinks over to a bench enjoying the best view over the garden of local flora and down to the sea – shaded, rather appropriately, by a beautiful big *higuera*, like the fig tree she remembered in Grandie's garden. He listened with charming interest as she told him about the garden, how it had inspired her to become a garden designer, and her experience at the rental agency.

'Oh dear. But I'm not sure how much I'll be able to help – I never met the owner, just a friend of hers who'd been asked to let me in with the key. And it was the inner courtyard they wanted sorting – "dressing" for potential renters – not the garden.'

'When was that?'

'Oh… three or four weeks ago. It's the guy renting it you'd have to ask now, and… well, I've heard he's a bit of a weirdo. And a right surly so-and-so, according to a builder friend of mine who had to fix the gate.'

'Oh.'

'Doesn't sound like a chap who'd readily give you a tour of his garden. Not that you'd be able to see much of it anyway, without a machete.'

Andie leant back on the bench and sighed.

Ben patted her arm. 'Tell you what, come with me to a pool barbecue lunch at my builder friend Marcelo's this Sunday. You can ask him about the guy – and others there might also know something.'

Andie sat on her little balcony with a melon lolly. She'd had an hour in the sea, a cold shower, and sunset was only about an hour and a half away – but there was no cooling down. Grandie's ten a.m. rule, together with Valentina's suggestion of leaving the walk up the hill until tomorrow morning, were making sense. But although she'd waited twenty years to have a peep at Grandie's garden again, she couldn't wait any longer.

She went inside, and having wasted battery and time on an unsatisfying WhatsApp chat with Johnny, and plugged in her phone so that it would have enough charge for the photos she hoped to take. After changing into thin, denim shorts, an orange vest, and trainers, and combing her fair hair into a pineapple top, she caught sight of herself in the mirror on the back of the bathroom door and realised she'd dressed for work. Well – it was work, in a way; maybe remembering this garden could get her back on track.

She seemed to be the only person going up the hill, everyone else coming down – arm in arm or in a laughing group – to the bars, restaurants and shops selling floaty dresses, leather bracelets and beachy stuff. Up and up she went, leaving the village centre behind her, the houses starting to give way to stretches of stubbled, orange hill and views over the beach. Eventually she came round the hill and could make out the rocky promontory and the profile of Grandie's seaside balcony up ahead. Her heart raced. Probably just another ten minutes' walk. It was further than she'd thought, but by the time it was dark on her return, she'd be among the sporadic houses and occasional street lamps. She finished the water bottle tucked into her running belt, wiped the stinging sweat from her eyes with a tissue, and unzipped her bag to take out her phone for a long shot… but damn – it was still charging on the bedside table. Never mind, this was just a recce. She'd come back in the morning.

She carried on up the hill until it mercifully started to level out. She remembered it so well: on one side that stunning view back over to the village and its small marina, and on the other, the top of the hill – fuzzy with dry esparto grass – that she and Grandie had once climbed. The sun was low now, shadowing the hills, flooding the sky and the silky, flat sea with pink and orange. You'd think there'd be lots of romantic couples walking up there, but every time she thought she could hear someone behind her, it turned out to be just the squeak of her water bottle, the rattle of the wooden key fob in her bag, or the snuffle of a stray dog.

She passed the last house before Grandie's. It used to be the brilliant-white second home of an elderly couple from Granada, but was now faded and crumbling, with a rusty old car covered in eucalyptus leaves in its driveway.

That snuffle again. A little whine. Was that gentle-looking dog she saw earlier injured? She didn't know what she'd do if he *was*, especially without a phone, but maybe tomorrow... She walked round the side of the old car – and gasped.

A giant... pig. *Wild boar*. Staring at her, huge, fluffy ears raised. Two humbug-striped piglets, fixing with beady eyes. Strong, honeyed muskiness filled the air. She could hardly breathe. Eyeing the mother's tusks, she edged backwards – but a curious piglet trotted forward. 'No, no...' she said quietly, stepping back further, but her running bag caught the wing mirror, twanging it with a loud thwack.

The mother snorted, charged... bouldered into her thigh. A knife of pain. Andie screamed, hanging on to the mirror, heart pounding, then as the huge head lowered again, she leapt onto the bonnet, scrabbling around on the rough debris to get onto the roof. Sprawled there panting, locking eyes with the animal, she wondered if she was safe – if they could climb hills, could they... but the boar trotted back to her babies. There were grunts and little snorts but she couldn't see them now... Then they were on the slope next to the house, above her, watching her. She kept still – as still as she could, with her heart shaking her body at every beat. Surely they wouldn't jump down on her? The boar started rooting around in the earth, and one of the piglets started to suckle. It was over.

Her vision was cloudy, lips numb... she took deep, slow breaths, trying to calm down. She was all right. She just had to wait until a car went past. Or until the boar was far enough away that she dared run back down the hill. But *running*... didn't seem likely; the pain was getting worse, and... *God*. Her thigh had a red river of blood pooling down from it into and over her trainer, down the car, over the side, landing with a pat-pat on the leaves below.

She must have sat staring at this for a while; the sun was now touching the top of the hill. It would soon be dark. How long until someone came up here? There were no lights from Grandie's house. The house further along seemed to have a light coming from it, but when would they next drive down here? Tomorrow morning? Afternoon? She twisted to look back from where she'd come. It was hard to tell if any of those houses, several hundred yards away, had lights on or were just reflecting the sunset with their windows.

The blood river was widening, a tributary now reaching her hand. This couldn't wait until morning. She took the trainer and sock off her good leg, and winced as she pressed the sock against the wound. Wondered about taking off her vest to make a tourniquet, like they did in films, but supposing she made it worse? She needed help.

'*Ayuda!*' she shouted out, over and over. Waiting in between for any sign – a light coming on, an opening door, voices – anything suggesting she might have been heard. But only the boars had heard – and didn't seem to like it, six eyes shining at her in the gloom. She waited a while, until they'd moved a little further up the hill, and started shouting again. Then stopped; the effort was making her faint. Or was that the blood? She couldn't faint – she'd easily fall off, and if the boar came back, she'd be... She pressed harder on the wound, trying to squeeze its hideous open mouth shut. Maybe the river was easing a little. It was hard to tell. But this was what she had to do: concentrate on that, and keep awake. Help would come; she just had to wait.

She looked over at the profile of Grandie's house against the sunset, the jungle of trees arching over the driveway hiding the rest of the house. There could be lights on there she couldn't see. She shouted for help again, her face in this direction, in case it made a difference... and it did, in a way, because she heard Grandie's voice in her head, telling her to sing.

'It's nothing, just a sprain, maybe a little crack,' Grandie had said, her ankle already ballooning in size.

'What else can I do?' Andie had asked. She'd already called the ambulance.

'Sing.'

'What?'

'Er... how about that new Ketama song we were singing the other day. Let's...' she had winced as she'd moved her foot, trying to get comfortable '...see if we can remember the words.'

Andie looked over to Grandie's and sang it. 'Acaba de Nacer'. He/she/it had just been born. What? She la-la'd the verse, except for the bit about having much to learn. Maybe, but she'd learnt plenty, now, about over-aggression in protective mothers. Then the chorus, something about having a beautiful face. She looked over at the boar. 'Nobody's said that to you, have they,' she wanted to say, but nothing came out.

A car. Right there, beside her. What? Her head was spinning, hands painfully scrunching the sharp eucalyptus nuts to try and keep herself awake.

The driver's door opened, a dark figure coming around the front of it. Slim, cat-like. Male.

There was a snort above her. 'Boar!' she managed to say, pointing to it.

His low voice said something about it not hurting her.

''Ready has! Can you…' A ringing in her ears cut out what she was going to say next. She bent her head forward, trying to collect herself.

'Come.'

She seemed to be lying on the roof now, and could only manage to lift and turn her head towards him… He was right there. Eyes wide and shining in the car light, a sculptured Jesus face, with Jesus hair. He was reaching out his arms. She moved and fell… into them. Not a big man, but very strong.

He put her into the back of the car, her leg, wrapped up in something, on the seat. He disappeared for a moment, flung her trainer in the footwell, quickly got back into the

driver's seat. She wanted to lie down on the soft surface…
but there was something in the way. The edge of something,
and a small *hand*… a staring boy in a booster seat, saying
something like 'happily' and making horn-fingers next to
his mouth.

'Happily?' She decided she didn't like kids anymore.

The man finished talking quickly into his phone, then
hastily turned the car around. The boy's '*jabalí*', he explained
in accented English, was the Spanish for wild pig. He was
going to drive to the hospital – quicker than waiting for the
ambulance, they'd told him. It would take twenty minutes.

'Thank you,' she said, throat tightening, wiping her face
on her vest. She leant her head on the side of the booster
seat, the child tilting to the other side in revulsion – then
suddenly forward again with the tusk face, and reaching
towards the now dark and sopping towel.

Eyes in the back of his head, the man quickly said
something to him. The boy gave a manic little laugh, then
sat back in his seat, deflated.

She started to drift… then all at once there were bright
lights, he was helping her out, holding her up, walking her
into a building… and she was on a bed.

He put a hand on her arm. 'I can't stay. My boy… would
be difficult in the hospital.'

She nodded.

He started to move away.

'Wait!'

He was back, silhouetted against the light.

'You… Cas' Higuera?'

He hesitated a moment. 'Yes.'

'Saved my life,' she said. Maybe she meant not just him,

but Grandie, and the profile of Casa Higuera against the sunset. But as he leant forward as if to say something, she saw his eyes widen behind his glasses. As if he hadn't realised that was what he'd done. Or saving a life was something he'd waited a long time to do. Then he was gone.

4

'So how are you today?' Shefali asked, from her Zakynthos holiday pool garden. Her voice had the usual calm lilt, but her gentle features still showed concern.

'It's good to be back at the apartment, and Valentina's been amazing. These anti-sick things seem to be working now, thank God. Can't complain.' Andie pointed the phone around the shaded balcony: her bandaged leg raised on pillows on the other chair, the remains of a nectarine, a bowl of pistachios, water bottle, and escapist Spanish holiday read beside her on the table.

'Lots of water with all those vaccines, antibiotics and painkillers.'

'I'm trying.'

Shefali shook her head. 'I don't know, you go out there to relax, get away from one hysterical mother – and go up a dark hill to run into another. What were you *thinking*? You could have been—'

'Wild boars aren't common here, and the nurses said they

hadn't seen a casualty from one in *years*. It was just awful luck.'

'And an awful shock. I'm sure you still keep getting flashbacks.'

'Yes.' Those tusks, the car roof river of blood. Also, the serious Jesus-in-glasses and his odd little son – but they were very blurred.

'What did Johnny say? Surely he can spare a few days to come and join you *now*. You shouldn't be alone.'

'I'm not. As I say, Valentina's looking after me, and—'

'You haven't told him, have you.'

Andie hesitated. How did Shefali guess that? 'I told Gerard, when I had to explain a delay in answering him, and – he called Johnny without asking me.'

'The old busybody! And?'

'Johnny rang... and was appalled, obviously.'

'And?'

'Said he wished he could come over, but what with Jazzy...'

Shefali frowned. 'He should have been the first person you wanted to tell. There's something wrong here.' Shefali had been sceptical about the relationship with Johnny for some while. 'I'm coming over. It's just a question of which days I can clear.'

'What?' Andie burst into a grin. 'But—'

'How does this Saturday sound? Three or four days. Maybe five. We get back on Tuesday, and if I can swap my days in the practice... Oh hold on, David's calling me, back in a minute.'

She disappeared. Shefali – so wise, serene and self-assured – had a blind spot when it came to the men in her family.

Her father – despite showing himself to be a superb Indian dancer at family weddings – had persuaded her to leave ballet as a hobby and study optometry so she could join the family optician business; and older brother Vijay, inheriting the practice on their father's death, always seemed to have her working there more than her agreed two days a week. In her one act of defiance, she'd upset the family by marrying non-Indian David, a web designer – but overlooked that he was even more of a control freak than her father and brother put together.

She was back. 'I've cleared it with David – Saturday to Thursday.'

'Well done!' Andie said. 'I mean, *great!*'

'I'll talk to Vijay as soon as I can and let you know. I was down to do some extra days during Zara's Multisports camp week.'

'Oh, it would be wonderful!' A message floated over the screen. 'Ah, I'm going to have to call someone back quickly. Talk again soon!'

They waved and blew each other kisses, and then Andie looked at Ben's message. He'd sent her some kind words through Valentina when she was in the hospital, but she'd assumed he'd gone off the idea of taking her to his friend's Sunday pool barbecue, now she was a dopey and limping non-swimmer.

'Ben! I'd love to come.'

'Great! I could pick you up in an hour?'

'Wonderful. What should I bring?'

'Andie, nobody wants you hobbling to a shop. Just your lovely, brave self.'

'Ah… okay!'

Such a charmer. After a hair wash and an inexplicably long deliberation over her sundresses, she sat back on the balcony to wait for him. She was aware that jealous Johnny would be unhappy about this. Obviously, she was mainly going along to find out the likelihood of the mysterious man who saved her letting her visit Grandie's garden. And obviously, in the extremely unlikely event that young Ben had any interest in her beyond fellow-gardener friendship, she would let him know that she wasn't one for holiday romances and was, anyway, in a relationship. Then a small van arrived below and Ben got out of it – wearing a Hawaiian shirt with white-and-pink orchids against sky-blue, just like her dress; they were going to turn up looking like a shop-window perfect couple.

Luckily, he didn't seem to notice, more concerned with her leg and offering her an arm to lean on. 'You poor thing. How are you doing?'

'I'm really not too bad, thanks,' she said. He didn't need to know she was spaced out on the high dose of ibuprofen that was apparently standard here. Inside the van there was the usual smell of earth with a trace of male sweat, familiar from the vehicles of her series of horticultural boyfriends. Even Ben seemed familiar; he could be the blonde little brother of her previous boyfriend, Dutch nurseryman Fabian.

He looked over at her with a winning smile as he started the engine.

'Does your builder friend who went to my grandmother's old house live in San José?' she asked, for something to say.

'Yes. In the development on the right as you come into the village.'

'Ah.' She'd seen them: three or four terraced roads of blocky houses, the top one looking like a row of gappy teeth digging into the poor mountain.

'You probably don't approve; it must be hard, remembering San José from all those years ago.'

She made a face and gritted her teeth.

He glanced over and chuckled, then set off along the main road of restaurants filled with happy-looking Sunday Spaniards. 'The houses look better close up. Certainly Marcelo's place does, anyway.'

He was right. Unlike some of the swanky but stark new 'second home' developments up on the hill, pot plants and cute post boxes suggested many of these houses were lived in all year round; the distance from the beach and the lack of sea view probably made them more affordable for local families. The view they did have – particularly Marcelo, with his corner plot – was one of endless rounded orangey hills of *palmito* and scrub against a backdrop of distant mountains. The sort of scenery that made you want to put on hiking boots and backpack and go for it – unless you'd already been gored by one of its inhabitants.

Ben followed her gaze and patted her arm. 'Don't worry,' he said gently, 'the few there are only come down from the mountains at dusk.'

His reassurance was welcome, even if, according to Google, that couldn't be completely relied upon. She found herself checking the height of Marcelo's garden wall. 'I hope I'm not going to spend the entire lunch having to talk about it.' Even the busy hospital nurses hadn't been able to help themselves, stopping by to ask her how exactly it had happened, impressed by her car-jumping agility and wanting to know more about her saviour than she could tell them.

'I'll make sure you don't.'

They went through a side gate to a shady, AstroTurfed garden with a small pool and lots of child-friendly, potted succulents. There was a cherubic seven-or-eight-year-old girl playing with boats, two men busy with a barbecue, two smiling Spanish women, and an English-looking couple in their fifties or sixties. The burlier man at the barbecue turned around, grinned, wiped his hands on a towel, and came over to give her the two-cheek Spanish kiss. 'Andie! I am Marcelo. Welcome! Allow me present you... my wife, Beatriz; Jaime and Ana from the shop of plants; and Phil and Jen from San José Service Propie—'

'Property Services!' his wife corrected him with a laugh.

Double kisses from everyone followed.

'My name is Lucía!' the little girl called out, and Andie smiled and waved to her.

'Please, *siéntate*... we made special chair for swim with one leg!' Marcelo pointed to a low beach chair on a towel, with a cushion for her leg, next to the pool.

'Oh *perfect*! Thank you!' She lowered herself onto it, kicked off her flip-flops and put her good leg into the pool with a sigh.

They all cheered and started asking how she was.

'A bit sore. I can't swim until a week tomorrow at the earliest, and I've gone right off pigs. Otherwise fine!'

The inevitable wild boar stories followed, some of which she'd heard in the hospital: Phil and Jen had nearly driven into one the size of a baby elephant; Marcelo had once come across a docile group of them when he was on a hike;

and all but Ben remembered when a solitary one took up residence in the village park in broad daylight, being hand-fed by the surrounding residents.

Ben put a hand to his face.

'Oh no, I thought I was safe in the daytime!' Andie said.

'It's only if they feel threatened, and a mother with young would—' Jaime started.

'Okay, I think Andie would rather talk about something else now!' Ben said, patting her shoulder and then going over to hear out Lucía's wild boar story and put an end to it.

They all smiled and nodded in agreement, and Beatriz came over with what looked like a sangria for herself and Andie.

'Oh…'

'Don' worry, I was thinking you will be on *medicación*; I made one *sin alcohol* – enjoy!'

She thanked her and took a sip: peachy, delicious. 'Mm!'

'I have it too, because of the baby,' she said, patting a tiny bump beneath her loose floral dress, then sitting down next to her with her feet in the pool.

'Oh, wonderful! I'm sure Lucía is excited.'

'Of course. And Marcelo too, especially because it is the first for him.'

'Ah! And I was thinking how Lucía looked just like him.'

'I know, and they are very close. With Marcelo's father too, he adores her. And talking of grandparents, I hear you wanted to see the garden of your grandmother, no?'

'I still do. But Ben says the man living there is a bit…'

'*Muy raro*. Very strange. When went Marcelo to do the gate the man was very angry, saying *don' come here, I don' ask you to come here, go!* Is like, he is there with secret, no?'

Marcelo turned around from the barbecue. 'I think is that my brother in the *guardia civil* made many questions after died his wife there when he was living there before, a few years ago. Anyway, I mend gate and go away, very quick!' He made a flying movement with his hand and a whooshing sound.

'That was a good plan, because the man obviously has a temper,' Jaime the plant shop man said, in Spanish. 'There was a problem with some delivery too, I heard.' He lowered his voice. 'I think he pushed that poor wife.' He was then talking too quickly for Andie, saying something about how spoilt flamenco dancers are, and having had an injury of some kind, unable to dance and tour for a while, he'd probably got fed up with her and pushed her off the cliff.

Beatriz started shaking her head. Phil, who'd been telling Lucía he used to have a boat exactly like one of her toy ones, leant over with a grin. 'Wouldn't it have been easier to just divorce her?' He repeated this in Spanish.

Ana the plant shop woman said something about how Vicente Vargas Ortega didn't dance anymore because he could now just hole up in the house with the life insurance.

Surely he didn't dance anymore because he had a young son to look after? How awful to have had to give up dancing, as well as lose his wife and the mother of his son. She was shocked that Ana and Jaime were so quick to assume the worst about him, and wished her Spanish was up to defending him against their rattling onslaught.

Jen leant forward and whispered to her with a wink. 'There's not exactly much crime in the village, so the villagers love exaggerating and making up stories!'

'I understood that!' Ana said in Spanish, laughing. 'Look,

I know he took Andie to hospital, but that doesn't mean he's a good man. You have to ask: why would his older son, just after the death of his mother, want to escape to live in Granada with his uncle immediately afterwards? Like he blamed his father.'

So there was a bigger son too. 'How old was he at the time?' Andie asked.

'Let me think,' Beatriz said. 'Sebastián was having English lessons at Kim's school at the same time as us, with the adults, so he must have been eighteen or so.'

'So that's why you speak such good English,' Andie said.

'Oh, I don' know...' Beatriz said, 'but Kim is very, very good teacher. She was coming today, but her mother was ill. Another time you can ask her about Sebastián and his father.'

'You'd think a boy that age would stand by his father, at such a time,' Ana persisted. 'There's definitely something going on there.'

'Yes, but San José is not good place for the son, for to study flamenco,' Beatriz said.

'He's a flamenco dancer too?' Andie asked.

'Yes. Very good, I have seen him dance in Almería. He will be... twenty-two years now.'

So... the little son was just a toddler when his mother died. Maybe even there when it happened. Poor little chap.

Andie changed the subject, and learnt how Beatriz was a nurse in Níjar, a pretty town famous for its ceramics and rugs; Jaime and Ana were looking for a bigger place for their plant shop; Phil and Jen had lived there for fifteen years, looking after and renting out clients' second homes, and unable to think how they would manage without such a fabulous, English-speaking builder and odd-job man like Marcelo.

Andie told them she worked for a garden design company, but didn't mention *Challenging Gardens*; there was no point, when they wouldn't have heard of it out here, she probably wasn't going to continue, and she certainly didn't want to go into what happened.

Ben, who'd been helping with the barbecue once Jaime got so distracted by the talk about Vicente that he was no use, fixed her a plate of swordfish, rather dry bread and a salad with too much oil – but it was heavenly after the tasteless hospital food.

He sat down next to her with his plate, and touched her arm. 'Andie, it sounds like your saviour isn't too hospitable. If you really must call on him to try and look round the garden, I think I should come with you.'

'That's very kind, but wouldn't that make him feel even more invaded?'

'Maybe, but I don't think you should go on your own. What a pity you didn't mention the garden on the night!'

'I know, but by the time he came along I was barely...' She did a spinning motion with her hand.

'God, how awful...' His hand moved to stroke her back. It was a bit too tactile for fellow-gardener friends, but... well, she had been gored by a wild boar. 'You know, if at some point you want to go over what happened, I promise I'd neither ooh-ah like a village sensationalist or tick you off for having gone up there.'

She looked into those dark blue eyes, something she'd been avoiding at this proximity, and smiled. 'That... sounds good. I might take you up on it.'

Could Ana have possibly overheard and understood? She seemed to want to have the last word, a hand on both their shoulders. 'Ben, look after her,' she said in Spanish. 'Vicente could be dangerous for all we know. Please be careful.' Then she smiled. 'And keep dressing in the same colours, you blondies – very cute!'

5

What was his name? Vicente... Ravas? Ragas? Might have had a 'b'. *Bravas*. As in *patatas bravas*, those spicy potatoes... *Bragas* sounded right – but no, didn't that mean knickers?

She was lying on the bed, having got too hot on the balcony, and thought it would be fun to look at YouTubes of Vicente in his dancing days. Had he been one of those dancers with a bit of humour and charisma, or one of those surly all-stamping ones? It wasn't hard to guess which.

Riveras. Riveros. Maybe the 'b' was a 'v'; they sounded much the same in Spanish. Vicente Var... *Vazquez*. *Velázquez*. Yes. But maybe just sounds familiar because of the famous painter. Or because of...

She put down her phone and looked out of the window towards the beach. *Fernando Velázquez*. Even after all this time, his name had music and romance – although of course he'd just called himself *Nando*. She and a Spanish girl had been doing crazy dancing to an upbeat song on someone's radio on the beach, and he'd joined in. Apparently they'd met before – two summers earlier, when boys were just annoying – and she'd thought, how could she not remember this chap, who looked like Robbie from Take That and listened so intently when she talked? He became one of the Spanish kids she had round to Grandie's – and her first boyfriend. Well, her first kiss anyway, although she only tolerated that because she liked the cuddles and gazing into those black-brown eyes. They were going to write, and see each other again the following summer when his family hopefully came down again from Madrid. But back in England, there were months of misery and incomprehension when he never replied to her two letters.

Much later, she'd learnt that male non-response was common. It was a man's way of saying something without having to find the words – letting you eventually find them for him and force the inevitable.

A message flashed up on her phone. Johnny. Case in point. How sick she was of his dutiful daily WhatsApps. Why was it *never* a good moment to talk? It was time she… well, told him what was on his mind. But not now, because she'd got to drive to the hospital for her check-up.

She got up and changed into a dress. Tried to ignore the peals of several more WhatsApp messages – but then decided to check they weren't from anyone else. Ben, for example, fixing a late afternoon to drive up to Casa Higuera with her.

But they were all from Johnny: he was missing her, worrying about her, still wanting to come over – but it all just felt like words.

She checked her bag, went to the loo, picked up her keys. Then her phone rang.

'Why aren't you answering? Are you okay?' he said in his gentle Irish lilt. Video call. There he was: lively blue eyes, soft brown hair, the broad chest she snuggled into... Her heart ached for him; this was not good.

'Is something wrong?' he asked. 'You don't look very happy.'

'No, no, it's just I've got my hospital appointment now,' she said, holding up the car keys as if he might not believe her. 'Need to leave...' She looked at her watch. 'In five minutes.'

'Okay. How did it go at the barbecue? Can anyone introduce you to the man renting the house, so you can see the garden?'

'Er... no. They just said he was grumpy and unlikely to help.'

'Ah, but *you* know better.'

'What d'you mean.'

'He helped you before, carried you to his car.'

'No, he caught me when I came off the car roof.'

'Must be very strong.'

Good God, surely he wasn't considering being jealous of Señor Patatas Bravas? 'I don't know. On the short side. Glasses.' Best not to mention he was an ex-flamenco dancer, after all those stupid comments when she and Shefali joined a flamenco class with a male teacher. 'Anyway, seems like I'll just have to see what I can see from the road. Look, I better go.'

'Okay, let me know what they say. Love you, baby.'

'Love you too.'

She went out to the oven-like car, switched on the air con and set off down the road. Breathed out heavily. She *did* love him – well, broadly speaking. But try as she might, she didn't see a future with him. It seemed too dependent on too many other things: her career aligning with his; Caroline's forgiveness and willingness to finalise the divorce; her still un-discussed relationship with the girls; her never-discussed possible infertility. And she had to agree with Shefali that a chap who who'd had an open marriage didn't seem like a good choice for a closed one – should he ever even want that.

Love you, baby. She was short, accident-prone, given to laughing things off, liked a cuddle, and often taken for younger than her thirty-five years, with her childish features and silly, fly-away, fair hair – but she wasn't a *baby*. Surely there must be a man out there who could one day... take her seriously.

There was a beep from the car behind her as she hesitated at the roundabout, distracted by both her thoughts and the gorgeous boat-with-waves structure in the middle of the thing. They really went overboard with their roundabouts here, as if stressing the importance of the decision you were making. Here, for example, it felt like it was asking if she really wanted to leave the seaside tranquillity of San José. Or maybe the waves were rugs, among other beautiful things, that she could be missing out on in Níjar. She took the third prong, towards the city of Almería. The one she would have to take at the end of month to go back to the airport and England – something she already didn't want to think about.

She was nearly back at the roundabout. She should go to the apartment, tell Johnny how the appointment went, as promised, and then – it would be a call, not a video call, God help her – tell him their relationship was over, but she wanted to stay friends. Opposition to that idea, she reckoned, would be strong but short-lived. Probably shorter-lived than her own feelings of loss. But oh, the relief.

On the other hand, she was relieved and elated by the hospital appointment; her leg was healing well, she could swim after her stitches came out next Monday, and she'd managed the whole visit in Spanish. She'd been attacked by a boar but hadn't lost life or limb; celebration was in order. She turned left to Níjar.

It was the town in charge of San José and the smaller villages dotted over a wide area, but not much more than a village itself. Narrow streets of ancient, white houses wound up the hill and would have to be explored at a less baking time of the day – as would the Butterfly Centre and a cactus nursery on the outskirts. Today she was here for the local ceramics and shaggy '*jarapa*' rugs – and soon found herself in a colourphilic (as she and Shefali called their colour-passionate selves) heaven. Blues and orange-to-russet colours seemed to predominate, as if the sea, sky and rusty-coloured volcanic terrain had seeped into the souls and hands of the artisans. Along with sandy-yellow and cactus-green. Earthy, muted and delicious shades – often in stripes, the colours zinging together. And all reminding her of crockery and rugs at Grandie's.

Halfway up the road, she already had a selection of bowls from hairgrip to cereal size, egg cups, two mugs and three *jarapa* bathmats. Bustling into one last ceramic shop, she asked to put her bags down by the till in case she broke something. The middle-aged, lady shopkeeper smiled, took her bags, and asked what she was looking for.

'I don't know, I love it all!'

The woman laughed again, and pointed out an exquisite design made by her uncle's workshop. It was the ultimate, the stripes overlaid by delicate hand-painted whirls. Andie picked out a suitcase-challenging fruit bowl. Adding a couple of free ceramic fridge magnets, the shopkeeper started wrapping them in newspaper. 'You're on holiday? You want me to wrap it in bubble?' she asked in sloweddown Spanish.

'Yes, please.' Andie delved in her bag for her purse.

The woman tutted and asked what had happened to her leg.

'Oh... an accident, getting better,' Andie said.

The woman looked at her carefully, down at the desk, and up again. Then turned a newspaper round towards Andie and put a finger on it. 'You look like...' Her mouth opened in surprise. 'You *are* the girl who got attacked by a—'

'Oh...' Andie stared at the paper. It had seemed a good idea at the time, to stop others going up a hill on their own at dusk, but the journalist from the weekly local paper hadn't emailed the copy to her, so Andie had assumed they weren't going to use it. There was an unflattering photo of her in the hospital bed, hair round her head like a stupid halo. It reported that she was a thirty-five-year-old gardener, and no, she wouldn't want a hunting group to track down the boar, who was only protecting her young.

'Poor thing!' the woman said, and came from behind the counter to do the Spanish double-kiss thing. She then tried to give Andie a huge discount on the already ludicrously cheap bowl, but Andie wouldn't agree to it, settling instead for a tour and photos of the pots and urns for sale in an inner courtyard – some inspiration at last for the Mediterranean projects.

Then she went to the café the woman recommended, and was soon sitting down in front of a finely crafted chocolate and banana crepe. As promised, she sent Hilary snaps of the newspaper article – not that it would make any difference to anything in England. Between delicious mouthfuls, she peeked at her purchases and grinned. No doubt she'd be back again soon, if keen potter and fellow colourphile Shefali came over.

'Goodness, you setting up house?' An English voice. Northern.

Andie looked up. A freckled, blue-eyed woman with a light brown bob, about her age, but considerably more stylishly dressed. 'Sorry?'

The woman pointed to Andie's bags and book. 'Sorry, take it you're English?'

'Yes.'

'Oh listen to us with our *sorrys*!'

'I know!' Andie said. The woman was holding a heavily Post-it-tabbed English textbook. 'Hey, you wouldn't be Kim, would you?'

'Yes!' She glanced down at her leg. 'And you've got to be Andie; I've heard *all* about you!' She looked at her watch. 'Just time for another coffee. Can I join you?'

'Please do!' Andie said, putting her book away.

Andie learnt that five years ago Kim had escaped a series of tedious jobs and boyfriends in Leeds. She now had her own English school here, and lived in San José with her Spanish accountant boyfriend. After asking how Andie's leg was doing, she wanted to know how long she was out for.

'Oh, just until the end of the month.'

'No! You don't want to go back to Blighty. Ask Ben to get you a job at the botanical garden, find yourself a little apartment where you can put all these lovely things. He's a great chap; time he had a lovely gardening girlfriend!'

'Oh no, no! Ben and I are just friends.'

'Of course, you've got...' They looked at each other. 'Okay, my mother's been out here for three years, but still watches all those English gardening programmes – and reads the trashiest of newspapers.'

'Ah.' Andie left the last bit of crêpe and looked down at the table. 'Can you... not let that get around? It's probably all over now anyway – both the show and Johnny.'

Kim put a hand to her mouth. 'Er... I did sort of mention it... But don't worry, everyone'll be completely on your side. Sorry to hear it's come to an end – so unfair. But onwards and upwards, right? And meanwhile, you get romantically rescued by a flamenco dancer!'

'Well... I don't know about that. It was dark and messy, and I can't remember much about it. I gather you used to teach his son?'

'Yes. Sebastián. Wanted English so he could tour the world. Bright boy, but an arrogant little sod. Probably spoilt by his adoring mother. Estefanía was lovely, used to make all his flamenco outfits. Then when the poor woman died, he stopped coming. I think he went to live with the property developer uncle in Granada he was always going on about.'

'What about his father?' And odd little brother.

She shrugged. 'Never met him. Poor chap, left on his own with a tiny son. Awful.' She winked. 'Until Andie dropped into his arms!' She looked at her watch again. 'Oops, better go. Give me a call if you want to meet up at the expat bar on Thursday nights.' She put a language school card with her phone number on the table. 'There are only a few of us, but it's great. Honorary – and potential – expats welcome!'

Back at the apartment, she decided to unwrap her purchases and use them, and after poring over the photos of the exquisite urns she sent some to a delighted Gerard. Then she lay on the bed and started sketching a design in which urns, plant pots and wall ceramics inspired the plants, rather than the other way round... until the rhythm of the ceiling fan lulled her to sleep. She dreamed about Grandie, beckoning to her, telling her to come and see the colourful broken ceramic tiles she was using to decorate the garden's amphitheatre...

She woke with a start and looked at her phone. Nearly five, but still nothing from Ben about going up to Casa Higuera with her. She couldn't complain – he'd been kind enough already, and would no doubt contact her sooner or later. But really, she couldn't believe there was anything to be afraid of; Vicente hadn't caught her in his arms and taken her to hospital just to throw her over the cliff for thanking him and asking to see his garden.

She showered and put on a no-nonsense, taupe T-shirt with the more modest pair of denim shorts: gardening girl rather than flamenco fan.

Down in the car, she checked she had her phone; she wasn't making that mistake again. Then she set off up the hill.

It was almost too quick, not giving her enough time to practise what she would say if he just happened to be in the driveway and saw her peering in. She slowed down as she passed her other saviour, the abandoned car – that looked like someone had washed it. Who would have done that? The council? Vicente? She drove on, her heart patting as she went past the tops of the trees marking the edge of Grandie's garden below, and onwards to the end of the road before it looped back the other side of the hill towards the village. She turned the car round and crawled down the side of the road with the garden – except of course the driving seat was now on the wrong side, so she still wasn't going to see much.

After the neighbour's neat, paved garden, there was a bit of rocky coast and then the *rambla* – a dry riverbed – that marked the top of Grandie's garden. After that there was the open area nearly as high as the road where she used to play rounders. From here there'd been steps down through a Hottentot-fig, ground-covered slope to the amphitheatre – but dense rubber tree and acacia foliage blocked any view from the road.

Then she saw the giant fig tree, and had to stop and get out to touch its dark green leaves. An old girl now, well past her wonderful fig-producing days, but she was still there. Andie leant over the brick wall, and could just make out the thick ropes of the swing. She smiled to herself and walked on. A mound among the foliage was probably the rocky Lookout Post, the winding path up to it totally overgrown... Finally, the massive, crimson-red spread of the old bougainvillea, hiding the house beyond, except for the small roof terrace next to what used to be her bedroom – and a waving boy.

Her heart thudded. It was like turning up at Johnny's, but this little peering face looked agitated, and quickly disappeared...

'*Hola?*' A woman's voice beneath her.

'Oh, *hola,..*' Andie tried to explain in Spanish that she was admiring the garden.

The woman replied something about not understanding her.

She could see her now, through the branches: round-faced and matronly, hair an unlikely strawberry blonde. Andie added that she'd also like to thank the *señor* for taking her to hospital last week.

The woman put a hand to her ear, made a beckoning and pointing gesture, and then with a '*momentito*' turned as if going back into the house.

Andie stood, dumbfounded, heart beating... but then heard the grind and squeak of the gates opening. She rushed down the hill towards the entrance, and down the driveway that forked from the road and through the tunnel of over-reaching trees. Then there she was in front of the old house – smaller than she remembered, really just a three-bedroom Sixties house with Spanish arches, little roof terrace, that inner courtyard. She tried to make out what the woman was saying, but her gaze was drawn over to Grandie's old stone bench under the olive tree at the start of the garden.

Making out the *jabalí* boar word, Andie answered in Spanish that yes, she was the woman attacked by the boar, and she'd like to say thank you to the man.

The boy came out of the house. He was a bit older than she'd thought, about seven, a little *The Jungle Book* Mowgli of a chap, with tiny shorts, a mop of shiny black hair, and the wide-eyed look of a boy brought up in a jungle – or not quite right.

'*Hola!*' Andie said, but his eyes avoided her – until they fixed on her leg with the interest of a child cannibal.

Then the woman held up a finger, turned and went inside, the boy following her.

Were they going to fetch the man? She waited so long, she started to wondered if the held-up finger had meant *no* rather than *wait here*, and she was supposed to be leaving through the still-open gates. She went over to the stone bench under the now mature olive tree. *This wasn't a good place for this bench, Grandie*, she imagined herself saying, and could almost see Grandie further up the now weedy gravel path, shrugging, laughing and beckoning her to follow...

'*Señora.*' A low, resonant voice.

She turned round. 'Oh...'

Dark. Darker than she remembered, even though they were now in daylight. Black, serious eyes, no glasses today, and the black Jesus hair tied back. A face all cheekbones and seriousness. A grown-up Mowgli maybe – although thankfully not bare-chested – with a panther-like stroll as he came towards her. Rather unnerving.

He said something she couldn't follow – in Spanish, and as if to himself. With absolutely no smile. A cold fish. Fish? She thought *fish* because... unbelievably, there was a fish on his white T-shirt. *A blue, cartoon fish.* How bad or grim could a man be, if he wore a cartoon fish?

'I... wanted to thank you for taking me to the hospital,' she managed in Spanish.

He put up a stop-sign hand. '*De nada.*' It was nothing. 'How is the leg?' She'd forgotten he could speak English.

'Oh... it's good,' she said.

He nodded. '*Me alegro.*' He was glad – although by God he didn't look it. There was no reason to think he'd look any gladder about letting her see the garden, but this was her chance.

'I would be glad,' she said in over-polite Spanish, 'if I could see your garden?' She then went into how her grandmother had planted much of it over twenty years ago, and she used to come and stay every August – but the tenses were tripping her up, and he was staring at the gravel, eyebrows knitted in hopefully concentration rather than irritation. 'Oh, it's difficult to explain in my awful Spanish!' she ended, with a grin.

Cue the indulgent smiles she was accustomed to, on and off camera – but they weren't happening here.

'In Ingleesh.'

She started again, but halfway through, the boy came out again, making a worrying rush with an outstretched hand towards her leg. Vicente quickly took his arm, seemed to be talking calmly but firmly to him, but the boy wailed, twisted, and flapped his hands in frustration.

Andie bent down to the boy. 'Listen, did you know... did you know there's a...' What was the Spanish for swing? 'Something marvellous in the big fig tree over there?' She waved her arm at the tangled garden; it could well be they never discovered it when they were here before.

His little face relaxed for a moment.

'It's a...' She swung her hand from side to side.

'*Un columpio,*' Vicente translated for the boy.

'You just have to cut some plants a little to go to it!' she said in Spanish.

The boy started pulling at his father's arm and pointing into the garden. Vicente promised him they would find a gardener to come and...

'*I'm* a gardener,' Andie said, back in English, her heart beating. 'If you have tools in there...' She pointed to the shed. '*I* can do it.'

'No, no,' Vicente said, shaking his head. 'It is strong work.'

'I *am* strong. I'm a gardener. *Profesional.*' He still looked utterly unconvinced, the macho sod. 'I'm even on a television programme, as a gardener,' she added in desperation.

He raised his eyebrows. 'But why do you want to do this? You are on holidays.'

'Because my grandmother's garden means everything to me. It changed my life.' And hopefully it would change her life again.

The boy continued to pull at his father's arm; it looked like he couldn't speak.

He muttered something soothing to the boy, then turned to Andie. 'If there are things you need in the...' He pointed to the shed.

'If not, I have a friend who could maybe let me use some of his.'

'Okay. But I will pay you for this. Come early, before it is too hot. Just an hour. Maybe for a few days. We will see. But... only if it doesn't make the leg worse,' he said, pointing to her bandage.

She was going to work in Grandie's garden. She struggled to contain herself; a burst of manic happiness in this place could be more than either of these two could cope with. 'I'll be careful, and it'll be fine.'

6

Tuesday 7th August

'Not too early, am I?' Ben asked with a grin. He was wearing his green uniform Botanical Garden T-shirt and shorts, like when she first met him.

'No – perfect! Just need to switch the coffee on and set the toaster off. Come and sit down.' She'd laid the table in the kitchen.

He pointed towards the balcony. 'Lovely out there. Shouldn't we—'

She smiled with gritted teeth.

'Ah... okay! Perhaps wouldn't look good at eight fifteen in the morning. I get you. Well, it *would* be good, but... bit revealing.'

Heavens, what did *that* mean? *What* would be good? She was going to have to somehow let her age drop into the conversation somewhere. She busied herself setting out the breakfast.

'Wow, this'll set us up,' he said, helping himself to boiled eggs, avocado, tomatoes, and toast and eyeing the croissants. 'Those gardens of ours won't know what's hit them! Although I'd rather join you in yours – a lot better hourly pay than I'm getting.'

'Really? Well, I suppose Vicente was just guessing at the rate.'

'No, he's paying top rate for what he's got – a TV garden designer!'

She put a hand over her face.

'I don't know why you didn't tell me.'

'Uh… partly because I'm probably *not* one anymore.'

'But there'll be something else, you'll see. I had a look; you've *got* something, Andie. Something else'll come up.'

'I honestly think I'm happier just designing for my boss's company, which I've continued part-time. Anyway… what's in that bag?'

'Ah yes. The tools are in the van – I'll put them in your car in a moment – and I brought an old towel to put on the back seat. But I thought I'd bring these up to show you – some clothes you could use, so you don't ruin your own. You need *trousers*, or you'll unzip that leg of yours.'

Andie held up the two pairs of loose, tie-dye trousers against herself – one in greens, one in blues. 'Bit glam – but they'll work. Thanks! Where did you…?'

'Let's just say, you're doing me a favour, finally getting them out of my wardrobe!'

'Oh, I see! Oh dear.'

'Don't worry, it was a couple of summers ago now.'

She pulled out a couple of T-shirts that were probably shrunken ones of his. 'Great, thanks so much. And oh look, the colours go with the trousers! And what's…' A pair of long-arm gardening gloves with the botanical garden's agave logo on them. 'Ah!'

'They won't know and if they did they wouldn't mind for a week or so. There's bound to be some really prickly buggers in there.'

'Okay! Thanks, Ben, this is brilliant.'

They moved on to the nectarines, croissants, and apricot jam while he told her a few cactus injury tales from work, and then she got up to take their empty plates to the sink. She'd been looking forward to wearing *Grandie's* gardening gloves; unbelievably, they were still there in the shed – as were several of her tools, and even her old straw hat. She'd gasped, exclaimed she couldn't believe it. How could they still be here, after at least three families had lived in the house since her grandmother? Vicente hadn't responded to her excitement, but politely answered the direct question by telling her that it was common in Spain to leave belongings behind in a house when you sell it. Then he'd gone back to staring at her with knitted brows, as if she were a very strange specimen – or a person keeping him from whatever he'd been doing, because he'd then closed the shed door, asked if nine o'clock was okay, and abruptly turned and strode back into the house.

'And you're going to be okay there? Alone with a strange man in the garden? I suppose the housekeeper'll be around.'

'I'll be fine.'

'So, he seemed all right to you? You got on with him?'

'Yeah.' Probably not, and… no. Well, she didn't *not* get on with him – she couldn't say that; it was more a question of there being *no human communication whatsoever*. Just as you wouldn't say you hadn't got on with... an animal at the zoo. Yes, that was about it. The gap between them felt more than cultural; it was more like a glaring, staring inter-species one.

And yet... there was something about how he was with his son, Rafi – something she even noticed when half-conscious in his car: intuitive, patient, firm... but gentle. You had to have a bit of awe for somebody who seemed so at ease with the burden of rearing a child like that. The least the two of them deserved was an accessible and working garden swing.

With a second coffee, they went through the possible snakes she might be seeing – with the predicable joke that Vicente was the only one she had to worry about. Then they packed up her car and Spanish-kissed each other goodbye with vague plans for pizza later in the week.

She drove off – and once again felt like she was going to arrive too soon, without having time to prepare herself. Prepare herself for what? She was going to *garden*, for heaven's sake; it wasn't as if Señor Serioso was likely to draw up a garden chair and converse with her while she worked.

As it happened, he didn't seem to be there at all. The gates opened, she drove straight in through the tunnel of arching trees, parked in the drive, and was greeted by the half-smiling woman. A small white car – definitely not the one Vicente had taken her to hospital in – was the only other vehicle there, although it was possible Vicente had put his in the garage at the side of the house. The woman showed her the hook under the eaves of the shed where they kept the key, and another to an outside loo – perhaps so that tomorrow her visit didn't need to involve anyone at all – and left her to get on with it.

Well! She realised she was accustomed to arriving on set – or even, since the show, at a client's garden – to a shower of greetings, admiration, and a choice of drinks and snacks. Here she was just an odd girl with a thing about her grandmother's garden, but that was okay.

She put shears, long-handled loppers, and long-armed gloves into the battered old wheelbarrow; put on the tool belt for the secateurs and her water bottle; and after shaking out any possible inhabitants, smiled to herself and put on Grandie's gloves.

She looked along the now sparse and weedy gravel path and could almost see Grandie up ahead, hands on hips, saying, *So! You took your time!*

I suppose I thought it would make me miserable to see it, but I hadn't expected you to be so... here.

Despite my ashes being in some dreary crematorium garden in West London, you mean.

I'm sorry about that. I did try to persuade Mum and Dad that you'd rather be here in the garden.

Nah, made no difference – as you can see!

God, she was going to have to snap out of this or they'd come out after an hour and see that, just as Vicente suspected, she wasn't strong enough to get anywhere at all with these plants. So, first up, the beautiful but beastly bougainvillea, totally blocking the path.

Use those long-armed gloves, you twit, Grandie was saying.

Oh, okay.

She remembered Grandie swearing as she cut herself on

69

the vicious spines, so she changed gloves and set to work. *Bougies*, Grandie used to call them, and she had one in every colour she could get her hands on, but this crimson-red one – Big Bella – was in full sun and always the giant. She cut a rather enchanting tunnel through where the path had been and, standing back to admire the effect, could almost feel Grandie pat her on the back.

Leaving a large heap of red and green to deal with later, she attacked the next obstacle: a shower of rocks that had tumbled down from the old Lookout Post. Or the Walnut Whip, as Andie had called it: you walked round and round the conical lump of rosemary and russet rock until you got to the all-seeing bench at the top... but it was now totally overgrown and impassable. She lifted the rocks on the path to one side, and gasped as she saw a small scorpion scuttle away, just as Ben had warned her.

Onwards. Jesus, the size of Eve these days! The Eve's pin cactus she thought was enormous then had now totally outgrown the stone wall Grandie had built around her. She carefully lopped off a few branches that could scratch that poor little boy as he trotted past. It was hard, hot work; she stopped and sat down on the bench under the fig tree, swigged from her bottle, and wiped the stinging sweat from her eyes on her T-shirt sleeve.

It was already gone ten, but she just had to cut back a few fig branches so she could at least see the swing... there it was. She released it from where it had been hooked over a lower branch, let it go to and fro with that old familiar squeak-squeak. She pulled hard on the ropes, then tentatively tried her weight on it. She'd happily swung here like this so many times… *I can hear where you are!* Grandie would say…

Twenty past; she really needed to stop. She walked back along the path, past all the mountains of clippings she was going to have to bag up. With that and the further work needed on the fig tree and Eve, there was probably another two hours' work to do. Two more mornings of an hour each. Two more visits with Grandie. Maybe three.

Back on the driveway, she noticed that the housekeeper had left a now warm water bottle and a packet of nuts on the stone bench. How come she hadn't been shown that? This seemed to be a household where speaking was kept to the absolute minimum. She tipped the peanuts into her mouth, enjoyed their super-saltiness, then went to the dark wooden door and knocked.

The woman opened it – quickly, as if she'd been watching out for her – and Andie told her she'd finished for today, but would like to come back tomorrow.

A nod suggested that was in order, and a further one, while opening the door wider, seemed to be inviting her in.

Andie came out of the heat into the hallway, where as a child she would run in and lie down on the terracotta tiles to cool down.

The woman said she was fetching *dinero*, money – or did she say *dueño*, the owner? Except he wasn't the owner, he was only renting. She gazed through the door at the end of the hall to the old living room and its balcony with a view for miles over the bay… until she felt a soft but uncomfortable tapping, through her green baggy trousers, on her wound.

She looked down. It was being kissed – or more likely *pecked* – by the beak of a cuddly toy bird. An exotic green one, camouflaging nicely with the trousers, and with a shiny black head like its owner.

'Um...'

The bird was made to look up at her, and when the boy pressed on its chest, out came a realistic jaunty little two-tone chirrup.

'Oh! That's lov— *Que bonito*!' She then tried to explain that she had a bird at home that did the same, but a different type.

He looked up but slightly past her with his wide, dark eyes.

'Mine is a robin,' she said in Spanish, hoping 'robin' was one of those Spanish words that was just the same as English but with an acute accent and stress on the vowel.

Judging from the boy's knitted brows, it wasn't.

'Er... a bird with a red...' She patted her chest, and was delighted to see his little face briefly break into a gappy smile.

He set the bird chirping again, held it up to her and said '*Carbonero!*'

As she repeated the word and smiled back, the housekeeper behind her was doing the same, patting him and gabbling something enthusiastic that unfortunately she couldn't understand.

Then with a fuller smile than she'd seen before, the woman introduced herself as María Ángeles and asked for Andie's name, before giving her an envelope and saying thank you, they'd see her tomorrow.

Back at the apartment, she discovered that *carbonero*

was a great tit. A canny, funny bird as well as a looker – as maybe Rafi could be, in his own way, one day.

She started stripping off to get into the shower – then saw the envelope, half out of the unzipped tool bag, and picked it up. On the front it said *Jardinera*, underlined. Female gardener. Then *Como te llamas?* He wanted to know her name. Well, that was a start. She took out the generous notes and put them in her purse, even though she would happily have done this for nothing, and poked the envelope into the paper bag she was using for recycling. Then pulled it out again. He had very large, whirly-elegant writing for a miserable sod.

7

She turned up a bit early, with stupid butterflies about Vicente being there, wanting to know her name – but was greeted by María Ángeles again. Followed by a smiling-to-himself Rafi, coming out of the kitchen with a piece of toast in one hand and a fluffy pink flamingo with dangly legs under the other arm.

'Oh! He's lovely!' Andie said, in Spanish. 'I saw… birds like these yesterday, look…' She got out her phone, found a photo she'd taken of flamingos at the salt flats, and held it towards him – but he made a little growl and flinched. María Ángeles whispered that Rafi didn't like people coming near his food.

'Ah… okay.'

On her own in the shed this time, she could look around and see if there was anything else of Grandie's. Ha! Hanging up and unreachable due to a broken folding table, the 'his and hers' blue and red secateurs that Grandie had bought to stop her and the gardener arguing about whose was

74

whose. Gardener? José Luis was probably nearly as old as Grandie, but when Andie's parents had suggested getting someone younger, Grandie wouldn't hear of it. Apparently he'd worked there even when Grandpa was still alive, and his widely-grinning, lined face felt so much like part of the garden that a small Andie had once asked if he lived in it.

She shook herself back into the present, and reached up to unhook the broom for the path – managing to knock two jars of nails or screws off the shelf with it. Fortunately they landed on an old doormat, but they had spilled their contents all over the place. Damn, why was she always so clumsy? But then, it didn't help that shelves and cupboards were always too bloody high for her. She considered leaving them there. Vicente wasn't likely to notice; she couldn't imagine him getting his elegant, flamenco hands dirty with some DIY. Hm, but if he came in here to fetch something... She bent down and started refilling the jars, cursing that it was too sweaty here to be bothering with this. Good God, there was a second, lower shelf of these jars of bits; you would have thought one of the occupiers of this house would have thought, sod this, let's buy a toolbox and get rid of...

Oh. Among the jars there was a golden, Twinings Earl Grey tea tin. All the way from England, one of the things Grandie wanted bringing over every year; it had to be hers. She picked it up and looked inside – just garden centre plant tags, by the look of it. She put the mostly refilled jars back on the second shelf and put Grandie's on the higher one, where it could be admired – even if only by her, for today and maybe tomorrow.

Then she set to work – further control of Eve, to stop

her scratching Rafi with her prickly arms, and then clipping back more fig branches and sanding down the swing seat. She cooled off with her water on the bench, smiling as she imagined little Rafi sitting on the swing – possibly with his bright pink flamingo still under his arm. How many macho flamenco dancers would buy their son one of those? Hats off to him for that anyway.

Movement in the garden, nearer to the cliff.

Her heart thudded. Surely wild boars couldn't get in here? Maybe through the rounders' pitch, down the slope and... She stood up and looked around for trees to climb – but she couldn't spend her precious time here paralysed with fear. She needed to see what it was. Or more likely, *who* it was, for heaven's sake.

She pushed through the old swingball circle, now invaded by rubber plants and acacias, to the dilapidated and weedy amphitheatre. Carefully climbing up a couple of rows, she could see... ah. Not a wild boar. Wild, but... *beautiful*. Vicente, over on the diving rock, in swimmer's trunks, stretching his perfect statue of a self in preparation for a dive. Then swinging his arms up and over to be airborne, arcing, his body tight, toes pointed, perfection, a tiny clip of a sound on entry, as if the water was grateful to receive him. She realised she was holding her breath.

He was surfacing. She could just possibly be visible from the sea, and it wouldn't look good to be standing there, watching with her mouth open. She went back through the bushes, but this time enjoying the feathered leaves of the acacia in her hand, the stroke of the thick rubber tree leaves on her arms. Going back for the broom, she swept the path, rhythmically, enjoying the control of her movements, like how she *used* to feel when gardening, and hadn't for some time. The dancing gardener, Shefali once called her.

She'd be back tomorrow, unless they told her not to worry about getting rid of the piles of debris, but she wondered if she could suggest another garden-clearing project for them. The Lookout was too dangerous for the little chap, but the clearing for the swingball? Maybe, if she could find the Spanish words.

It was gone ten, and time to show them what she'd done. Well, Rafi and María Ángeles anyway, because Vicente was probably still in the sea. Maybe that was just as well; having seen him like that, she'd find it hard to look him in the eye without blushing. What? Oh dear. Surely she wasn't developing a little bit of a thing about this exquisitely miserable man? Hilarious really: in Johnny she constantly looked for moments of seriousness, and here she was looking for signs of levity – a small, cartoon fish on a T-shirt, a pink flamingo, some whirly writing – in Señor Serioso. Although why she cared, in either case, was a total mystery; one was about to be told how they both knew it was over, and the other was a blatant non-starter.

The door was open, so she called out *hola* and pushed through the fly curtain beads to find Rafi and María Ángeles getting ready for the beach.

Feeling a little put out that they didn't look desperate to come and check out the swing, she tentatively said it was ready; did they want to see?

They did; it seemed they thought it would take longer to do. They followed her out, and then Rafi trotted and jumped along in front of them in a way that made Andie glad she'd done so much on the sides of the path.

He made a little noise when he saw the swing, and got up onto it, his legs barely long enough to reach the ground. While María Ángeles pushed him, she enjoyed seeing that little gappy smile again.

A low voice said something to Rafi, mentioning her name. Vicente had somehow, panther-like, crept up behind her.

'*Papi!*' Rafi called out.

Vicente repeated what he'd said.

'Thank you, Andie!' Rafi called out, as his father took over the pushing and he went higher. Then looking round at his father, he seemed troubled, and Vicente slowed the swing to a stop. The boy said a word and pointed to his father's arms, which had a long scratch and several smaller ones.

'You look like you've been in a battle with a lion,' Andie said.

A half-smile. 'Yes. The path is bad.' He patted Rafi's shoulder and reassured him. 'He hates... *heridas*,' he said, pointed to his arm, and Andie's leg. 'Hates, but also he is fascinated.'

'Yes.' She could hardly have missed that. 'Well... maybe I could sort out that path too.'

'The path to the place for diving. Yes, if you want to, this would be good. Thank you, Andie.'

'*Oh my God, where are you?!*' Shefali had written in response to the WhatsApped photo of Andie's ornate silver platter of little cakes in the *tetería*.

'*Moroccan tea shop in Almería city. Just underneath the*

romantic Alcazaba castle thing on the hill. As near as I'm getting today – too hot for it.'

'Let's hope for a cloudy day when I'm there then.'

'You're coming??!!' Andie hadn't heard from her the day before, and had started to think either the brother or husband, or both, were going to stop her coming.

'Saturday, flying back Thursday morning! Hope that's okay, now you've got yourself a flamenco gardening job.'

'Of COURSE it is!!! And the garden's only an hour in the morning and will probably have stopped by then.' And if it had, having Shefali there was going to be the perfect way to take her mind off it.

'Did you sort out the swing? Did the little boy like it?'

'Yes!'

'And did Vicente give you a kiss on each cheek for it?'

'NO!!!'

'Very poor form. And now what?'

'And now I'm going to do another path,' Andie wrote, not wanting to go into a discussion of Vicente's diving.

'Aha. There's still hope then!'

Andie sent an eyes-to-heaven emoji.

'Seriously though, this is the ultimate Challenging Gardens project. Wonderful thing to do for that troubled man and boy. Very special. Now get on and eat those cakes. You deserve every one of them.'

Then Shefali's patient arrived, and Andie enjoyed the rest of her cakes while looking for a flamenco show for her friend, unable to believe her luck when she saw there was one on Saturday in the beautiful Cathedral Square she'd walked through earlier.

★

After a sofa siesta, she worked on her design for the Hampton Court Palace Garden Festival display, now taking shape nicely in the app – and sent off the latest version to Gerard. She was just finishing her tea, when he called.

'Andie! Not at the beach? Oh no, I suppose…'

It was great to hear that plummy old jolly voice, rather than just read the exclamation-marked emails. 'Oh, hello! No, no, I always go for a bit, paddle if it's not too wavy, and then loll on a sunbed under an umbrella. Hopefully next Monday they'll say I can swim! So how are you doing?'

'Ah good. Me? Fine. All good here.'

'And Hughie's finding the time to help you out okay? I still can't believe your ex-rival is now shacked up with you.'

'I know, I know. But actually… we're not going to be garden design rivals anymore – we've decided to pool our resources and become Summerby *Snow* Garden Design! Sounds brilliant doesn't it, like it was always meant to be!'

'Oh!' Actually it sounded like a weird oxymoron of a company, pulling in opposite directions – and wasn't it a bit soon in their relationship to do this? Even more of a commitment than—

'And before you ask, yes, we're getting married!'

'Gerard! Oh… I'm so happy for you! When? Where?'

'October the sixth, at Hampton Court House, right opposite the palace and gardens! I told Hughie we have to wait; I have to have Andie back for it.'

'What? I'll be back at the end of the month.'

'Well, just in case you want to stay on. Your garden's fine, by the way. I watered it yesterday. As for the Hampton

Court garden design – Andie, you're surpassing yourself, and I think we'll have to put it in *your* name, not the company's.'

'No, I'm not hearing of that, I told you. So glad you like it. But I'm not sure we can call it the *Mediterranean* garden anymore. Bit too semi-desert Almería.'

'The *Almerían* Garden?'

'Not sure anybody knows where Almería is.'

'Er... the *Spaghetti Western* Garden?' She imagined his face creasing into a grin. 'Now you've got that bit of *corral*.'

'Gerard, that's a bit of *amphitheatre*, as labelled! Although you're right, it *could* be a corral.'

'But seriously, all that terracotta among the planting – and those urns! I *want* those urns. Can we import them?'

'They're made by the family of the lovely woman who runs the shop. Don't see why not.'

'We could end up importing them for clients. A whole new side business could develop – giving you a reason to pop over there all the time to liaise.'

'Mm, sounds good to me!'

'Anyway, keep up the good work, but off you go to the beach now. Don't know what's happening in Grandma's old garden there, but it seems to be doing you a world of good.'

8

She was just about to drive off to the garden when her phone rang. 'Marcelo, hello!'

'Good morning! Ben say you like use my er... *máquina* for to cut...?'

'Your garden shredder! Oh, yes please!'

'I can bring it after half hour? You can have for some days, a week, *no problema*.'

'Brilliant! *Estupendo!*'

'Ben told me of what you do for the boy, is very good.'

When she'd briefly bumped into Ben on the beach, he'd loved hearing about the swing – but she'd then learnt that, like his father, Rafi had been the subject of rumours.

'I don't believe the story about him,' she said. 'He looks *exactly* like Vicente.'

'I don' believe neither, Andie. Stupid peoples saying this! See you soon.'

She drove off up the hill, trying to forget the gossip Ben had told her: that his wife could have conceived Rafi from an affair with Vicente's apparently unbelievably handsome and charming young Uncle Juanito, a frequent visitor when Vicente was away on tour. Apparently the police had even looked into it, as a possible motive for him to push Estefanía from the cliff in anger, but Vicente had refused to do a paternity test. Well, why *should* he do one? It would have felt like an insult to his poor dead wife. And if Marcelo didn't believe any of this, with a brother in the Guardia Civil who was involved in the case, she certainly wasn't going to. Poor Vicente, having to cope with this speculation while grieving for his wife; it wasn't surprising that he wanted to keep to himself.

She parked and waved at María Ángeles and Rafi through the kitchen window. They looked like they were still having breakfast – maybe Vicente was there too, out of view – so she decided to let them finish before interrupting to tell them about Marcelo dropping off the shredder. Meanwhile, she'd get her tools out of the shed.

She noticed immediately. It was there, but not quite where or how she'd left it: the golden tin now casually angled, its Royal Appointment sensibilities flinching at the proximity of a dusty jar of wall plugs. She straightened it, ran her finger along the bobbly emblem on the lid. María Ángeles had probably come in here for something, picked it up to admire it and put it back again; no mystery really. Or maybe it was Vicente who had done that, because she was fairly sure there used to be two windsurfing boards, and now there was only one.

She heard a car coming into the drive. Wasn't Marcelo going to be half an hour? She came out of the shed and, sure enough, there was the battered white van with the red writing on, Marcelo grinning as he came to a stop – and Lucía's little round face beside him.

'This is great, thank you so much,' she said, as he lifted the shredder out of the back of the van. 'Helping Daddy today?' she asked Lucía, in Spanish.

Lucía shrugged, giving Andie a resigned smile, but while her father was explaining about how she was with him because Beatriz had had to cover for a fellow nurse who was off sick, Lucía's face suddenly lit up and she jumped out of the van. 'Is it true Andie made a secret swing deep in your garden?' she asked.

Andie followed Lucía's gaze over to Rafi, standing next to a worried-looking María Ángeles at the front door.

Andie quickly explained that Marcelo was just here for a minute to lend her a machine that would make her work faster in the garden, while Marcelo tried to persuade Lucía to get back into the van. But some kind of wordless communication had gone on between the children, because they'd sneaked behind the van and started dashing down the path, Rafi leading the way, towards the swing.

María Ángeles and Marcelo called their names, but the children just squealed and ran on. There was nothing for the adults to do but follow them, and when they caught up, try to stop themselves laughing as they watched slim little Rafi pulling back a heavily Lucía-laden swing seat to get her started.

Lucía was soon whooping as she swung higher and higher, but looked at Rafi and then put down her foot to slow herself to a stop. She moved over and patted the small bit of remaining seat next to her. 'Come and sit here – we won't go too high,' she said.

Rafi glanced at her wide-eyed and then looked down at the path, toeing the gravel.

'D'you speak Spanish?' she asked him.

'He understands everything,' María Ángeles put in, 'he's just…'

Lucía nodded several times. 'I know. Like my friend Doina Romanescu at school,' she said to Marcelo, then smiled at Rafi and patted the seat again. 'Come on.'

Rafi didn't look too certain, but came over and sat next to her, and as María Ángeles told them to hold on tight as she pushed, they laughed and kicked their legs.

Marcelo, like Andie, was anxiously looking to see if Vicente might be around, and started trying to persuade Lucía that it was time to go. Bribing her with a hidden bag of fruit chews, Marcelo eventually managed to get Lucía back to the car, and Rafi managed an 'adios!' with his wave as they drove out.

'How sweet!' Andie said, smiling at María Ángeles, but although she got a nod and a quick smile back, the woman started looking worried again. Andie looked at her watch. 'I'll make a start.'

After shredding the piles of debris from the previous days, Andie had a look at her next task.

From the olive tree bench, the path curved around the yellow bougainvillea leaning against the house and then through dwarf palms, rosemary, lavender, and other low shrubs towards the steps going down to the beach some ten metres below. This path must have been well used by previous residents; it had been cut well back, and its sandy surface was worn with use. A little way along, however, the path forking from it to go along the cliff towards the diving rock was a different story; you'd think Vicente was the first to use it since her father.

She started walking down it carefully, remembering her father turning to remind her that she could watch but then had to go straight back to Grandie. There'd been a high gate at the end – and a fence along the path – presumably to keep an adventurous little Andie from the edge. She was yet to see if the gate was still there, but the fencing had gone. There was no need for it; nobody would climb over Grandie's low stone wall to cross over to the cliff edge now, through all those giant sproutings of sword-like *Agave americana* leaves. She paused to admire the woody flower spike they each sent up, branching delicately at the top to produce their tiny yellow flowers. The emblems of Almería, gracing every postcard against a blue-sky background.

They're called PITAS, Grandie seemed to be saying beside her, *as if you could whistle with them. Remember?*

Certainly she remembered something about people making instruments out of them, among other things. She'd seen painted ones in pots in little front gardens in the village. Grandie always used to use one as a Christmas tree…

She needed to get on. There were lots of spent *pitas* leaning over the path, or totally collapsed across it and needing to be hurdled or ducked under; this must have been how Vicente had scratched himself. Turning back to fetch the saw from the shed, this time she looked past the agave *pita* silhouettes and out to sea, towards what she'd only half noticed before: a windsurfer, slim, strong but graceful… and now heading towards the beach. Black hair tied back. *Vicente.* Well, that explained the strength of those arms she'd fallen into that night.

Then she couldn't see him; he must have come up onto the beach. Maybe he'd soon climb up the steps. Flustered, she tried to work out whether she wanted to encounter him where the two paths met, his perfect body wet and glistening from the sea, or whether she should quickly fetch the handsaw and get back here out of sight. She decided on the latter, and in her rush, soon had a collection of scratches similar to Vicente's.

Back with the handsaw, she could hear Grandie telling her to be careful; the poor woman had learnt the hard way that these agaves had toxic sap. Mostly, however, Andie was just cutting off the harmless dead poles. It was taking ages, partly because she was treating them with ridiculous respect. She'd chopped up disintegrated ones of course, but also made what looked like a logging pile – asking to be used in some creation, a little wigwam perhaps – and a smaller, carefully laid out collection of fully branched poles that deserved to be painted and decorating that inner courtyard.

It was way past her hour, and she'd drunk all her water. She took off her gloves and put her tools and the shredder in the shed, looked forward to a shower and then a little trip out in the car to visit the flamingos in the salt flats again, or maybe this time drive up to the lighthouse. She knocked on the door.

It was opened, after a few minutes but very abruptly, by Vicente. Now in dark shorts and T-shirt – no cartoon fish or any other sign of levity – and looking seriously annoyed.

'Why did you bring your friend to my house?'

'He's a builder, lending me—'

'Why did you bring your *builder* to my house, without asking me?' Eyebrows furiously forced together, eyes wild.

'I'm sorry. I was going—'

'You are not on television programme now!'

She looked down at the gravel, unable to meet those eyes anymore. Then over at the olive tree bench, Big Bella, the top of the giant fig, taking them in maybe for the last time, because he was now rattling on in Spanish about privacy, and something – or somebody – *not working*.

'D'you mean...' She looked up – but he'd disappeared. Like some kind of theatre trick. What? Was she supposed to leave? Her heart patted away.

He was back, holding out an envelope.

She put up a stop-sign hand.

'*No, no, tómalo,*' he said, flapping it at her rudely.

She took it, wanting to say she would have done the work for nothing; it was enough just to be here with memories of Grandie, see Rafi's smile on the swing... María Ángeles must have told him about Marcelo, but didn't she mention how Rafi seemed to get on so well with Lucía?

'D'you... want me to finish the other path?' she asked in Spanish, not quite managing to stop a tremble in her voice. She didn't want it to end like this.

'That has already been agreed,' he said in Spanish, as if they were locked into some formal contract.

'Okay... good. I'm sorry about this. *Hasta mañana.*'

Back at the apartment, she closed her eyes in the shower, heart still beating too fast, keen to wash off the memory of that angry face. But soon *she* was starting to feel angry – about his over-reaction to a builder's van in his drive, for God's sake, but also with herself, for letting him down.

It wasn't like she didn't well know the feeling of people invading her privacy – even if in her case it was usually only online or in a pile of post screened by her agent. Anyway, *hasta mañana*. Until tomorrow.

Andie wiped pizza from her mouth, looked out at the golden beach now striped with the long shadows of the promenade's *Washingtonia* palms, and back at Ben. 'This is *such* a treat.'

'And it's *my* treat,' he said, smiling at her.

'*Absolutely* not. You've done far too much for me already; mine, and that's final.'

'Hm…' He scratched his chin. 'Not sure how we're going to resolve this… other than doing this more often and taking turns?'

Andie smiled then busied herself cutting her last slice. 'Well… yes, although it looks like you're quite in demand, so I wouldn't want to… er…' At least three young Spanish girls had stopped by to say hello to them on their restaurant pavement table – with varying degrees of friendliness and suspicion; no wonder he'd suggested eating inside.

He laughed and shook his head. 'I'm single. I can choose my pizza companion!'

'I'm sure, but you have to admit that last one looked a bit put out.'

He shrugged. 'I'm always honest with them. They just don't want to believe it.'

'So… you've been here three years but… haven't been in a relationship?'

He nodded his head slowly. 'That's right. None of them

have ever matched up to Florrie. You know, the girl at college I was telling you about.'

'Oh… and she really didn't want to come out here, even just to visit?'

'No. She went off to do an extra diploma in London, and that's her scene now. We keep in contact, but we want different things. Nothing would persuade me to go to back to freezing, soggy UK, let alone *London*.' He pulled a disgusted face, then laughed. 'Oh God, I always do this with English visitors, forgetting their *lives* are there. Sorry!'

'No, no, I can see your point. I mean, if you want to *garden*, spend the majority of your life outdoors, why choose to live in a country with such an utterly miserable climate? I often think my perpetual grimace at the elements is going to wrinkle me way before my time.'

'What wrinkles?' he said, laughing. 'Doesn't seem to be doing you *any* harm. Although obviously you *should* consider joining me here in sunny Almería. Just think, no more dreading January: here it's like a sunny English late spring – just glorious.'

'Gawd, yes I had read that.'

'But then you have ties in England, and a good job…'

'Well, some of that's up in the air now. As for Johnny and me… we also want different things.'

'It's over?' he asked with sweet concern.

Just in case he thought anything more than friendship was possible between them, she considered lying – but that didn't seem right after he'd bared his heart about Florrie.

'Not yet, but it's heading that way.' Possibly soon; they hadn't been in contact now for three days, as if both were waiting for the other to make the break.

'He's jealous about Vicente?'

'What? No, no.'

'I mean, he's only got to google and check him out...' He raised his eyebrows.

She looked at him, waiting for him to continue. 'He can't, doesn't know his full name. In fact, nor do I.'

'Vicente Vargas Ortega. You should have a look, if you like dancing. Bound to be something on there. Probably also something about him and La Soleá.'

'Where's that?' she asked, thinking it sounded like a flamenco club.

He laughed. '*Who*, Andie! La Soleá is a flamenco singer diva. Loves being interviewed all over the place. Think they've been an item for a while now – or at least, as far as *she's* concerned; flamenco men are absolute animals, apparently.'

'Oh.' She realised she'd been sitting there with her mouth open in surprise.

'And of course, Vicente's a *flamenco* with a temper too – even the great La Soleá might not be a match for that.'

An image of Vicente's wild, dark eyes came back to her. He hadn't shouted, but the steeliness of his anger was somehow even more frightening.

'It's good you got to see that today,' he said, patting her hand.

'*Good?*'

'Yes. I knew even just hearing about Marcelo being there would set him off.' He put a hand to his face, looked down.

'Hang on. You... *arranged* it? Come to think of it, you must have a shredder yourself, could have brought it round rather than sending Marcelo in to... provoke a reaction!'

He smiled with gritted teeth and put his hands up as if he'd been rumbled. It was a cute gesture, he was a cute chap, and had been so kind – but this was out of order.

She glared at him, not returning his smile.

He put his hand on hers again. 'I'm sorry. I just thought you needed to see him as he is. I'm worried you're just a bit taken with him – and don't want to see you get hurt.'

'Hurt? Look, I'm not here to get taken with anyone; nobody – other than that wild boar, and the odd agave – is going to hurt me. I'm here for the garden, which means everything to me, even though I do realise that sounds completely crazy.'

'It *isn't* crazy; I love the way you feel like that, and I'll do anything I can to help you. But be careful, because you might not be the only one who feels that garden might hold memories and secrets.'

9

Friday 10th August

She turned up as María Ángeles and Rafi were coming out of the door, leaving for an appointment somewhere. Vicente was giving Rafi a squeeze, some friendly instructions, and tucking a stray flamingo leg into the boy's backpack.

Then they were gone – and so was his sweetness. 'Come.'

She followed him to the kitchen. He seemed to have just showered in something dark and piney. His hair – in one of those bun things favoured by footballers, flamenco dancers or men who'd given up on haircuts – was shiny and blacker than ever. He would have been *all* serious black, had his neat *culo* not been in a pair of swim shorts covered in *tiny parrots*. She raised her gaze just as he turned around.

'*Siéntate,*' he said, pointing to a chair.

She sat down. Bloody hell, was there really any more to say about yesterday? The kitchen was white and sleek now; only the old wooden wall clock remained. Under it was a pinboard covered in Rafi's pictures of the garden or the sea – watercolour, felt pen, crayon… and an interesting

93

pencil one on the back of an envelope, with a big bird in the foreground and a smaller one flying over a cliff full of what could be clumpy agaves.

Vicente was saying something she didn't catch, his voice low and quiet. She turned her head to find him holding out a can of lemon tea in one hand and a bottle of iced coffee in the other.

'Oh!' Good grief: *hospitality*. She pointed to the can.

He poured the drinks into glasses and joined her at the table. 'Andie...'

Hands together as if in prayer – or about to fire someone. If that was the case, she was going to go full tribunal, because she was only trying to—

'I'm sorry about yesterday. I have been thinking, maybe is my fault. You don't have my number, so you can't send a message to ask about the builder.'

'Oh...'

'And I was *too* angry. Can you pardon me?' Head on one side, mouth nearest she'd seen to a smile.

She put up a hand. 'Look... it's fine, I completely understand, really.'

Then he *did* smile. Like sun coming out after a storm. Wide, softening those scary dark eyes, and revealing a surprisingly neat row of teeth, for the wild creature she thought he was.

Finding herself staring and grinning back at him for far too long, she took a sip of her lemony drink. 'This is delicious.'

'I know, but Rafi can't have it. The sugar makes him...' He twirled his finger in the air.

'Ah, yes,' she said, afraid it would do the same to her;

full concentration was needed to deal with this man. She pointed to the pinboard. 'He seems to love being here.'

'He made these in Almería. It surprised me, that he remembers so much. This is why I returned here for August – I was thinking it could help him.'

'And… *has* it helped?'

'Yes. He's talking a little more, and more… *tranquilo*.'

Calmer. 'Oh, that's good,' she said, nodding, wanting to ask more. What was wrong with Rafi? Did he go to a regular school? 'He writes well. How old is he?' She pointed to where he'd written his name and the Spanish for beach.

'Seven this month. Yes, he has just started to write a few words – although he still says no to numbers.' He tapped his temple with a finger. 'The brain is all working, just… different; the doctors said he was a little *autista*. But when his mother died four years ago… he stopped talking.'

'Oh dear, I'm sorry… poor little thing. But… you should have seen him with Marcelo's daughter yesterday.'

'Yes, María Ángeles told me of Lucía, and Rafi wants her to see her again. I wanted to ask you, can you give me the father's number, so we can invite her?'

'Of course! I'm sure she'd love to come. She's a friendly, confident girl – happy to do all the talking if necessary!'

'*Perfecto.*' They get out their phones for him to take Marcelo's number, and then he gave her his number.

Well, who would have thought, Vicente was in her phone now, complete with WhatsApp profile selfie of him and Rafi with an ostrich.

'And yours?' he asked.

'Ah… yes.' She told him the numbers, for some reason feeling she had to give them in Spanish.

'Okay...' His face had clouded a little, as if he'd said too much. 'I need to work. See you later.' Then he did one of his theatrical disappearing acts through the other kitchen door, which went off to a room Grandie had used as a study, to do whatever he did now he didn't dance.

She washed up the glasses and, briefly stopping to peep into the old living room looking over the sea, she went out to get on with the path.

She was probably only halfway along, but now they were talking, almost friends, with phone numbers, it was surely more likely that he'd give her all the time she needed for it – and possibly more projects in the garden.

Just as she was thinking that, she reached the place where a path came into the cliff one all the way from the swing. Grandie loved making paths; it felt like every summer she and her parents came over, there was a new one. But as Grandie used to say, paths get quickly reclaimed unless you look after them, and that had definitely happened here.

She pushed through the lower branches of pines and rubber trees to see if the Secret Bench was still there... and breathed out heavily: it was. A wooden two-seater in its own little rocky clearing in a kink in the path, a lovely place to sit when the heat got too much, *'fresquito'* – cool – with its dense shade and breeze from the sea. Or a place to hide with someone, of course. Nobody would want to sit on it now, in that state, but maybe it could be mended, because how could you get rid of it when it had not just her and Nando's 'A+N', but several other initials... including 'E+J' followed by a kiss. Vicente's wife Estefanía and his Uncle Juanito? No, that was just more of Ana's negativity about Vicente, and anyway, it would have been pretty dumb to scratch that on here, if they were trying to have a secret affair. She shook her head, and then tried to see further through the branches. From memory, the path also went past the fairy statue – that her mother thought was 'just awful' – before reaching the fig tree swing.

Give them a nice little circuit to stroll, she could hear Grandie saying.

I know, that's what I'm thinking.

She went back to the '*pitas*' path; she might suggest it, but she needed to get *señor*'s route to his diving rock done first.

She sawed and dragged the dead giant flower spikes until she was out of water and energy, and decided to stop after just one more *pita*. It was a beauty, and rather than lay it down in the upcycling pile with the others, she stood it up against a eucalyptus trunk, looked up at its dried flowers, patted and stroked its smooth girth while trying to ignore the inevitable smutty comments Johnny would have made.

'You like it? *Pita* of Almería?'

Good God, Vicente had noiselessly padded up the path. 'I do,' she said, then pointed to the different piles to distract him away from her blushing cheeks. 'Those could be used for making something on the beach, perhaps? And these are ones you could paint. Especially this one. Maybe for your courtyard?'

A lopsided smile. 'I don't paint.'

'What, *never*?'

'Never in my life.'

'Really?' A first flat? An old chair? *Nothing ever?*

'Is that so bad?' he asked with an intense concern that made her want to laugh.

'Well... I suppose there are some things I've never done.'

'*Ah sí*, what things?'

There was quite a choice – mostly girly things like lipstick and high heels, but also...

'I've never used an oven.'

'*Qué?* You don't cook? How do you eat?'

'I can *boil* things,' she said indignantly, and when his eyebrows crinkled with confusion, she mimed holding a saucepan over some waggly-finger heat. 'Then there's Thai takeaway, and lots of jam sandwiches.'

His eyebrows went up. 'Jam? You don't make jam?'

'No!' Her feminist hackles started to rise. 'Why, do *you*?' she asked.

'Yes.'

'You make jam.' This conversation was becoming surreal.

He put a finger up, as if about to make an important point. 'At one time, maybe three years ago, I make more money from make jam than music.'

'You make jam and music. How lovely! What kind? Of... er... both?'

He listed a number of Spanish fruits and their combinations, followed by a number of music styles – mainly flamenco combined with pop, blues or jazz.

She looked over at the study. 'Ha! Wonderful. But how d'you...?' She pointed over to the house.

'Most of the time I play everything myself. Here I only have some equipment, but it is enough until October, and sometimes I go to Almería for recording.'

'October?'

'I have just spoken with the owner... we will stay another

month. Even I will have to drive every day to take Rafi to the school in Almería. Oh, and she is happy we are doing the garden!'

'Thank goodness for that – I was wondering! Actually, now you're going to be here longer, there's a pretty path going from here to the swing, so you and Rafi could walk round in a circle. It's got a bench and a lovely statue. Would you—'

'Yes! If you want to do it, that would be very good!'

'And… maybe I could ask Marcelo to help me mend the bench? If he's going to bring Lucía?'

'Of course.' He looked along the path, then over towards the top of the giant fig. 'Your grandmother *made* this garden, you say?'

'She planted at least half of it, and made all the paths and little "rooms".'

He looked confused. 'Nobody was helping her?'

'She had a gardener, but he was nearly as old as she was! They were funny, always teasing and laughing at each other.'

He nodded slowly, with a slight smile. 'Ah, more a garden *companion*, because she was… *solita*, no?'

Solita. The Andalusians loved to make everything little, cute or more agreeable by adding *–ito* or *–ita* to the ends of words. In this case, alone became 'alone-y' – a surely more bearable-sounding situation.

'She was, for ten years or so after my grandfather died, but she took José Luis on… well, I think soon after they arrived here in 1980. He'd been here forever. Grandpa was happy to leave them to it, spent his whole time in the sea.'

He nodded again, then pointed along the rest of the path and told her he'd let her finish.

'What?' She looked at her watch. 'Time's up, *señor*, too hot and too much.'

He laughed. 'No, no, I mean to say for today, until tomorrow…'

'Ha! And *I* mean to say, I've done enough today.'

He lifted his chin in mock irritation. 'You laugh at my English, and we will see how you like to speak Spanish, from this moment!'

'*No me cuesta nada!*' she said, laughing, even though she *would* find it hard. 'But your English is amazing.'

'No, no – but not bad, because I need it for work with English and American production companies.'

'Aha.'

'*Hasta mañana,*' he said, turning to leave.

'I can't come tomorrow; I'm collecting a friend from the airport.'

He stopped and looked at her, face back in super serious mode.

'And Sunday morning won't be good, after a late night, but I could come on Monday.'

He nodded. '*Bueno*. But your friend, what will he do?'

'She'll be fine, and she *wants* me to do this.'

He smiled again. 'And… I'm sorry again about yesterday,' he said, patting her arm.

'I've already forgotten about that.' Especially now her arm tingled where his hand had been.

Then one of those massive black bees floated past, with its low, throbbing buzz – this time within inches of her face.

She flinched back, letting out a little scream. 'Oh God, I *hate* those!'

'I'm sorry also about our local *fauna*! But this one, he is not going to hurt you. He just *zzzumba* a lot and look dark and bad, but he is nice.'

IO

Saturday 11th August

Andie sat on the sofa with her tea, smiling at one of those big black bees floating over her balcony; she'd still have to keep her wits about her, dealing with *señor*, but it had been a huge step forward – meaning weeks more of rediscovering and opening up the garden were likely. It was a shame she couldn't celebrate with jam, but she'd run out.

She picked up her phone. According to the app, Shefali was currently more than halfway down over Spain, and due to arrive on time. She got up and had a last look around: everything was clean and tidy for her friend's arrival, and the second bedroom was kitted out with a cactus design tissue box, ceramic bowls for all Shefali's bracelets and unnecessary beauty products, and a jug with a beautiful little branch of dried agave spike that she wished she'd had time to paint. She sat back down again and looked at her watch; she'd finish her tea and go to the airport, even though she'd be ridiculously early.

Her phone twanged the arrival of an email. Hilary,

breaking her rule of no weekend contact; things must be desperate. Something about *what was she meant to do for her, if she wouldn't listen* and so on and so on. She could suggest exactly what Hilary should do for her, and it involved the bridge next to the woman's swanky office and the Thames bank sludge beneath it.

Then the phone rang, with Johnny's name across it. She was going to have to answer it this time, or she'd be dealing with him when Shefali was here.

'Andie! What's going on? Are you all right?' he asked. 'I was literally going to call the local police if you didn't answer this morning. I've been worried *sick* about you.' He was breathing heavily; you'd think he'd heard that *Challenging Gardens* had sent a hit man out after her, rather than just let her know, through Hilary, that she wouldn't be needed for next season's show, the previous presenter having decided – or more likely, been coerced – to come back early from maternity leave.

'I'm fine. I had to switch the phone off. Hilary kept giving me an earful about not wanting to do the Mediterranean garden book—'

'*What?* Don't start making decisions when you must be in shock. Take it easy, think—'

'Oh come on, Johnny, are we really surprised? Honestly, I'm okay with it. It's actually a relief, to be honest.'

'A *relief*? How can you *say* that? We've had such a wonderful time together on the show. How can you be happy to see all that end?'

He seemed to be confusing her feelings about their relationship with her feelings about being in the programme. Or maybe, as she'd often suspected, their relationship *depended* on her being in it. 'I'm not, but I've had time to think about it, and I really think I'll be happier just working for Gerard. I'm so enjoying designing this—'

'*Gerard?* I wouldn't put all your eggs in *that* old basket! Now he's teamed up with Hughie they're going to be overstaffed and probably downsizing themselves into a romantic retirement. Didn't you think it was odd he could manage without you for the whole of August?'

No, but she'd been surprised he'd suggested she might want to stay longer. A little seed of doubt entered her head; perhaps it had been unwise to immediately have gone and booked a further two weeks at Valentina's. 'Well... eventually maybe, but for now we're busy with several designs, and particularly the Hampton Court Palace Garden Festival.'

'Well, good, good... but Hilary's got some other ideas for you. You should listen to her... I'm still hoping to come out and see you. We could talk about these when—'

'She called you?'

'Of course.'

'Didn't she tell you what else she advised?' Andie asked. 'That we shouldn't be seen together until your divorce is finalised and made public?'

Silence.

She wished she could check his face. 'But surely that can't be much longer now.'

'Well... everything's been a bit on hold. You know, what with Jazzy.'

'If we're going to listen to Hilary, we should put our relationship on hold too.'

'What? Andie! What does a piece of paper matter? It's never made any difference to us before.'

'Well of *course* it has; I'd never have even *started* a relationship with you, if you hadn't already been in the process of divorcing.'

'Ha! Such an old-fashioned girl. Love it. But don't worry. Hilary? It's just a generational thing.'

'But... what d'you mean, the divorce has been "put on hold?"' Then the idea came to her, tumbling down on her like a pile of bricks. Like it should have done, if she'd let it, many months ago. The lack of moaning about paperwork, cost, division of belongings or childcare; surely even the most amicable divorce proceedings threw up little snags, irritation or hurt – but... nothing. It was only ever discussed on the rare occasions she mentioned it – and then with a dismissive quip or two followed by distraction. 'Maybe it was never put in motion in the first place.'

Another hesitation. He should never have attempted to hoodwink her on this; he was clearly an appalling liar. 'It was... discussed, I promise. Decided. We just didn't actually...'

A blow to the stomach. The Ball considered making an appearance, until she reminded it that this news, like her being dropped from *Challenging Gardens*, was actually the turning point she needed.

'You told me you were *getting* a divorce, not just *discussing* it. That's a huge difference – and a *massive* lie.' He was protesting, gently and soothingly, but she was suddenly completely done with his charming Irish blarney. 'I mean, at what point *were* you going to tell me? Divorces don't normally take this long, do they? Or maybe you calculated that by the time I cottoned on, you'd have finished with me and moved on to the next season's affair.'

'*What? No!* That's *not* what I—'

'Sorry, Johnny, but that's it. You've completely broken my trust in you. And even without this, I think you and I both know… it's over.'

'No, no, we need to *talk*. You can't just—'

'We should have talked five months ago. Look, I've really got to go now.'

'I can't believe you're doing this on the *phone*! Please, let's have a WhatsApp video call later. There's things I… want to say.'

His voice sounded a bit trembly; she hadn't expected that. Her throat tightened. She took a deep breath. 'I'm going to pick up Shefali now. Please, don't contact me while she's here. We'll talk, of course we will. But Johnny… I'm not going to change my mind.'

There are a number of things you shouldn't do before driving a car, and dumping your lying but tearful boyfriend was definitely one of them. She pulled off the road and went to a café, blew her nose and drank a strong coffee. After a *tostada* with peach jam, she had the energy to fight off, or at least delay, the flow of painful memories of times with Johnny – and try to embrace the idea of now being *solita*. She just needed time. Meanwhile, she had the mission to reveal Grandie's garden to Vicente and Rafi, and five days of Shefali's calming influence.

She drove to the airport, parked and rushed to the Arrivals gate – just as Shefali was coming through, looking serene in a flowing, aqua, bird-print dress, hair in a shiny, plaited ponytail.

'*Shefali!*' Andie cried out, and saw her friend's face break into a smile. They rushed to hug each other, laughed at their telepathic colour coordination, and went into a finale of one of their little dance routines that ended in a hip bump and a high-five. 'How are you doing? D'you need anything before we set off?'

'No, no, take me to the famous Grandie village, *todo directo*.' They went out to the car, parked just metres from the airport entrance. 'God, it's more like a village station – or a garden centre,' Shefali said, admiring the giant cacti.

'I know, amazing isn't it.'

'How's the leg? You seem to be scampering about okay.'

'Sometimes aches. Mostly just itchy; can't wait to have the stitches out tomorrow.'

'And then you can swim again?'

'Hopefully!'

They got into the car, but before Andie could get her sunglasses on, Shefali had studied her and put a hand on her arm. 'You've been crying. What's happened? Or rather, has anything *else* happened?'

Andie had already told her about *Challenging Gardens* when they'd spoken the night before. 'I finished with Johnny this morning. He was lying about the divorce – they never even started it. You were right about him all along.'

'Oh *no*... even I didn't suspect that. That's really quite... *conclusively* awful behaviour. Poor Andie – another wound to heal. Goodness me, woman,' she said, pulling her into a hug.

'I'm okay, really.'

'D'you want me to drive?'

'No, it's fine.'

'I'll make you a good lunch later. You're not going to heal on jam sandwiches.'

'I've run out of jam.'

Shefali let go of her. 'Oh dear Lord, we'll have to sort that out! So... apartment, cup of tea, shop, beach, Spanish-time lunch, siesta... then flamenco! Is that right?'

'Absolutely!'

Andie came out of the bathroom in her towel and found Shefali where she'd left her at the laptop. 'Anything? I could only find a couple of blurred—'

'*Oh* yes.'

'What?'

'You have to look at the groups he was attached to – like somebody searching *Challenging Gardens* to find you. He danced a lot for this guitarist Nico Talavante, and before that there was a singer he toured with. Come and look,' she said, as she clicked on a YouTube clip.

Andie sat down next to her. There was Vicente, responding to the guitarist, the hand-clapping singers, but also lost in his own moment, taut, intense, rattling off the thundering footwork, but with movements not confined to the flamenco tradition.

'He's definitely had some ballet training. Look at those lines,' Shefali said, as they watched him doing multiple turns and forming himself into a statue.

'Lovely arms.'

'All the better to fall into,' Shefali said with a wink.

'Oh don't start.'

Shefali grinned at her, then looked back at Vicente sadly.

'Can't believe he gave up – such a beautiful dancer. I've saved the links in a file called V among your designs.'

'Thanks.'

'Not that I'm suggesting you should have designs on *him*. Although he er… does come highly recommended.' She clicked on a *Hello!*-like interview article.

Andie read a few lines and then put a hand to her face. 'Oh God, can I *un*-read that? Can't believe he'd let her write it – privacy seems so important to him.'

'Maybe he didn't, and she was swiftly dismissed.'

Andie looked at the name in the caption to a striking-looking dark woman in a low-cut and well-filled spotted blouse. 'La Soleá. Local gossip has it that they're still a thing. Uh, this is tacky… put his dancing back on.'

A faster number. A different evening and setting, and maybe later in the show, jacket off, white shirt sticking to his damp chest. Bursts of irascible footwork alternating with irresistible smiles – in a very Vicente kind of way.

Shefali must have seen her smiling, and nudged her. 'You wouldn't be just the teensiest bit smitten, would you? Let's be honest here; this talented gentleman is exquisitely made.'

'Well, that hasn't gone unnoticed. But he's moody and weird, not someone I could feel comfortable with. I mean, go on a date with him, a little burp after your rum and Coke, and pff… he'd disappear into thin air.'

'Then drink something burpless.'

'He'd also have to be interested in spending more than five minutes in my company.'

'But Andie, give it time. You said he *makes jam*; this is a match made in heaven.'

'Really, you've got to stop this,' Andie said, but then leant forward to study the still photo of Vicente. 'Although, I have to say, it's nice being able to shamelessly gawp at him. I like his haughty nose. Roman, I'd think you'd call it.'

'Is he short?' Shefali asked, eyebrows raised in hope. They'd always said they were the only two women in the world who preferred their men petite.

Andie put a flat hand ten to fifteen centimetres above her head and nodded, her mouth in a resigned line.

'They're *all* short, aren't they? The Spanish men,' Shefali said, looking around the golden-lit, ancient Cathedral Square of milling Spaniards from their chairs in the tenth row in front of the stage.

'So maybe you've got David's Spanish grandfather to thank for his stature. Actually, given his heritage, why isn't he interested in *Spain* for this holiday flat you're going to buy?'

'I think both of us thought anywhere south with a decent beach would be too full of Irish pubs and English expats. But there's an undiscovered paradise going on here in Almería. I'll have to bring David out to have a look.'

'Definitely,' Andie said, although she couldn't imagine Shefali persuading him to do that; David might be small in stature but he was big on having his own way.

'You wait 'til I show you Níjar where they make all the ceramics.' She told Shefali all about it, as well as the spaghetti western film studios that might lure film buff David here.

Then, half an hour later than billed, the show began. They usually went to one of the shows in the annual

London Flamenco Festival, so they weren't put off when legendary guitarist Tomatito started with one of those slow rather inaccessible solos. But then the rest of the band came on – a second guitarist, a *cajón* player rapping his fingers on the wooden box beneath him, the singers and the *palmeros* clappers – and they soon recognised some of the numbers from their flamenco dance class. Later, they were joined by the dancers: a sassy lady in a red-spotted, black dress; a heavy older man with an earthy, macho energy; and a handsome young man with a more modern style, looking understandably mightily chuffed with himself for getting such a break in this company.

Afterwards, Shefali looked for their favourites – her female dancer and Andie's sweaty, balding but heart-rending singer – in a programme leaflet she picked up from the floor. 'Oh... what was Vicente's surname? Could the young dancer be that older son of his?' She handed it to Andie.

'Sebastián Vargas – yes! Wow, he's doing well.' She scanned the rows in front, full of people finishing drinks and collecting their things and standing up... 'And oh my God, there's his dad. End of third row on the left.' She bent down and started fussing with her almost empty plastic cup of Coke.

'You should say hello.'

'No. What's he doing?' Andie asked, keeping her head down.

Shefali looked over. 'He's with a friend. Could be that guitarist in the video, but I can't... Ah, Sebastián's come through. Talking to the friend more than his dad. There's a boy with them.'

Andie glanced up. Rafi? If he was there, she'd say hello.

But no, a slightly older, more self-assured boy, the friend's hand on his shoulder. She looked down again, picking up her bag. She could hear one of them – Sebastián presumably, complaining loudly that Rafi hadn't come. Didn't he realise that his little brother couldn't possibly have coped with all these people and sitting down for so long? He'd be making one of his birds chirrup and flap its wings up and down the aisles.

Then a girl with a flamenco event T-shirt, keen to start stacking the chairs, shooed them down the row... straight into Sebastián.

'Andie!' Vicente exclaimed, eyes wide with amazement behind his glasses, as if she only inhabited gardens.

'Oh, hello! Wonderful show, wasn't it!' she said in Spanish.

Still looking dumbfounded, Vicente explained to the others that Andie had been doing wonderful things in his garden in San José.

The friend looked surprised but said hello, Sebastián ignored her and seemed to be waiting for an introduction to Shefali, and the boy wanted a promise from his father that he'd be seeing the garden soon.

'This is Shefali,' Andie said, patting her friend's arm. 'It was a real treat for us, because we don't get enough flamenco in England.'

'You *dance* flamenco?' Sebastián directed at Shefali, in a voice nearly as deep as his father's. He was taller, hair short at the sides like most guys his age, rather than the usual flamenco locks. Handsome, but in a harder, male-model kind of way.

Shefali showed off her recently revised GCSE Spanish

and said they'd had a year of flamenco – including learning the traditional street party dance *sevillanas* – until their lovely flamenco teacher went back to his native Seville.

'Perfect! You can come tomorrow to my *sevillanas* masterclass here,' Sebastián replied in English, smiling widely at her. 'They will tell you is all sold, but you will be my *invitadas*, no problem.'

Andie and Shefali looked at each other, while Vicente and Nico made encouraging-sounding comments. 'Okay!'

11

Sunday 12th August

'I can't believe you brought your flamenco shoes,' Andie said, watching Shefali put them in her dance bag. Her friend was also wearing a light but full skirt that was going to look gorgeous as she did all those *sevillanas* twirls.

'I can't believe you *didn't*.'

'I was only thinking about Grandie's garden when I packed.'

'But you said you didn't bring the right stuff for that either!' Shefali looked at Andie's feet. 'You're *not* turning up in Crocs.'

'I've got trainers in my bag.'

'The white ones that've gone orange and frayed from volcanic cactus gardening?'

'The very same. I know. I wasn't really thinking *at all* when I came out here; I just wanted Grandie.'

Shefali nodded gently. 'And... have you found her?'

'Yes. Well... gradually.'

They went down to the car and set off, Shefali asking for a detour to pass Grandie's garden.

Gradually finding Grandie. What had she meant by that? *Mostly*, might be the word. Sometimes she was there; sometimes she wasn't. Like the last two summers. Once her parents had gone off on their travels and left her with Grandie, there'd been the usual music, gardening and beaches, the usual adventures and laughs, but there'd also been hours – sometimes a whole afternoon – when she was left on her own or with her friends. So that Grandie could carry out undescribed errands in the village that she said wouldn't interest her.

'This has got to be it!' Shefali said, leaning out of the window.

'You can't see much from the road.'

'Wow. The Secret Garden. And look at the *size* of it!' Shefali exclaimed. 'I'd love to have a look. D'you think he'd mind? I don't want him furious with you again, like he was after the builder chap came round.'

'No, no, I'm sure it'd be fine. Maybe you could drop me off, take the car for a wander if you like, and pick me up after an hour or so? Tomorrow, maybe. Although I'll be going earlier than usual, as I've got to go to the hospital to have my stitches removed.'

'Okay! And I'll come with you to that, of course.'

'Oh, that would be nice. You don't seem to have to wait long there – it's not like back home.'

'Really? My God, is there *anything* wrong with this place?'

'Once you adjust to living in an oven for a couple of months of the year, no!'

They drove off to the city, taking the seaside road again. For the concert the night before they'd parked the car at the seafront and taken a taxi rather than cope with the ancient, narrow alleys around the Cathedral Square. This time, all they had to do was cross the road to the dance studio at the university.

'Now you see why I said bring your swim stuff!' Andie said.

'Great! But, Andie, are you sure your leg is okay for three hours of stamping?'

'No. And I think I slept on it funny last night. I'll see how I am at the break; I might have to leave you to do the "stylisation" second half on your own.'

'Oh…'

'I happen to know there's good carrot cake to be had in a shady café terrace just up the road. Anyway, let's go in and see if this boy can teach.'

There were already at least twenty ladies and a couple of men in the mirrored and thankfully air-conditioned dance studio. A couple of flustered-looking girls were taking names and giving out receipts, while also making heavy weather of dealing with a few students paying in cash. When it was their turn, Shefali politely explained that they were '*invitadas*' – guests who didn't have to pay – but the girls weren't happy, and there was no sign of Sebastián.

'I had a feeling this would happen,' Andie muttered to Shefali, putting notes on the table to cover their fees. 'All mouth and tight trousers.'

Shefali laughed, and they went to change their shoes and get into the middle row of dancers.

With just a minute to go, Sebastián made an appearance from some back room, and seemed to enjoy the hush this brought about. His welcome speech was too fast for Andie and Shefali's Spanish, but seemed to charm their fellow students. Then they were off, going through the steps for each 'verse' of the dance on their own, and then with their partner.

He explained clearly and loudly, but the music he'd chosen was fast, and any help for strugglers was provided as best they could by the two girls who'd taken the money. Sebastián then went through the class partnering some of the dancers – mostly the very young and pretty ones, but also the pretty but much-too-old-for-him Shefali. For a partner dance that was supposed to be non-contact until the last chord, he seemed to be managing quite a few touches of her waist and arm, much to Shefali's obvious embarrassment.

At drinks and biscuits time, they found a quiet corner and compared notes.

'Lovely to see *sevillanas* danced so beautifully by a pro,' Shefali said, 'but can't he help some of the older ladies at the back? It would make their day. Well, if he kept his hands to himself.'

'I know! But I'm quite happy to pass up my chance; my leg's aching. I've had enough.'

'Oh no. But he's annoying – maybe I'll come with you.'

'No! The next bit is probably the best. You can pass it on to me later. I'm off for cake, and will come back and prise you out of his arms at the end.'

Fifteen minutes later, Andie was sitting in front of a soya cappuccino and – the popular carrot cake all gone – a slice of red velvet. Nothing in life was ever certain. Other than, for her at the moment, a phone full of more communications than she could handle. Back in the UK, she used to see them as birds landing on a telegraph line that you had to shoot at regularly – before you were Hitchcock-like overwhelmed by them. Here, the birds were confined to their app cages, only to burst out at her alarmingly when she opened them.

On the top of the chair where she'd put her Croc-ed foot to rest her leg, a sparrow looked at her with alarm, and cocked its head on one side in a Rafi-like way. She was going to have to find a new image for her chaotic communications. And there was one important communication she was going to make now, before she forgot.

'*Hola, I hope you don't mind, but Shefali would like a quick look at the garden when she leaves me there tomorrow? Also, I need to come half an hour earlier, as I have an appointment.*' She inserted tree, bougainvillea flower and nurse emojis and sent it off.

He hadn't been online since a few hours earlier – he and Rafi were probably swimming – so she went through her other WhatsApps: Gerard asking about buying five of those urns from the Níjar shop; could she talk to the woman. *Yes, okay!* Steve from *Challenging Gardens* asking how the heck she was now, which she was about to answer with a *Great! How was Turkey?* when she noticed it was the last of five messages.

He'd sent links to three newspaper articles. '*I can't believe this happened to you. How terrifying it must have been. Please look after yourself! On the plus side, Twitter seems to have loved your comment. Come over for dinner with me and Sal when you get back – no pork on the menu, I promise ;-)*'

Some newspapers had somehow got hold of the story about her wild boar accident in the local Spanish newspaper. Hilary? Without asking her first? Bloody hell, maybe this was what she'd wanted to discuss so urgently. She looked at the articles. Oddly, the emphasis was all on how she didn't want the attacking boar hunted down, because she understood the mother's need to protect her young – even though this almost certainly wasn't a serious question that had been put to her in the hospital. Good grief, they were translating it as forgiveness for Caroline's over-reactive media assault on her! And yes, a brief look on Twitter suggested the aggressive tide had turned away from her – for now, anyway. She closed Twitter, and looked at the sparrow. Out here in Spain – gardening, designing and healing – she really didn't care if they loved or hated her. 'It's all such rubbish,' she said to the bird, took another mouthful of cake, and replied to Steve.

Then Vicente's name flashed across the screen. '*Of course, no problem.*'

She sent a thumbs-up.

'*You are not in the Sevillanas class?*'

'*My leg started hurting.*' She snapped a picture of her leg out on the chair with the three sparrows and a pair of pale grey dove-like creatures in the shot. '*I'm resting here with friends.*'

'*Ha! Momentito.*'

He wanted her to wait a little moment. She hoped he was showing Rafi her picture.

He was. A video call came through with Rafi on his bed, perhaps being put down for a siesta, surrounded by stuffed birds and other animals. '*Gorriones!*' he said, holding up a sparrow and making it chirrup. '*Dilo!*'

She repeated the word, as asked.

Rafi shook his head. '*No, no! Gorrrr-iones!*' he said, with lots of rolled 'r'.

She sent back an improved effort, and asked about the other two birds.

He held up what was probably a pigeon, and told her it was a *tórtola* – a turtledove. Then he scratched at his little slim arm, looked at what could be a felt pen mark, and said in slow Spanish as if she were a bit stupid: 'We have a surprise for you.'

Vincente laughed and seemed to be telling him surprises were supposed to be a surprise.

'I'm not *saying*, *Papi*,' he said indignantly, 'only it's blue!'

Could they have painted the *pita*? '*OH!*' she sent back in a message, because some loud people were sitting down at the next table. '*You didn't do some PAINTING?!*'

Vicente sent a zipped-mouth emoji, a laughing one and a goodbye hand-wave – and before she could reply, he was offline – in that way he had of disappearing.

Walking back, she found she was smiling to herself, daydreaming about how maybe Vicente and Rafi might start coming to the house every summer, and every August she'd come out and do a little more on the garden for them. There'd be the odd little funny WhatsApp during the year, a Christmas robin message for Rafi... An unexpected little friendship. Just maybe, if he wasn't with La Soleá anymore, and she could start thinking of him as being completely human and normal, they could be *more* than friends... but no! What was she thinking? How much demand for garden designers could there be in this semi-desert? And there'd been nothing to suggest he even saw her as a *woman*, let alone one he could love. Ridiculous.

Meanwhile, she had to make sure his older son didn't think she was rude leaving his class – especially as she already somehow felt they'd started out on the wrong foot, as it were.

She was just in time to watch the final run-through of the entire dance, with the advanced variations in steps and some students – including Shefali – using castanets. There was a round of enthusiastic cheering and clapping from the students, and Sebastián blowing them all a kiss and telling them they'd been marvellous.

She sat down with Shefali while she changed her shoes. 'Well?'

'You were right; he was better at teaching the advanced stuff than the basics. Shame you missed it.'

'Ah well. We'll have to book a course again back home.'

Black trousers and a pair of black suede flamenco shoes were suddenly standing in front of them. They looked up, perhaps expecting a goodbye and thank-you smile, but he was looking rather serious.

They got to their feet and thanked him for the class.

'They teach you flamenco well, in England – or you are just very *natural*,' he said to Shefali.

'Thank you,' Shefali answered. 'Although when it comes to flamenco, rather than *sevillanas*, *Andie*'s the natural one. Maybe because she's a gardener; isn't there that saying that flamenco has to be danced *a tierra*, into the earth?' she said with a laugh.

It was half true; Andie surprised herself at how easily she managed the footwork and rhythms, and she loved all the floating sea anemone hands. 'But I'm useless with all the props: fans flying everywhere, shawls in knots!' she said, but he looked at her without a trace of a smile. 'I'm sorry I couldn't manage the second half; I've got a wound just above my knee that started bothering me.'

He stared at her for a moment. 'You are the English girl who was attacked by the *jabalí*?'

'Yes, but it's—'

'Didn't your father tell you he was the hero of that night?' Shefali asked.

'What?'

'He took me to hospital,' Andie said, surprised he didn't know.

'So, this is why you do things for my father's garden? Even if you have injury?' He looked unhappy about this for some reason.

'Well obviously I'm very grateful, but no, I actually came out here to return to that garden. My grandmother created most of it.'

Now he looked appalled, eyebrows pinched together with concern. Anger, even. Good God, why was everything so complicated for this family?

'But this is all much time ago,' he said slowly. 'You have seen, and now this enough, no? This attack... maybe is a warning, a sign to move on.'

12

Monday 13th August

'Well, he doesn't seem to have stayed over at his dad's. Thank God for that,' Andie said to Shefali, as they parked in the drive and saw only Vicente's blue car. She was still bristling at Sebastián's comment about her boar attack 'being a sign'.

'Let it go, Andie. He's just an arrogant youth with parental hang-ups. Wow, look at this place! Where do we start?'

There was no sign of anyone in the kitchen; Vicente must have pressed the button to open the gates and decided to leave them to it. She got out and led Shefali to the swing and round along the still rather rough bench path.

'Oh my God, I *love* this fairy. How could your mother have thought she was awful?'

'She was an arrogant woman with parenting hang-ups?'

Shefali raised her eyebrows; she was one of those people who didn't like to speak ill of the dead, even if she'd watched

Mrs Butts being a confidence-sapping parent to her friend, and for at least a year been 'the Indian girl' whose friendship was *not* to be encouraged. 'And yet she liked to see *you* as a fairy! Still envious of those amazing tutus she bought you.'

Mother's encouragement of ballet and the arts in general (provided you didn't think of earning a living from them), and possibly her gooseberry pie, had been the only good things about her.

'What did your dad think about all this?'

'The garden? Thought Grandie was overdoing it, but was also vaguely disapproving of José Luis being here to help her so much. Dad's usual contradictions about everything!' They came to the cliff path. 'And along there is where he used to dive, and now Vicente does. Well, I've seen him do it once, anyway.'

'And will never forget it,' she said with raised eyebrows, nodding slowly.

'I'm trying to! Anyway, it now looks like I might be able to open up other areas, like the amphitheatre. Great place for Rafi to play.'

'We would have loved that for putting on all our little dance shows,' Shefali said.

'Well, we *could* have, if my parents had ever let me bring you out here with me.'

Andie took her back round the cliff path.

'Oh... this is heaven,' Shefali said. 'D'you swim down there? Paddle, I mean?'

'No.'

'What? Other than the sight of Vicente in his trunks, and the odd bag of er... *nuts*, there've been no perks to this job?'

'Shh! He has a way of suddenly appearing, like a panther creeping up on silent paws,' Andie whispered.

'Ooh-er!' Shefali said with a laugh. 'I'll let you get on. I'm going to go and check out those wild beaches for the stitch-free swim you'll hopefully be having later. I'll be back at quarter to.'

'Make it ten, just in case Marcelo's late. He's coming over to look at the bench. We're going to see what it needs and then maybe he'll make a start on it, while Lucía plays with Rafi for an hour.'

'Ah, sounds good. See you at ten.'

The moment Shefali had driven off, as if he'd been watching from the window, Rafi came running outside, beckoning to her to follow him. '*Sorpresa!*' Ah yes, the surprise. As they went in, he called out to his *papi*.

Vicente appeared in the doorway to the living room. 'A-ha! Come and look!' They went through the side door to the inner patio, with its little bubbling water fountain, potted shrubs and cacti that Ben must have sorted, and… a large pot of painted *pitas* branches – sapphire blue, sky blue and canary yellow.

'Oh!' She patted each one. 'They're gorgeous! *Deliciosos! Increíbles!*' They'd even used a tiny brush to paint the little dead flowers white. 'And I *love* the colours!'

'Rafi and his blue and yellow for everything – there was no choice,' Vicente said with a smile, hand on the boy's shoulder, and yes, Rafi was in blue trunks with a blue-and-yellow Dory fish on his T-shirt. Andie realised she'd never seen him in any other colours.

María Ángeles had arrived and, coming through to see what was going on, was full of congratulations. There was talk about what they might build with the pile of *pita* poles she'd left, and then Andie said she needed to get on with finishing the bench path for them.

Rafi seemed to be asking if that was the one with the fairy statue, judging by his wing movements.

'Yes! She's all clean now – she enjoyed her shower! Maybe you can introduce her to Lucía,' Andie said in Spanish.

He nodded.

María Ángeles asked if she needed a drink.

'No, no, I've got one, thanks,' Andie said, and went off to the shed for tools and the wheelbarrow.

The path was nearly finished – she just needed to dig some fiendishly trip-threatening roots out of it. She chopped with the spade, pulled, unearthed a tennis ball... and then sensed a presence behind her – and heard a giggle.

She turned. 'What are *you* up to?' she said, having picked up the Spanish for this from María Ángeles.

Rafi went up to the fairy, much the same height as him, and then went behind her and draped his arm round the statue and smiled in bliss. Andie quickly took her phone out and got a photo, which she showed him. But then he looked past her along the path, where you could just see the agaves giving way to the blue sky at the cliff, and his smile vanished, his eyes widening. She wondered if he was remembering his mother's accident.

'Look what I found,' she said in Spanish, trying to distract him with the tennis ball.

He took it but carried on staring along the path, his little chest rising and falling. Was he going to go into one of his tantrums? How would she cope with that... and in Spanish? He shouldn't be here; she shouldn't be in charge of him – especially if he was upset – but he looked fixed to the spot.

'Look over there!' she said in Spanish, pointing in the opposite direction. 'I once did something amazing with my grandmother. We went *all* the way to the top!'

She was relieved to see him turn, his gaze following her arm.

'*Colinita?*' he said, pointing to the Lookout Post.

'No, no, not the little hill, the *big* hill, behind!'

His eyes went up to the top of the perfectly rounded hill covered in esparto grass and *palmitos*, his mouth opening in awe.

'You can see all the garden from there, and the girl who was unkind to me on the beach didn't matter anymore.'

'*Niñita.*'

'Yes! From there, the girl was tiny.'

He continued to stare at the hill. It was better than him staring at the cliff edge.

'Now Rafi… let's go and find María—'

He shook his head.

'But…' She remembered Marcelo luring a stubborn Lucía with car sweets. 'I'm hungry, have you got biscuits? Biscuits with… jam? Let's go and have some.'

He glanced at her – or rather the top of her head – then nodded and led the way, padding along in his flip-flops more slowly than usual.

She could hear María Ángeles calling his name now, and Andie shouted out that they were coming.

'Lucía will be here soon,' Andie said.

That seemed to make him pick up the pace a bit.

They arrived back with a relieved María Ángeles, and

had oat and raisin biscuits that they dipped in a little Níjar bowl of his father's blueberry jam. She complimented Rafi on his pictures of the garden, sea and birds, then went back out to work.

Grandie's voice reminded her about a smooth, low fig branch she used to sit on with a jam sandwich. She found it and sawed off a few of its smaller branches, so that Rafi could get up there and dangle his little legs from it, looking more Mowgli from *The Jungle Book* than ever. Chopping up the branches, she found a piece of blue plastic. Another treasure for Rafi? But it just looked like a child-size handle to something. There was a piece of nylon trailing from it, so maybe a handle to a pull-along toy, or... a kite.

It was an odd place to use a kite, with all these trees, but then...

Remember yours? Grandie seemed to ask.

She'd had a little red aeroplane kite, with wings that rotated and buzzed in the air as she pulled at the string, like a little pet in the sky above her. Grandie was forever having to get a broom to poke it out of trees. One time, Andie let go and they had to retrieve the little plane and the handle from the beach.

Her heart thudded. Could Rafi and his mother have been playing with a kite like that here, and... She walked along the path, poking around either side with the spade, until she reached the T-junction with the path going to the diving rock – and the huge agaves along the cliff the other side of the low stone wall, that she was going to have to look through. There was no point in telling Vicente and asking him to help her; he'd say, *Don't you think the police looked at the area?* And it was very likely he'd be angry with her for even bringing it up; it sounded like he'd been persecuted enough about it all at the time. She'd have a look, then get back to work.

She got over the wall and started digging around, apologising to the agave for some probably needless dismembering. Sweat was stinging her eyes, the agave fought back with a scratch, her heard started to spin in the full sun... Maybe this was what had happened to Estefanía for it then... God, she was less than a metre from the edge. How firm was the edge? She couldn't go any nearer. This was starting to feel crazy, dangerous and – with the burning of the scratch on her arm – very uncomfortable. She didn't even know if this was anywhere near where Estefanía had fallen. Although, by the stressed sound of the shout from Vicente below, it probably was.

Steadying herself with her hand on a rock, she put down her spade to wave to him – but he'd already disappeared, no doubt on his way up to ask her what the hell she was doing. She had a quick sip from her water bottle, then had a last desperate look around her, and considered giving the agave on the very edge a poke.

But she didn't have to. Right by her hand, there was what could be a sideways-on, tiny, blue tail fin sticking out from between two rocks. She leant over and pulled... pulled harder... and out it came – unbelievably, still with two wings attached. The same colour as the handle in her belt bag – but with two yellow stripes on each wing.

She stumbled back over the wall to the path and found a bit of dappled shade under the eucalyptus, sipped water again, and poured some on to her arm scratch, which seemed to be taking fire. Now would be a good time to be invited down to that beach, but Vicente, towel over his shoulder and advancing at speed, didn't look too hospitable.

'What were you *doing*? You want to *die*?' he shouted at her.

She held out the plane, and pulled the handle out of her bag. 'I found these.' Her heart sank when he didn't seem to recognise them. 'Rafi was here, looking down the path, seemed upset… and then I found the handle…' she said, feeling giddy with nerves. He still looked furious. She wished she hadn't started this… but then something came to her. 'Maybe in that drawing, the big bird is the fairy statue, and the bird in the sky is this little kite. And maybe…'

'Where was it?' he asked quietly, his face softening.

She showed him where she'd found the two pieces. His eyes went from the rock and back to the little plane. He took them from her, hands a bit shaky. 'I don't… remember these,' he said, turning them over in his hands.

'I'm sorry – they could be anybody's. Who do I think I am, playing detective? I just wanted to help.'

He looked up. 'Of course you did. You are good person, helping us. But also you are having a lot of danger for a holiday! Don't go on edge again, Andie, or you don't come here to do garden again. I can't permit this.' He looked at her for a moment. 'Are you… okay?'

She'd started hanging on to the eucalyptus for dear life; the fire on her arm scratch from the agave seemed to have spread to her brain, confusing her, threatening to fell her just like she felled the agave's *pitas*.

'Come, let's go in the house. You need to wash this,' he said, pointing to her arm. 'Juice of agave is very, very bad.'

He put an arm round her waist and led her along the

path. Good God, Accident Andie again, once more in her saviour's arms but too squiffy to enjoy it. But more than squiffy this time; could the agave poison have reached her stomach? Possible or not, The Ball was there, and had made an executive decision that rejection was in order.

'Oh, sorry…' She stopped and bent over, hoping to miss Vicente's feet with the projectile of this morning's breakfast. *Never mind burping after a rum and Coke*, she imagined herself telling Shefali later, *I only went and barfed on his toes*. But he was like her dad used to be, mumbling soothing words, unclipping her waist belt and handing her tissues and water bottle for a mouth rinse.

'*Pobrecita*,' he said. Poor little thing. Somehow the 'little' for once sounded nice, coming from him. 'Come, let's go inside.'

He helped her rinse her arm in the kitchen sink. 'Do you want to shower? But it has to be cold water, or you make it worse.' The scratch was bubbling up into red blotches.

She nodded.

'It's a good idea, because maybe you have juice on the shirt. Call Shefali to bring new clothes.'

She rang her, and Shefali said she could probably be there in about fifteen minutes.

Rafi was at once horrified and fascinated by Andie's bubbly arm, and had to be taken off to the swing by María Ángeles to stop him touching it. So when Andie emerged from the downstairs bathroom, wrapped as modestly as possible in an oversized beach towel, it was just her and Vicente. He took her to the sofa in the living room, with a glass of pineapple-and-coconut water.

'How is it now?' he asked. He'd given her an antihistamine

tablet that had either helped or just made her drowsy enough not to care.

'Bit better.' She looked over at the beautifully painted *pitas* in the courtyard. 'I'm having a bit of a love-hate relationship with these agaves.'

He smiled briefly. 'You are. And again, I'm sorry I was so angry, but to see you there... I will show Rafi the aeroplane. I have looked again at his picture, and I think you are right; soon he will talk of what happened.'

She nodded, not knowing what to say.

He looked at the floor. 'It was a difficult time. I was on tour so much, and then I was here with an injury. Estefi and I were having to become used to being together all the time... and then there was all the *estrés* with Sebastián, always complaining, never listening, and that day he had had an argument with us, and taken the train to Granada to go to his uncle. Estefi was upset. This accident... should never to have happened.'

'Oh God. I'm sorry. It must be so hard to feel that. But... it's okay now, with Sebastián?' she asked, despite her own reservations about him. She could easily imagine him having been an awful teenager.

'Er...' He looked sad, made a tipping motion with his hand, and stared back at the floor. 'I try. Sometimes he tries. But...' He shook his head. 'I never had doubt it was an accident, not for a moment, but Sebastián still thinks Estefi ended her life... which of course he says is my fault. So we blame each the other. On and on. Even if we not talk about it. But now...' He looked back at her, his dark eyes shiny. 'What you have found... this could help Rafi at last talk about what he saw, Sebastián will finally believe it was accident, and the three of us can heal at last.' He looked up to the ceiling, hands together as if in prayer. 'Thank you, God, Andie-grandmother, *jabalí*-pig or whoever sent us this garden girl!' he said with a laugh, but his eyes still brimming with tears.

Wiping her eyes on the towel, Andie was lost for words.

There was a distinctive 'Hell-oo! *Hola!*' and a knock at the door coming from outside.

Vicente patted Andie's arm and smiled, then they went to let Shefali in. Andie went off to the bathroom with the bag of clothes. When she emerged in the sunflower sundress, Vicente looked at her in surprise, as he had at the concert, and then collected himself. Did he really think she spent her whole life in gardening clothes?

'Ask the hospital to give you something for your arm as well as take the *puntos* from your leg,' he said, giving her the Spanish double kiss. Then he briefly hugged her and whispered, 'Thank you, Andie.'

13

This time, Sebastián *had* stayed over at his father's, a flashy red car and a loud male voice inside suggesting he was still there. She closed her car door quietly, rushed to the shed for her things, and went into the garden.

Vicente's WhatsApp yesterday suggested all was well; Rafi had cried when he finally managed to tell him and Sebastián what had happened, and had wished his mama hadn't tried to reach the plane and tripped, but was soon concerned with which shampoo would be best for washing it. Vicente imagined they would talk about it more when Rafi was ready. Sebastián, who Vicente had called to come over, had apparently been sceptical initially, but hearing Rafi talk about it, even with few words, had finally reassured him that his mother hadn't taken her own life. He and Vicente had talked long into the night, shed some tears, and Vicente hoped it would be a new start – but it was going to take time to heal the hurt between them.

Andie was tearfully happy at the thought of this, but had

no expectation of any change in Sebastián's attitude to *her*; she had a hunch that having to be grateful to her would only make him find her even more annoying.

Her arm was still itchy and sore, but she'd put on an extra layer of the cream from the hospital and planned to spend just half an hour digging up the last roots in the bench path so she could start with something new next time. After she'd helped Marcelo with the bench, of course. But… 'Oh!' she exclaimed; Marcelo had completely done it: replaced the broken slats, strengthened the joints, and coated but not obliterated the initials on the back support.

She sat down on it, her arm on the rest, then looked behind her and wondered if it might have been a good idea to ask him to rub down the E-and-J-kiss; now Vicente had hinted that things were strained between him and his wife just before she died, the affair with his charming and handsome young Uncle Juanito didn't seem quite so impossible.

Vicente appeared, pointing at her arm. '*Madre mía*, maybe you should have one more day resting.'

'It now looks worse than it feels. I thought I'd just come for a bit and finish this… if that's okay?'

'Of course, Andie. Why didn't you say hello? Oh… don't worry, Sebastián is showing Rafi a stupid game on the iPad. But he's very relieved, and I'm sure he will thank you for finding that plane.'

'Well, let's not push that. I just want to hear that he stops blaming you and giving you a difficult time.'

'Well, let's not push that either; it's going to be a hard habit to break!' He sat down next to her and patted the bench. 'So what d'you think?'

'I can't believe what a good job he's done – and nobody told me!'

'He wanted to surprise you.'

'Seems a shame to leave it here. Maybe you could ask to take it back to Almería with you when you go.' And then see the E&J initials? Perhaps not. She moved over a bit so she could put an arm over the worrying initials.

'Well…' He smiled and crossed his fingers with both hands. 'I have put the price lower for my grandmother's house in Granada that I am selling, so that maybe I can buy the house and the bench!'

'Oh! Really? I didn't know it was for sale!' Andie said, excitedly.

'It isn't. But it *was*, last year, so I *hope* the owner will be interested.'

'Ah, it would be wonderful. I'd so love it to be yours!'

'We will see. And… there is another person who would be happy. My grandfather. Because… he is José Luis, your grandmother's gardener.'

'What? Why on *earth* didn't you tell me this before?' she asked, trying to process this.

'Because I wasn't sure how you feel about them.'

'They were great friends. I really liked him – even though my Spanish wasn't really up to talking to him. How could I *not* feel happy about them?'

'Ah… I think we have to talk about this. But first…' He pointed to her good arm resting over the back of the bench. 'Is okay – you can put your arm down. These letters are okay.'

She put it down and waited for him to go on.

'This story about my wife and Juanito…' He shook his head. 'The truth is he was visiting a lot because he was having a secret love with manager of the bank... now his husband. Estefi was helping him.'

'Oh!'

'So now you know it's not them, you can guess who they *were* for,' he said.

'E and J...' She shrugged. 'I've no idea.'

'It's E and J*L*.'

'Oh – I thought that last thing was a kiss,' she said, tracing it with her finger. 'So... José Luis was having an affair with someone, here in the garden? Really? With Grandie helping him?'

Vicente laughed. 'Andie! Your grandmother was H-elen, no? But what did he call her, José Luis?'

Andie's heart fluttered. Those last years when Grandie had seemed distracted, sometimes leaving her on her own... 'Eleni,' she said quietly. 'Sometimes Elenita. But I would have known. Why wouldn't she have told me? I don't know...'

'For the same reason José Luis didn't tell everyone; nobody believed they waited until his wife had died. Only my uncle Juanito and me. My father was very angry – and Seb, for some reason, has continued with this. This is why he is cold with you; he thinks you are like your grandmother, and...'

'That's ridiculous,' she said, then put a hand to her face to hide her embarrassment.

'Come, I want to show you something.'

She followed him back to the shed, where he opened the door and took the Earl Grey tin off the shelf and gave it to her.

'I know,' Andie said. 'It's Grandie's... my grandmother's. We used to bring a tin every year.'

'Look inside.'

'I have.'

'*Pues*... look again.'

She opened the tin. Paper plant tags. She flicked through them.

He was standing very close to her. He had nice arms: strong, brown, a light covering of silky black hair. She imagined Grandie in José Luis' dark arms and smiled.

'Andie!' Losing patience with her, one of those arms brushed against her to grab the labels and turn them over... where there were words in faint biro. *Te amo... cariño... mi Elenita...* I love you... darling... my little Eleni...

'Oh my God!' Andie said. 'And José Luis, is he still here in the village?'

'No, he's in a *residencia* for old persons in Almería.'

'D'you think... I could visit him? Would he remember me?'

Vicente shook his head and looked sad. 'Sometimes he doesn't remember his own family.'

'Oh *no*...'

'But take this,' he said, handing her the tin. 'It's yours. Your "Grandie" would be so happy.'

She felt the sting of tears, nodded. Seeing this, he squeezed her arm. She had a feeling Grandie was watching.

Someone else was also watching. 'Ah, *The English Gardener*, like the film.' Sebastián, standing there with hands on his hips, lip curled in disgust.

While Vicente asked him what he meant, she put the tin down and took out her phone to quickly go into Google. 'No such thing,' she said. 'Maybe you're thinking of *The Constant Gardener*. Or *The Spanish Gardener*. Either way, the gardeners were misunderstood and treated very badly. As they are in most films.'

Sebastián's mouth fell open for a moment, then went into a closed smile. 'They should make film called *The Holiday Gardener!* Ha!' He looked pleased with himself. 'In the last week of the Spanish holiday now?'

'No, actually. I'm here until the fifteenth of September.'

Vicente looked at her in surprise; she hadn't told him she'd extended her stay. Then in rapid Spanish he said something to Sebastián about her being the *detective* gardener, and reminded him that without her discovery, it might have been some time before Rafi talked about what happened.

Sebastián looked down at the ground for a moment and then moved towards her and took a hand to shake it with both of his. 'I think this is what they do in England... thank you, Andrea,' he said, looking her in the eyes properly for once. 'You are clever to see this in Rafi's picture and look for it, when nobody else did. To get Rafi talking... to get the three of us talking. Thank you.'

'It was lucky, that's all,' she said, joining in with this odd gesture then letting go.

They came out of the shed, Andie holding the Earl Grey tin, and there was Rafi, smiling and thanking her for the bird – presumably meaning the kite plane.

Then Rafi yelped at the sight of the bubbly red blobs on Andie's arm.

'Don't worry, Rafi,' she said, 'I'm going to take it home and get it better, so I can carry on with the garden soon.' She said her goodbyes and got into the car.

Vicente came to the window. 'I hope you and Shefali have a good last evening.'

'I'm sure we will, thanks.'

'We will write,' he said, which always sounded rather exciting but in fact just meant a few lines on WhatsApp about when she was next gardening or that he'd done an online payment.

Andie and Shefali sat on the balcony with wine and pistachios, wearing swirly little skirts of gorgeously light Indian fabrics from a village boutique – Andie in pink, Shefali in turquoise – and looking through Shefali's photos of the wild beach they'd driven to.

'You should send him *that*,' Andie said, pointing to the one of Shefali in front of a massive sand dune of flour-soft sand. The idea was to entice David, hopefully with pressure from little Zara if he showed her the pictures, to book a half-term trip in October.

'Too late. My selection has already gone. I'll use it for back-up ammunition if needed.'

She'd never heard Shefali sounding so positive about persuading David into anything. She'd so far given in to private education she didn't really believe in, and agreed to stopping at one child when she would have loved to have one more. Once they each inherited a bit of money when their parents had died, buying a second home had been Shefali's idea – but the project had soon been totally taken over by David. Until now.

The phone made a harp sound, so Andie handed it back to her.

'*Yes!* He agrees, and says he'll book the flights once I've talked to Valentina!'

'Oh *brilliant*!'

'Andie, you've *got* to come out again then too – even if only for a few days.'

'What? I'll only have been back five weeks. But… yes, I might ask about that single room Valentina's got!'

'Do it!' Shefali sent off a reply to David and put down her phone. 'Right. So what are we doing about your lost phone? If you're sure you left it in the shed, ring Vicente from mine,' she said, pushing it towards her.

'His number's in my phone.'

Shefali raises her eyes to the heavens. 'Honestly, you and your phone.'

'Don't,' Andie said, shaking her head. 'But to be fair, I had just been knocked for six by a series of tidal-wave revelations, not to mention the proximity of Vicente in a confined space.'

'Well, this is true. Let me ring it again – maybe he or the housekeeper will hear it.'

'And then what? I suppose he could call Marcelo and ask where I'm staying.'

'It would be much easier if we just popped round. He's not going to mind.'

Andie leant back in her chair and finished her wine. 'The truth is, I can't handle any more Casa Higuera today. I mean, among other things, I need time to get used to our grandparents having been lovers – and why I'm the last to know about it.'

'Does it make you feel… even more attracted to him?' Shefali asked quietly.

Andie looked up. What was the point in denying this anymore? To herself *or* Shefali? She raised her eyebrows and sighed. 'Yes! Oh God...' She breathed out heavily. 'I've had crushes and fancies before but... this is on another *level*. It's... *painful*. Doesn't matter how much I reason with myself, I just can't...'

Shefali put her hand on Andie's and sang '"I can't fight this feeling anymore...!"'

Andie laughed. 'What film was that song from again?'

'I can't remember... but I think they stopped fighting it and got it together.'

'Yeah, well lucky them. I think this is going to be more like that awful Lorca quote. What was it? "To burn with desire and keep quiet..."'

Shefali tapped on her phone. '"...and keep quiet about it, is the greatest punishment we can bring on ourselves." Dear God, what a misery Lorca could be! Forget that. Your feelings for Vicente are a *gift*. At worst, you've probably got a fascinating friend for life. At best... well, imagine... a man who dances, makes jam and can deal with The Ball throwing back your breakfast! Just hang on in there.'

'Yup, that's me, hanging! Although sooner or later I'll probably have to let go. But the phone... look, apart from anything else, I don't want to take time out of our last evening.'

'Okay. If you're really sure it's in the shed.'

'I am. I took it out of my bag to try and fit the Earl Grey tea tin in. So, what d'you want to do? Take a stroll before we have dinner on the seafront? Have a drink at that place overlooking the marina we never got round to? You choose.'

'I'm really enjoying just sitting here, trying not to have

too many nuts before the paella! But I might get my packing out of the way; it's going to take some skill getting all those ceramics in.'

'Okay.'

Shefali went off to her bedroom, and Andie fetched her book. Irritated by the clichéd Mediterranean hunk in her last summer read, she was finding the distraction she needed in a quirky woman's slow-burn romance for a Cornish chap who wore thick glasses and made quilts.

She could hear Shefali singing to herself as she got her suitcase down, and then, connecting her Spotify to Andie's Bluetooth speaker, filling the flat with REO's 'Can't Fight This Feeling'.

'Oy! Turn that off!' Andie shouted out to her. 'Or at least until there's a prayer of him having the same—'

'A *prayer*, you say?' Shefali called out. 'Coming up!'

On came Take That's 'Pray'.

'Oh my God.' Andie put down her book and went through to Shefali. 'Wish I hadn't told you, now!'

'I *knew*! *Way* ahead of you. And I've got a good feeling about it.'

Andie started dancing to the music.

'Can you remember the dance?' Shefali asked. Aged eleven, they'd made up moves to it – the first of years of choreographed songs they'd done together, in local dance school shows or, more often, just in their living rooms.

'Sort of!'

Shefali pushed her into the main room and restarted the song. They got through a verse, but Andie complained that there wasn't enough room, so they started again after shoving the tables and chairs to the side. They were soon in tears of laughter at the corny acting out of the words, and singing along at the tops of their voices.

Then Andie spotted Valentina at the door. 'I'm sorry, wait!' Andie said, going to the speaker, turning it right down and coming back to her. 'Are we making too much noise?'

'Too much to hear the telephone, yes,' Valentina said, pointing to the clumpy hotel one on the table. 'I was tryin' to call you. You have a visitor.'

'Oh,' the two girls said in chorus, as Valentina stepped to one side and they saw an amused-looking Vicente, holding up Andie's phone.

Valentina smiled and disappeared.

'I was going to pick it up tomorrow… no, the next day…' Andie said to Vicente, aware she was sounding rather daft. 'Thanks.'

Vicente looked round the room. 'So this is where you are. Very good. And space for dancing!'

Andie and Shefali exchanged a lip-biting glance and laughed.

'I saw from street. Do it again!' He pointed at the two small sofas. 'Which is for the audience?'

'We made it up when we were eleven; you *really* don't want to see it,' Andie said.

'But I do! I remember the song, is Take That, no?'

'Yes, but…'

He sat down and put her phone behind him. 'No dance, no phone.' He was in his glasses and wearing the T-shirt with the cartoon fish – and a cheeky smile she would never have believed possible two weeks ago.

'Well… don't say we didn't warn you,' Shefali said, going over to the speaker.

The music came on, and off they went... laughing but throwing themselves into the corny pop steps that had evolved a bit over the years.

'Yes, yes, *more*! I love this!' Vincente said when it finished. 'How do you dance so completely together? *Increíble*. And with you looking like photograph negative of the other, it's very nice.'

'Aha, we're blood sisters, pricked our fingers in the first year of school!' Andie said, miming the action.

'This is why! Another? Then I have to go.'

The girls looked at each other. Their newest creation was the obvious choice, counteracting the Take That cheese with a bit of ultra-cool.

'"*You Don't Have to Call*", Erykah Buda – d'you know it?' Andie asked.

Vicente nodded. 'Of course.'

The quirky soul music came on, and they enjoyed their hip-hop and lyrical jazz to it, Andie trying not to catch Vicente's eye when they mouthed along with Erykah asking what planet the boy was from.

Then they lost their cool and did a daft little curtsey at the end.

'*Qué arte!* You should put this on Instagram or TikTok, you soon won't need to work again!'

'Well...' Shefali started. They'd been going to, but David had objected.

Vicente looked at his watch. 'Ah. I have to take Sebastián to the station in Almería.'

'Oh? I thought that was *his* red car,' Andie said.

'No, no. He will have to be on flamenco stages a few more years before that. His car is in the *taller* to mend... he came from Granada with her in the car, and now is talking about this car *all* the time.' He made a bored face and chuckled, to show flash cars didn't interest him.

Andie and Shefali waited for him to go on. *Her*. And the car had still been there this morning, so she'd stayed the night. This *flamenca* from Granada – who'd been on stages for many years – had to be La Soleá.

14

Thursday 16th August

Andie came back from the airport and, not yet ready for the Shefali-less apartment waiting for her, walked to a blue-and-white café on the seafront that Valentina had mentioned. She only just managed to find a table among the happy groups of Spaniards enjoying their breakfast *tostadas*. She ordered a multi-fruit smoothie, even though it was going to take a while to get even half of it down; without Shefali, there was nobody to jolly her along, and The Ball was rubbing his hands in anticipation of her Soleá-shaped misery.

Gardening might have helped – it was still early, she could have finally finished that path – but Marcelo was there doing fencing along the cliff and some tree work; she would have been in the way. Also, La Soleá could still be there. In fact, she might be there tomorrow. The rest of the week. She could have moved in for good, for all she knew. After Vicente left, Andie and Shefali had kicked themselves for not having casually asked about the flamenco owner of the car. *Oh? Anyone we would have heard of? Is she here for a show in Almería? A holiday?* But the earlier evening's chat about Andie and Vicente had somehow blithely assumed La Soleá was no longer in the picture; hearing that she was not only in it but had just slept in his house and presumably in his bed had knocked them sideways.

The smoothie arrived, a large slice of watermelon precariously balanced on the edge threatening to topple the thing. She didn't want to spoil what she did have with Vicente. As Shefali said, they might be friends for life – she could come over a few times a year, and after all the rediscovering of the garden, develop it further. *Friends.* But friends discuss their love lives, so they obviously weren't yet friends *enough*; he'd never mentioned Soleá, and she'd never mentioned Johnny – although, if he were interested, a malicious and out-of-date account of her relationship was available on social media. But they still had another month. Just as importantly, *she* had another month, to decide what she really wanted to do, and even, possibly, where she wanted to be...

Today, however, she needed to regroup – a bit of work for Gerard later, but mostly just enjoying the heavenly cornflour-blue day. There was a light breeze over the sea's gently curling waves. She'd get one of those loungers under a sunshade and spend most of the day on the beach, swimming and reading. *That's the spirit, hang on in there*, she could hear Grandie say – and she should know, because she hung on for some fifteen years for José Luis.

'Andie! Look at the colour of you these days!' Kim, in lacy, white, cover-up dress and carrying beach stuff; of course, she didn't teach until mid-afternoon.

'Hi!'

'You look amazing, this place – that *garden* – must be doing you the world of good. I heard you had a friend staying. Has she gone now?'

'Yes, it was great having her here. I've just come back from the airport.'

'Ah… well I'm having a couple of hours on the beach before I do some lesson planning. Want to join me?'

'That's where I'm headed! Just need to go back and get changed – and pick up one of those,' she said, pointing to Kim's lilo.

'Right you are! The sunbeds by the kayaks?'

'Perfect.'

Half an hour later they were bobbing about on their lime and orange lilos, paddling them around the anchored boats and deciding which one they'd want, and then gently lilo-surfing back to the beach.

Once they were on the sunbeds with ice lollies, Andie braced herself for the inevitable question.

'So how are you getting on with Vicente?' Kim asked. 'I hear you're doing his garden *every* morning.'

'Just an hour, most weekdays. He's fine, very grateful, pays me far too much.'

Kim looked over.

'No really, he's okay. And very sweet with his little son.' And gardeners who're sick on his toes.

'Well, I always thought people were being unfair about him. Poor chap. Does he help you?'

'Oh no, he works in his studio, produces music.'

'Ah.' Kim looked over at her, clearly wanting to know more. Hopefully she wasn't going to start going on again about her falling into his arms.

'Anyway, I wanted to ask you something. D'you know any local photographers? My garden design company boss is importing some urns from a shop in Níjar for a couple of projects, and wants to do a page on the website. I need some arty photos – and hopefully a video of them being made. Uh, and he wants me on there talking to the man and translating, God help me.'

'Oh, that sounds great! Let's see, professional ones, I don't know... but I'll tell you who's a superb amateur. Mónica, who works part-time at the estate agent's near the – ah, I think the one you used.'

'Mónica? Really?'

'She started out doing the photos for all the properties and then took a course I think... now has an *amazing* Instagram page. And she did a wedding video for some friends of mine, so she'd be good at that too.'

'Okay! But I'm not going to her office. Her boss was horrible.'

'Oh yes, the pugnacious Ignacio. Don't know how she stands him. But you don't have to go in there; I'll give you her number. Actually, she often comes to the expat group on Thursdays – one of several locals who like to use it as a free English conversation class. Give her a call and we'll meet her there tonight. High time you came along, anyway. Oh – and if you make it a morning for the photos, I could come along and help with translation. I'd love to see those things being made.'

Andie set off up the hill towards the bar. She was wearing her pink swirly skirt, forgetting it showed her ugly scar – but then maybe that was good, people could stop asking how it was and see for themselves.

She saw the blue octopus painted on the wall that Kim had told her about; she'd arrived. It was early for most Spaniards, so not too busy. She was just going up the steps when her phone rang. *Johnny*.

She went down them again, letting it ring, and pondered. If she didn't answer now, her phone would be buzzing distractingly all evening. She'd call him back, but keep it short.

'Johnny.'

'Hello, baby.' He was going to have to stop calling her that. 'Oh – sounds like you're in a bar.'

'*Outside* a bar. I'm going to the expat group... where there's a photographer I need to talk to. Hopefully she's going to take pictures of the urns for the website.'

'Ah. And how are you doing?' he said, in the downbeat way you use when the person you're asking couldn't possibly be doing well. As if *he*'d broken the relationship. But then, he *had*, in a way – or rather, he'd never fully committed to it in the first place.

'I'm... okay. I can swim again! I spent the whole day at the beach, making up for lost time.'

'I thought you gardened every morning – or has that stopped?'

'No, I still do an hour most days.'

'And how's *that* going?'

Kim was waving at her from the bar's terrace above the road. Andie pulled the phone away from her ear and looked up at the heavens for a moment, making Kim and Jen laugh and do throat-cutting and scissor movements.

Andie couldn't stop her chuckle.

'What's funny?'

'Sorry, some friends are making signs at me... Look, it's not a good time to talk. I'm fine, had a great time with Shefali, and now just trying to... get used to being single, okay?'

'Yes. Although you don't have to.'

'I've got to go. It's—'

'Wait! I've got something to tell you. I gave Jazzy your card and Tessie the turtle. She loved them... and wants to know when you're next coming round.'

Andie turned so she couldn't see the people in the bar, just the houses opposite and a calico cat sitting on one of their walls. 'But I'm not allowed to come over when they're there, remember? Not even *before*, let alone—'

'No. You *are*. Caroline's okay with it now. I think she was persuaded by the girls. As well as the way you defended her in the press, of course – and then your interview after the boar attack.'

'Oh.' Well, who would have thought. Why couldn't this have happened months ago? It was too late now.

'So I've told the girls you'll be here for a bit of Lilac's amazing apple pie as soon as you get back.'

'As a *friend*, Johnny. Not your *girlfriend*. You'd need to make that clear.'

'So I can tell them it'll just be a couple of weeks.'

'Four.'

'What?'

'I extended.'

'*What?* Is there something you're not telling me?'

'No, nothing to tell,' Andie said, which was true enough.

'I really need to go now. We'll talk again soon. Give the girls a kiss from me.'

Kim beckoned her over to their table, and put a chair between herself and Mónica. She waved a hand round the table. 'You remember Phil and Jen, rental royalty in the area, Ana your fellow plants woman, Mónica...' A tanned, blonde-haired arm put a Mosto grape juice in front of her. 'And Ben, of course.'

Ben patted her shoulders. 'Feels like I haven't seen you in *ages*.'

Kim tutted. 'Oh sit down, Ben, and stop being such a charmer.'

He put himself the other side of Mónica. 'So, how's it going at Vicente's?' he asked. Chatting among the others stopped; they all seemed to want to hear about that.

'Well, they've now got a swing, a statue and a lovely bench they didn't know about! Probably going to work on the old amphitheatre next.'

'Great!' Ben said. 'Marcelo has certainly been glad of the work and not had any more problems with him – and apparently Lucía's totally in love with Rafi.'

'Who wouldn't be!' Andie said.

'Rafi?' Ana asked.

'His little boy,' Andie answered. 'Nearly seven. Adorable. Vicente's amazing with him.' She wanted to tell them about how it was now certain that Estefi's death was an accident, put an end to Ana and Jaime's nasty suggestions, but Vicente wouldn't have liked her to be talking about his private family problems.

'Fine,' Ana said, 'but there's some gypsy blood there –

you've only got to look at him. I wouldn't get too… *close*, Andie,' Ana said in Spanish.

Mónica winced, and Phil and Jen frowned.

'You can't distrust someone just because of their roots,' Kim said. 'Especially when you're only guessing at them.'

'You don't even *know* him,' Andie said.

'No. But…' She got up with her empty glass, asked if anybody else wanted anything, but they didn't.

Once she'd gone, Jen leant forward. 'Just ignore her. She had years of appalling treatment from a flamenco dancer boyfriend, before she met Jaime. I'll have a word with her later.'

'Oh. Oh dear. Well that explains a lot,' Andie said.

'I gather you managed to find out he's making music for a living now,' Ben asked.

'Well, it came up.'

He put his beer down and tapped her hand. 'Right. While Ana's not here, we can ask you the big question: has he invited you on a date yet?'

'Ben!' Kim exclaimed, despite having tried to ask that herself earlier.

'No!' Andie said. 'And as I've already said, I'm not looking for a holiday romance.'

'Ah, but it wouldn't have to be that,' Phil put in. 'Ben, didn't you say the botanical garden is expanding? Maybe they'll need more gardeners.'

'There's talk of that, yes!' Ben said.

Kim nudged her. 'And with the urn-importing sideline your boss wants to set up, you could make a life here.'

'Well, it certainly sounds better than some of the options

my agent has been putting to me. Today it was some awful low-grade-celebrity survival thing.'

'What, *I'm a Celebrity, Get Me Out of Here*?' Kim asked, looking impressed.

'No, but similar – with even more desperate ex-celebrities. You can just imagine, they'd be constantly tripping me up and setting wild animals on me for a laugh.'

'Come out here then – you're safe with us!' Ben said.

'Maybe when my garden design company boss retires,' Andie said.

'Which is when?'

'Couple of years?'

'Right, that's that sorted then!' Kim said.

Ana was back with a large glass of something.

Andie realised Mónica had been a bit quiet. 'Can you understand all this?'

She smiled. 'Only if I use *all* the brain! Sometimes only I can listen, not speak. But, Andie, Kim says you want photographs in a *taller* in Níjar?'

They discussed what she needed and Mónica was startled by how much Gerard would pay. After Kim joined the conversation, they settled on Monday morning, if that was okay with the workshop.

Mónica put a hand on Andie's arm. 'I'm so happy it seems you have a good time here, after what happen with the house rental. It was strange, because I was going to take your deposit, and then Ignacio receive a call and he say, *stop*. He never explain why Vicente have the house, not you. But it was not Vicente who called – there was other name I heard.'

Ana had been listening intently. 'Hm. Probably somebody

calling for Antonio Moreno. Offered your boss a lot more money, or a bribe,' she said in Spanish.

'Who?' Mónica asked.

'Haven't you heard of him? Big property developer. He did that new road of houses cutting into the hill – although how he got permission, God knows. A hard man to say no to, probably. He's Vicente's brother-in-law.'

'God, I can't imagine the lovely Estefanía having such a bully of a brother,' Kim said.

'Doesn't sound like the sort of person who'd have time to help a brother-in-law sort out a short-term rental,' Andie said.

'Ah yes,' Ana continued, 'but a short rental can lead to a long rental... and then a purchase. Purchase of land the owner might not want to sell to a property dealer, but to someone who looks like he's fallen in love with the house and garden, maybe. Then later... family deal.'

Andie's heart thudded. Should she mention that she knew Vicente was trying to buy the house? No, she didn't want to encourage Ana's negativity towards him. 'Vicente wouldn't want to see the land developed, that garden means a lot to him.'

Ana gave a patronising chuckle, but then looked at Andie sympathetically. 'I'm sure it does. And I know it means a lot to *you*. But—'

'Well,' Mónica interrupted, 'the owner hasn't asked us to sell it, so don' worry!'

'Oh no, they wouldn't do it through an agent. Much too public. It would be a private deal. And as for Vicente... people can start to see things differently when there's a lot of money to be made, and the security that gives,' Ana said.

'Particularly people with children. Mónica will know this, in her business.'

Mónica nodded her head sadly. 'It's true.'

15

Friday 17th August

No red car. In fact, no cars at all. The gates had been left open for her, and a can of still coldish lemon tea on the olive tree table suggested she'd only just missed the last person to leave. But this was good, she told herself; she'd be able to quickly finish the bench path – without any further distractions along there – and move on to the swingball circle they'd discussed on WhatsApp.

She had just finished the path and was coming back to the swing area when a long, dark snake zig-zagged across the path in front of her.

She gasped.

He won't hurt you! she could hear Grandie saying.

I know. Just took me by surprise. How long do Montpelliers live? Maybe he's Monty the Pest Control Officer. Or a descendent. Oof, I could do with a sit-down after that.

She reached the fig tree swing and then pushed back some acacia branches to reach the old swingball circle.

Since Grandie had put a thick layer of gravel down, which carried on for the path to the old amphitheatre, it wasn't going to take long to cut back round the edges and reinstate it. She was sure there used to be a little two-seater stone bench here. *Where was it?* She sawed off a fig branch. *Ah*.

She sat down, pinged open the can and let the sweet tea revive her. It reminded her of collapsing here with Grandie after their tournaments. They were fierce opponents; she could still hear the whir of the string as the ball went round, the thwack of the bats, the comical screams and groans. Mum was always asking why Grandie didn't build a tennis court on the flat area beyond the amphitheatre; 'now that really *would* be something', she'd say, as if the rest of the garden wasn't. 'Because it's too hot to run around picking up balls! This is much better,' Grandie would reply, and Andie would agree.

She finished the can, leant back, and stretched her legs out. She now remembered this bench arriving, she and Grandie watching José Luis and Dad huffing and sweating as they carried it through and put it into place, with the old Spaniard then turning to them and saying something like: 'There you are, girls!' Once her parents had left on their travels, she'd sometimes sit here as a nut-munching, score-keeping spectator; she wasn't Grandie's only opponent. José Luis had awesomely quick, cat-like reactions, and was almost unbeatable – unless you could distract him with laughter. That wasn't difficult; Grandie and José Luis regularly laughed their heads off – the scrabbling competition for tools, their hilarious attempts at topiary… At some point, in their laughing friendship, those little plant tag messages started.

Why didn't you tell me, Grandie? She would have been happy for them, found it wonderfully romantic, pressed them to get married and have her as a bridesmaid.

You know why.

Of course she did. Her mother – and maybe Dad too – wouldn't have approved of the relationship. They would have told Grandie that their daughter wasn't to know, and if she found out, they couldn't let her stay there anymore. In the last three years, she'd stayed three weeks on her own with Grandie, some of the most precious time in her life; how awful it would have been to not have had that.

Couldn't you have got married?

We were waiting until we won round José Luis' son. But it wouldn't have made any difference to your mother; as far as she was concerned, José Luis was too uneducated, too rough, a Romani, an insult to her deceased father-in-law...

And Dad?

Linden had the heart to say he was happy for me – but then agreed with your mother! Where did I go wrong with that boy?

But... were you happy? A piece of paper probably wouldn't have been that important to Grandie.

What do you think?

Andie smiled. She remembered José Luis' noble profile, his slim, manly build, his face creased with smile lines.

And his son disapproved, just like Vicente's son disapproves of me. Although of course in my case, there's nothing to disapprove of.

There didn't seem to be a reply to that.

Oh, what's going to happen, Grandie?

Still no answer.

Oy, where did you go? Uh.

She got up and continued cutting back the branches. Her mind went back to Grandie and José Luis. If she'd known about them, Grandie wouldn't have had to sneak off on presumably fictitious errands; Andie would have given them time to themselves.

I'm sorry, Andie. I should have told you. I could have trusted you. Instead, I left you on your own – or with that little boyfriend of yours, unsupervised! – far too much.

No, no. It was fine. And I liked the way you trusted me. She looked over towards the Lookout Post, that she now preferred to think of as Rafi's *colinita. It's me who needs to be sorry.*

No, you don't.

She was grateful not to have to time to tussle with that thought; what sounded like a van had come into the drive, and it was now beeping its horn. The swingball game! Vicente said it would come today. She dropped her things and trotted back along the path to the driveway.

On seeing her, a man got out, opened the door of his van, and lifted a big box onto the olive tree table. He was asking her for some kind of number or ID. Luckily, Vicente's car came down the drive at that moment, and he provided what was needed.

'*Buenos días*, Andie. How is the dancing gardener today?' Vicente asked with the wide smile she was never going to get used to.

'Good!' She looked at the box. 'Wow, look at this. Looks like the super-super deluxe version – even has a scoring thing!'

'Tell me where. It's heavy.'

Probably not as heavy as some of those agave flower stalks she'd heaved along the path, but she let him do the gentlemanly thing. He followed her along the path. 'No María Ángeles today?' she asked.

'No. She's having a few days with her sons in Tabernas, not back until Tuesday.'

'Tabernas, where they make films?'

'Yes, there are two places for filming. Her sons work at Fort Tabernas Studios – one is builder, the other is manager of a bar.'

'Ah.'

'Rafi was invited to Lucía's for the morning, which is good because I have to visit José Luis today. The *residencia* say he has been a little... *inquieto* these days.'

'Oh. Oh dear.' She struggled to relate the agitated old man to the grinning, playful chap she'd just been remembering.

'I will show him more photos of the garden, see if they calm him.'

'You should add one of the swingball circle – I've nearly done it! He used to *love* playing it.'

They'd arrived. He put the box down on the bench.

'Here, you might need these,' she said, handing him the smaller secateurs from her belt bag. He looked appalled. 'To open the box,' she added, with a laugh.

He sat down next to it and started cutting the tapes, while she chopped up a branch and put it into the wheelbarrow.

'*Ya está.*'

She turned round. 'That's it' – as in he'd opened it, laid all the pieces out, and turned the instructions to the English page.

'D'you have to go now?' she asked.

'No... I can't be there before eleven.'

'Ah. Well I think you'll find there's...' She picked up the instructions. 'Yup.' She handed them to him, turned to the Spanish page.

'Oh no, no,' he said, shaking his head. 'I have no concentration for these.'

Admittedly there was a worryingly detailed anatomical drawing of the thing, but how hard could it be? It was just a pole with a spiral on top.

'Well nor do I. None at all. But I don't have a housekeeper; if I don't make things myself, I can't have them.'

'You live *solita*?'

'Yes.'

'Nobody helps you?'

'Not often, no.'

'Oh...' He looked down at the pieces.

'Have you played this?'

'As a child, a few times, at a friend's house. Not many toys – I was dancing or learning to play guitar all the time.' He picked up the base. 'This we fill with sand, no?'

She watched him go off with it towards the sandy beach path. Today he was in navy cargo shorts and a yellow T-shirt. She imagined a Rafi-like little Vicente having a brief play date between dance classes, a whole childhood taken up with learning to perform flamenco – that he'd now given up. How strange that must feel.

A bit later, finishing the rest of the trimming, she heard some Spanish swear words behind her; he was back, piecing the thing together.

'Grandie taught me *all* the Spanish *palabrotas* – just so you know.'

'Ha! She is extra-ordinary lady.'

'She is.' She could feel Grandie nodding at the use of the present tense for her.

She put the remaining debris in the wheelbarrow and turned to find a swingball, complete with scoreboard and little holders for the bats, fully assembled. '*Olé!* That was quick! D'you remember how to play?'

'I think so. But first, photo. Move the...' He pointed to the wheelbarrow.

She pushed it out of sight, and they took a series of selfies of the two of them, Andie making sure the stone bench was in there.

Then they picked up the bats to play.

'No, *I'm* orange,' Andie said.

'You have the yellow.'

'I like the orange.'

'I like it too. Orange is like yellow, but more.'

'Yes, and maybe I want more, too!'

He put the two bats behind his back and made her choose an arm – just like she'd seen José Luis and Grandie do with the two secateurs. She got yellow, but somehow managed to beat him at the game.

Then a phone rang. She fished hers out of her bag, but he was already answering his – and was breaking into a huge smile and making a thumbs-up sign to her. After some rapid Spanish he finished the call and stood there, grinning and speechless.

'What?' Andie asked, laughing.

He waved an arm, taking in the garden and the house. 'It's mine! The owner has agreed the sale!'

'Oh! Fant*a*stic!'

'I can't believe...' He was shaking his head. 'Only yesterday I accepted a price for my grandmother's house, quite low, but I wasn't wanting to wait and wait... and it was worth it!'

They smiled and nodded. In Spain it would be normal to hug about this – even in England – but maybe that felt too much, standing there in a secret garden room.

'So now what next for the garden?' he asked. 'For *my* garden!'

'Come this way!' She led him along the gravel path to where it opened out into the old amphitheatre.

'*Dios mío*, I had *no* idea!' he said, casting his eyes over the three levels of semicircles, each paved with a mixture of now dilapidated tiling and ceramics, that looked over a stage area backed by rocks and then the sea beyond. 'Your grandmother created *this*?'

'It was already here – I think she said the previous owners made it for big family parties and dancing. But she did the tiling, and planted more trees so it was hidden from the road,' she said, pointing at the rubber trees and acacias, 'and the luscious ground cover on the slope. Oh, and made the steps going up the slope – and the smooth slope further along – so we could go up and play ball games on the big flat bit before the dry riverbed.'

Vicente couldn't seem to see past the amphitheatre. He touched a piece of ceramic with his espadrille. 'We have to mend all this.'

'*We*? Are you going to help?'

'Well... maybe! Rafi too. He will love this. He and my

friend Nico's boy, Paulo, can do little shows for us of their flamenco – or just run around the levels! They are here tomorrow. I can show them. *Qué maravilla!'*

He jumped down on to the stage area, stamped his feet, whirled his arms above his head, clicking his fingers. Then beckoned to her.

She sat down on a rickety bench. 'I'm okay here, thanks.'

'*Sevillanas* – just the first *copla* – come, to celebrate!' He was going into Spotify on his phone.

'Well… maybe a *slow* one.'

On came a sweet plaintive song, something about 'I was wrong about you' – not very celebratory, but slow like he promised. Nice and easy – if she didn't get too distracted by those elegant arms, and the sensuality of the old courtship dance as they weaved around each other.

'Bravo, Andie, very good!' he said, doing the clapping before the next *copla*, but then his phone rang. He went over to it and smiled. 'Nico!' he said, putting it to his ear, and started telling him about the amphitheatre and how it was now his. They started excitedly talking about the house, but then Vicente looked a bit disappointed. There was something about Paulo, and the call ended.

'A guitarist has broken his hand, so now Nico has to go to Malaga tomorrow, to rehearse and play. We were all four going to the cowboy filming place in Tabernas that also has zoo, for Rafi's birthday – but now I have the two boys on my own all weekend. *Uf…*' Then he stopped nudging a tile back into place with his foot and looked up at her. 'Unless… Do you want to come with us?'

'Oh!'

'He's a good boy; he won't make you crazy. Paulo, I mean

to say. Rafi of course will be terrible, running everywhere. A cowboy will have to lend us a...' He mimed a lassoing movement that made Andie laugh. 'Also, it is in the Tabernas desert; it will be very hot, much dust – and with too many people.'

'Well! How could I say no?'

He laughed. 'Good! And if nobody is shooted, lost or eaten, there is a swimming pool at the end, so bring your things!'

16

Saturday, 18th August

'No, NOT *a date!*' she tapped out on her phone, in answer to a cheeky Ben. '*It's with two small boys! In car now.*'

'*Genoveses beach tomoz with Kim and Carlito? Pick you up about ten?*'

'*Great.*' She sent a beach umbrella and a thumbs-up, then put her phone away.

Behind her, Paulo had been trying to show Rafi his camera, but after some brief interest in one of the games on it, Rafi was ignoring him. When Paulo added that his dad had given it to him for an excellent school report, Rafi groaned loudly, flinging his head back and raising his eyes to the heavens. Andie faced forward and shook with silent laughter.

'Well done, Paulo,' Vicente said, 'that's—'

'Ki-ki-ki-ki, ki-ki-ki-ki-ki!' screamed the woodpecker Andie had given Rafi for his birthday.

'Uh… oh dear!' Andie said to Vicente. 'And that bird's no singer, is he?'

'He *heard*!' Rafi said in Spanish, and the bird started pecking at her neck, head and ears.

Meanwhile, Paulo had taken a cap gun out of his bag and was firing at it point-blank.

Rafi yelped, moved the bird out of reach – and when Andie put her hand behind her, let her take him for safekeeping.

'Boys, please! I'm trying to drive.' He glanced over at Andie. 'We have not yet arrived, and already I have enough,' he muttered with a chuckle. 'And sorry in advance about the *pistolas* – it is one time in the year I permit it.'

'At a Wild West park, fair enough.'

Andie cradled the soft toy in her hands. She'd WhatsApped Vicente from the shop in the village, with a photo of the green woodpecker, asking if Rafi already had one. '*No! We have been looking for that one! Well done, Andie, you don't need to do this, but thank you.*'

Then, just when the bird was reminding her of the singing robin Johnny had given her, Johnny rang.

'Hello! Can't really talk now, I'm in a car,' she said.

'You're early! Where are you off to?'

'Oh… bit of sightseeing.'

Vicente glanced over at her.

'FaceTime tonight? I want to talk to you about coming over.'

'*No*.'

'Why? I *said* I was going to, you just didn't believe—'

'You *know* why. Look, sorry, I'll talk to you later.'

She finished the call and stared at her phone in disbelief; how could he possibly think he could come over now?

'*Todo bien?*' Vicente asked.

'Yes, everything's okay. At least, it *will* be…' She was

probably going to be taking more calls like this, so maybe it was best to tell him. 'My boyfriend and I have broken up.'

Oddly, he just nodded solemnly, looking like he already knew this. 'And now you are in the desert.'

'What?' She put the phone away and looked out of the window. 'Oh, so I am!' The orange-to-russet earth had given way to a pale lunar landscape of bare rocky hills. 'Wow. You can see why they filmed those old westerns here.'

'Yes, and sometimes they still do, and other films too. It's why they call it Mini Hollywood. There are three of these places here; the one where the sons of María Ángeles work, where they do most of the films; this one where they added a zoo; and the little one, my favourite, with the house where lived the lady in *Once Upon a Time in the West*.'

'Oh yes, with that sad, sad music…'

'Yes… and they *play* that music, while you are going in her house! But for some years I have only gone to the one with the zoo, as you can imagine…'

'Lots of birds?'

'Of course. And *papagayo* show.'

'Parrots? That sounds fun.'

'Well, the first two times. Every year I suggest the Aquarium in Roquetas. Maybe next time!'

They turned off the motorway and were soon pulling into the car park. Rafi put the woodpecker in his backpack, and after Vicente had turned around and read the riot act to the boys about not running off, they all got out.

It wasn't yet ten but the heat beat down on her, and the slightest of breezes whipped up whorls of dust. She gasped as she took in a schoolhouse, a clapboard church, a barber's, a well-equipped smithy with a horse and a cowboy with jangling spurs on his boots and a long duster coat… it was like stepping into a western.

'*Rafi! Vente aquí!*' Vicente shouted beside her.

She turned to find the little boy had already scampered off and dived into one of the cordoned-off wigwams twenty metres away. Paulo was waiting for him on the edge of the road with folded arms and a long-suffering expression.

Rafi came back, grinning. She could see why Vicente had dressed him in a bright blue-and-yellow hyacinth macaw T-shirt with a red backpack – and had clearly developed bird-like peripheral vision to be able to cope with him.

They moved on through the Wild West town, and were soon at the boys' favourite – the jailhouse, where Vicente let them put his face in the *Wanted for Murder and Robbery* poster and place him behind the jail bars. Then Paulo asked if he could go back to the car because he'd left his camera behind.

'I will go,' Vicente said in Spanish. 'But you two have to stay right here and be good for Andie.'

She turned to him. 'Oh no, let's just all—'

'You *can*,' Vicente said, patting her arm. 'They'll just be playing with their guns in the jail and the…' He pointed to the haystack probably put there for the stunt actors to fall into later. 'You can watch them from this bench. Sit here like western woman, look.'

What if they were naughty or ran off and she couldn't find the Spanish words quickly enough? But the boys were looking at her; she couldn't really say no.

Once Vicente had gone, they started filling the air with the surprisingly attractive nutty smell of the cap guns, jumping off the wooden steps and landing in the haystack as Vicente had predicted. She fixed her eyes on them, a human hawk.

Rafi came over and asked her to refill his gun. Well, that was going to be a first. He seemed to be studying her while she fiddled around with it to get the little red ring in.

'Are you going to marry?' he suddenly asked in Spanish. You *singular*, so thankfully he could mean generally rather than to his father.

'Well! I don't know!' she said, laughing.

Paulo, man of the world that he was, tutted and then seemed to explain that she couldn't, because her house was in England, just like his father's last girlfriend Inge had had her house in Germany. Dad now had a Spanish girlfriend again, he added, as if that was for the best.

'Were they good?' Vicente was back, with the little blue camera and four ice lollies.

'Yes! Ooh...'

'Quick, before they melt,' he said in Spanish.

They sat in a row, the two boys in between her and Vicente. Rafi leant into his *papi* to whisper something to him.

'Yes, I know she has a house in England, Rafi. She's not going to live in a wigwam, is she?'

Rafi still looked puzzled, but the boys had finished their lollies and Paulo took him off to carry on with the game.

'You see? You can do it. Or at the least, as well as anybody of us can watch them. Two years ago, Rafi and I were here and just for a moment I talked with someone I used to know and pff... Rafi had disappeared. I could not find him. They had to make...' He put his hands together to make a loudspeaker. '*Qué vergüenza.*' He shook his head, remembering the shame of it.

She stopped concentrating on the remains of the melting lolly and looked at him.

'I know what happened to you,' he said. 'Nico told me. I said I had television gardener, and he looked on the internet. Leave it, Andie, you are natural with children; we have *all* made mistakes.'

Her eyes pricked with the start of tears. 'Thank you,' she said quietly.

He'd already turned his gaze back to the boys. 'There is a cactus garden, if you want to see. Also a cowboy show and can-can dancing. If you want break from these monkeys you can go to these. I will understand!'

'Oh no, it's fine. Although... I'll see how I go!'

He laughed, then looked at his watch. 'Okay, boys – parrots!' he said in English by mistake, but they seemed to understand, and Rafi had to be told there was no need to rush.

They went through into the zoo area. It was beautifully planted with cacti and succulents; she didn't need to see the separate garden. Next to the little open-air theatre, there were two cages of parrots, their vibrant, primary colours a delight for the eyes. Rafi slowed down and approached with reverence – then grabbed Vicente's arm. '*Papi*... still here!'

He pointed to the two smallest parrots, yellow-orange with green in their long tails, perching pressed close to each other on the branch in the aviary. They were chirping and shrugging their wings like they were having a chat.

'Oh!' Andie moved in for a closer look.

'Apparently, they are not couple, just very good friends,' Vicente said.

'Really? Ah! That somehow makes them even more special.'

They stood back for paparazzi Paulo to do his bit with the little blue camera.

Then the theatre started blasting out 'Circle of Life' from *The Lion King*, prompting them to take their seats – which, for Rafi, had to be in the front row. The music was even louder in the theatre. For Andie, it was one of those songs she usually ignored, having heard it far too many times – but maybe because it sounded more beautiful in Spanish, or because she was sitting next to Vicente and his cub, with their matching heads of shiny black hair – she was struggling not to be swept away by it.

Then on came the brassy *Hawaii Five-O* theme. Andie and Vicente looked at each other and laughed.

'Surfing in the desert, *fenomenal*!' Vicente said, laughing.

Her phone pealed a WhatsApp; rather than turning it to Silent, she seemed to have turned it up. She pulled it out and yes, it was Johnny – sending her a photo of Jazzy holding the turtle and waving. Bloody hell. She switched it off altogether and put it back in her bag.

'Ay... before much time you will have a new gardener boyfriend, I am sure,' he said, guessing who she'd heard from.

'What? Good God, I hope not. All of my boyfriends have been gardeners; it's clearly not the way to go.' Actually, Fabian was a seedsman – whose seeds had failed to get her pregnant – but she wouldn't go into that.

'Andie! You need more... *variedad*.'

True, variety was the spice of life, and all that. 'How about you?' She blushed. Did *he* have variety, or just La

Soleá? 'I mean, do you have a girlfriend?' Nothing wrong with that; friends ask each other these questions. So far, it was a bit one-sided.

He raised his eyebrows. 'Ah. Well... nothing to tell!' he said with a smile and a shrug.

Or nothing he *wanted* to tell. Hadn't he already told her and Shefali that Soleá had spent the night at the house? And they'd seen that article from a year or two ago. But... how naïve she was being! Maybe Soleá was on a casual basis, just one of several. For some reason this bothered her even more.

Hawaii Five-O had reached a final dramatic chord, and a smiling girl in a zoo T-shirt was now on the stage at a long workbench, with parrots on branches behind her. The Spanish was too fast for Andie, but there were parrots doing puzzles, riding bicycles, competing to put rings on hoops... and flying from the girl to another keeper on the top row, fortunately not dropping any bombs on the way. A silky white was available for stroking. Then an enormous red, green, and blue one was brought in by the other keeper, and Rafi stood up, even before the woman had asked for a child to help her, and confidently held the pole for the big bird to land on and fed it nuts like it was an old friend.

'Every year!' Vicente said to Andie.

It was time to see the rest of the zoo. Panther-like Vicente surprised her by being enthralled with the Thomson's gazelles and a baby zebra rather than the big cats; Paulo read all the information plaques for them; Rafi, after being dragged away from an emu, fell in love with a desert fox – until Paulo told him it ate birds' eggs; and a hyena took a worrying interest in Andie. Seeing this, Rafi beckoned her over to a well-fortified enclosure of warthogs, and made his fingers into tusks like when they first met.

Vicente tried to make Rafi understand that it was unkind to laugh about her experience, then turned to Andie. 'I'm sorry, when someone is hurt or upset he can't cope. He doesn't know how to react, so he can seem very cruel,' he whispered to her in Spanish.

As if to make amends, Rafi then took Andie's arm and insisted they all went up the hill to see '*suricatas*', whatever they were, but Vicente was enthusiastic, so it wasn't likely they'd have tusks.

They arrived at two enclosures of little holed hillocks, each with a meerkat on sentry duty while the others scrabbled about, groomed each other, or played. Both families of meerkats seemed to be peacefully sharing space with huge, bristly porcupines.

A keeper arrived with a wheelbarrow of buckets, and started talking to her charges and throwing out mealworms for them.

'Can they go down a hole and come up in the other cage?' Andie asked her in Spanish.

'Oh no,' the keeper answered, shaking her head. 'We had to split the family,' she said in slow Spanish. 'Never any problems with the porcupines, but their own relatives? Uf! I don't know... *families*!'

'Oh no!'

The keeper allowed the boys to help her fling out the mealworms.

Vicente got a call. He took one look at his phone and seemed uneasy, but, moving further away, greeted the caller politely.

She thought she heard him say Antonio. Wasn't that his brother-in-law? The other half of *their* family? She could make out him saying he was at the zoo, and something about this person and Sebastián coming for lunch for Rafi's birthday. But the voice on the end was so shouty and insistent, she could even pick out a few words of it: house… buying… Rafi… *Englishwoman*.

What? She then heard Vicente use Antonio's name in a furious retort, so it *was* him. Why was this man talking about her in that angry voice? They hadn't even met – and she'd be back in England in less than a month, for heaven's sake.

Vicente had said something else and finished the call, hitting the phone to 'off', by the look of it, before putting it away. He glanced over at the boys then folded his arms and breathed out heavily for a few minutes staring at the ground, face pinched in anger. Andie didn't dare ask '*Todo bien?*' like he'd asked her after Johnny's phone call, because it clearly wasn't.

Then he looked up, and made himself smile at Andie and the boys. 'Okay! Swimming pool, everybody?'

17

Andie pulled out another iced coffee from the ice box, leant back into her semi-shaded deck chair and, from one volcanic promontory to the other, took in the long curve of golden sand going into a shallow turquoise sea. Then she turned and looked behind her at the wide, orange-earth valley of *palmitos* and agaves backed by mountains that made it look like a film set – which, of course, it had often been. Further along the valley there was the stunning Mónsul beach that she had visited with Shefali, but also at least two others she needed to explore. In the other direction, pine trees shaded the path that took you up the hill to the old, conical windmill and then down back into the village. 'Oh my God, this is paradise,' she said, burying her feet in the soft warm sand.

'It is. Don't tell anybody!' Kim said, from her deck chair the other side of the umbrella pole.

'How come it's not *packed*? It must be the most beautiful beach in the world, let alone Spain.'

'Because once the car park for this beach and Mónsul are full, they close the entrance to the valley. Then you can only reach them with the little village beach bus, or on foot.'

'And being in the natural park, it's protected from any development?'

'Yes. For now, anyway.'

'And I can walk to it! I didn't realise.'

'As long as you bring enough water, yes! Up for another swim? Or maybe just a lilo float, after all that lunch!'

'Okay! Ah, here come the boys.'

Ben and Kim's boyfriend Carlito were walking back along the beach, having scaled the rocky hill for an apparently stunning view. They were quite a contrast – Ben with his mop of fair hair and shortest of shorts showing off his fine legs, next to the short-haired, modestly dressed Spanish accountant – but they seemed to get on well.

Ben smiled at Andie. He'd been doing a lot of that today, Andie realised, and had been very good – as had Kim – about not teasing her about her zoo date with Vicente. She'd told them he was buying the house, but hadn't mentioned the angry call from property developer brother-in-law Antonio. There was no way Vicente was going to sell it to him – he loved the place – but she did wonder how lunch with Antonio and Sebastián was going the other side of the hill.

'I took the most amazing panoramic from the top. I'll show you later,' Ben said, putting his phone away in one of the bags. 'I don't know why you didn't pick *me* for the Níjar pottery cameraman.'

'Perhaps because you don't have a *camera*?' Carlito suggested, with a grin.

'I've got tomorrow off. I could come along anyway.'

'*No*, Ben, there'll already be three of us,' Kim said. 'Maybe you'll get your chance next time.'

'Next time?' Ben asked. His eyes were hidden behind Ray-Bans, but his eyebrows went up with interest.

'Well, if it takes off as my boss thinks it will,' Andie said, 'I might be back again before long to arrange a bigger import.'

'Yes!' Ben said happily, 'and you'll see for yourself how lovely it is here in the winter. Or autumn, even!'

'Ha – that would be nice. How long can you swim in the sea?' Andie asked.

'October,' Carlito said. 'For normal people. The English into November. The *crazy* English,' he added, pointing to Ben, 'into December.'

Kim shook her head and pulled a face.

'Only if the weather's been good,' Ben said. 'After that, it's wetsuits until May.'

'Good God, so at least half the year you can swim in the sea. How lovely. And then there's all that year-round sunshine to walk and sit outside in…'

'Yes, so you may as well live here and visit *England* with the pots, rather than the other way round!' Ben said, sitting down on a towel next to her, while Carlito put his down next to Kim.

'Except… I'd have to think how I'd carry on designing gardens – in a semi-desert!'

'What?' said Ben indignantly. 'We *are* civilised here, you know! There's at least one superb garden design company in the city. There won't be many, it's true, but there won't be many garden designers either. Who knows, maybe they need another pair of hands.'

'Poor Andie,' Carlito said. 'Always you two are trying to move her from England. Maybe she *likes* England, maybe the English love to have gardens designed!'

'For the few weeks a year you can enjoy them, yes,' Kim said. 'No, you're right; we have to stop this.'

'It's okay,' Ben said, lying down on his back. 'We can just lie back and let San José work its magic, trust that it'll persuade her for us!'

'It already has, I can assure you,' Andie said.

Ben sat up and looked at her. 'What? Really?'

'And yes, I did notice there's a garden design company in Almería. And several further up the coast in Mojácar, where my being English could appeal to all those expats – although that wouldn't be the favourite. I've been thinking I could rent my house out for a year and give it a go. But I'd need to visit again in a few months' time and see how I feel about life here out of season – and find enough work to survive, of course.'

Ben and Kim punched the air like they'd just won a match.

Carlito nodded and told her he had a wonderful lawyer friend who could help her with all the paperwork.

Ben jumped to his feet and tilted his head at the sea. 'We all going in then?' he said, as if celebration was in order.

Carlito started taking off his T-shirt.

'I'm just going to put some more cream on,' Kim said. 'You should too, Andie.'

'Endless sun cream – only thing I don't like here,' Andie said.

Ben ran off into the sea, Carlito following him.

'Look at Ben!' Kim said. 'You've *seriously* raised his hopes now.'

'What?'

'I'll put money on him asking you out tonight – and it won't be the four of us.'

'He's too *young*.'

'A ten-year gap. But he's twenty-five; it's not like he's a teenager. Can't you see he adores you?'

'Kim! I really don't think he...' She'd been telling herself he was the sort of guy who adored *all* girls. 'Oh dear, have I been leading him on?' She suddenly felt really bad about him. Little things he'd said came back to her, like how he'd like to be sitting on her balcony at eight thirty in the morning, that time he came for breakfast. 'But he can't be serious – I mean, he's not exactly ready for a long-term commitment, is he?'

'He gets lots of female interest and *seems* happy as he is – but that doesn't mean he isn't looking for someone to share his life. I think underneath all the flirty charm, there's quite an old-fashioned boy who wants a wife and kid before thirty.'

'Hm.'

'Or maybe earlier, if the lady he's after has a ticking body clock!'

And if the lady couldn't produce any? How come she never seemed to interest any guys uninterested in having children? Shefali's David had to be talked into it for years, and an old friend of hers who'd been living with her chap since college days recently shared on Facebook Messenger that she'd had to settle for breeding dogs.

'Andie?'

'I'm not sure I can hear mine quite yet. How about you?'

'Oh definitely. Loud and clear. But I need another

couple of years to expand the school a bit, take on another member of staff. About the time Carlito hopes to become a partner at work. He's always going on about the freckled children we're going to have. Mind you, little sod's got to pop the question properly first, before he can have any of those.'

'Ha! *Will* he?'

'He's booked us a romantic long weekend in a hotel for my November birthday, near his parents in Granada, so fingers crossed!'

'Brilliant!'

'You'll have to tie in a Níjar urn trip with the wedding – unless you're living here by then, of course. Here, put this on,' Kim said, offering the cream while Andie was digging around in her bag.

Then Andie's phone rang in her hand. Vicente. Odd; he usually WhatsApped rather than called. She put it to her ear. 'Hello! How are—'

'Andie, I need you come here now.' He sounded angry. What had she done? 'Rafi... has gone. I can't find him. You come here help please.'

'*Gone?* When?'

'I don't know, half hour maybe. Please, *come*.'

'Of course. Ben could drive me – that would be quickest. I'm on Genoveses, came in his car.'

'Ben. Gardener man. Okay, but hurry.'

'We will.'

Kim had got up and called Ben in from the sea. Andie handed him a towel and quickly explained. Kim and Carlito wanted to help too, but Andie said she'd call if there was anything they could do.

'He should call the *police*,' Ben said, as they bumped along in the car much too quickly over the rough beach track.

'I'm sure he will. I don't know – how long should he wait? Rafi's a right monkey; he'll be hiding in the garden. That'll be why he wants my help; I know all the places.'

A pacing, anxious Vicente was waiting for them in the drive. As soon as they got out, he nodded to Ben and was saying in Spanish that Andie had to tell him if there was anywhere she thought he'd hide in the garden. He was making it sound like it was somehow her fault, but she ignored that.

'Okay, let's have a look,' Andie said. 'Ben, you could wait here in case he comes back to the house?'

Vicente followed her down all the paths, anxiously looking from side to side as Andie called Rafi's name.

'He'll come out if he hears you,' he said. But Rafi wasn't behind the statue, in the tree where he'd looked like Mowgli, behind the rock between the swingball circle and the amphitheatre, or anywhere else she could think of. They reached the amphitheatre and climbed up the hill to the wide flat space.

'He can't get out of here, surely; the wall's too high,' she said. 'You checked the beach?'

'Of course.'

They went over to the edge and peered down, just in case he'd moved down there.

'Then the only place he can get out is the driveway, if that was open.' Her heart started thumping as they exchanged a look. 'Ah, but what about the jungle of trees *in* the driveway...'

They strode back towards the house, still calling Rafi's name, but Vicente stopped at the overgrown Lookout Post. 'What about up here?'

'No, no, he's waiting for me to sort it out for him; too overgrown.' They rushed on, crossed the drive and started peering through the trees that sent branches over the driveway to make a tunnel.

'I already looked there,' Ben said. 'Should we call the police?'

Starting to panic, Andie was thinking the same.

Vicente got out his phone, but whoever he called wasn't answering. He dialled another number, but there was no reply from there either. 'I *knew* it. They've taken him,' he said quietly, while Ben was searching through the trees again.

'Who?' Andie asked.

'Antonio and Sebastián. We had an argument. They think they know...' He swore and started calling the numbers again.

But Andie was finally hearing something. Grandie? No, herself saying something to Rafi about how it wasn't the Lookout Post she and Grandie had climbed, when wanting problems to get smaller, but...

'The *hill*!' she shouted. 'If he disappeared when Antonio and Sebastián left, he could have sneaked out of the drive and gone up there. I told him about Grandie and me doing that, when I was upset.'

Ben had come back, and all three squinted up at the stubbled, rounded, and rocky hill the other side of the road.

'I can't see him,' Vicente said, shielding his glasses from the sun. 'We would see him.'

'Maybe not, if he was right at the top near that rocky bit,' Andie said.

'Let's go,' Vicente said.

'I'll come with you. Andie can't do it in flip-flops,' Ben said.

She watched them rush out of the driveway, and minutes later they were almost running up the hill.

Feeling faint, Andie got a water bottle out of the car, sat on the stone table, and fixed her eyes on the slope. Why had she told Rafi about going up there? She'd done it again, put another child in danger with her thoughtlessness. 'Oh God, please make him all right, please, *please*…' Vicente and Ben were near the top and seemed to be slowing… there were shouts… and then she saw Vicente lift something… Her heart pounded. Rafi? Was it Rafi, hurt? Oh God… It *was* Rafi – and he was waving at her! She burst into tears of relief, vigorously waving back with both arms.

Ben called her phone. 'He's fine, don't worry! Coming back now.'

She made some kind of noise in reply, then tried to get herself together before their return, washing the sea salt and the tears off her face with the hose.

Then they were there, coming down the drive, Rafi grubby but apparently okay, Vicente and Ben looking exhausted. The little boy was nodding as Vicente told him what he'd put them all through and what danger he could have been in, making him promise never to do it again.

'*You* have to promise not to sell the house,' Rafi said in Spanish.

'Okay, I promise,' Vicente said.

'And that Andie can always be in the garden.'

'What, am I not allowed in the house?' Andie said in Spanish, trying to lighten things.

Rafi folded his arms.

'Of course, she's always welcome here,' Vicente said. 'Now, let's get something to drink, come on.'

The four of them sat down in the kitchen with juice or a can of something and a piece of leftover blue-and-yellow birthday cake.

Vicente cleaned a scratch on Rafi's arm, put a plaster on it, and pulled bits out of his hair. 'You need to wash and cool down. Shower now or sea first?'

'Sea!' Rafi said, and looked round at Andie.

She smiled and gave a thumbs-up.

'And who is *he*?' Rafi asked her, pointing to Ben, who in his excellent Spanish had just wished Rafi a happy birthday and asked how old he was.

'He's a friend called Ben. He's a gardener too,' Andie explained.

Rafi looked Ben up and down. 'Does he have a house in England?'

'No!' Ben answered on his own behalf. 'I have an apartment in the village, near the park playground.'

Vicente pulled off Rafi's T-shirt. 'Come on, let's get you dipped in the sea.'

The four of them went down to the little sandy beach, where the water was even calmer than at Genoveses. On one side, there were rock pools and the remains of a sandcastle, and the other side had a small wooden lock-up, where Andie guessed Vicente must leave windsurfing and beach things.

'Ha – I've only seen this beach from a boat,' Ben said.

'Only nice people can borrow it,' Rafi said, as if he still hadn't fully made up his mind about Ben.

'Rafi! It's not *our* beach,' Vicente said. 'You can't *own* a beach in Spain; they're for everybody to enjoy.'

'And Ben *is* nice,' Andie said, with a laugh.

'A friend of Andie's is a friend of ours,' Vicente said, looking slightly embarrassed. Maybe he was wondering what kind of a friend Ben was becoming, whether she was about to have yet another gardening boyfriend after all.

The gentle water cooled and calmed them, and it wasn't long before Rafi started to look tired, putting a thumb in his mouth and clinging on to Vicente.

'Let's take you back for some quiet time on the sofa. Maybe watch a film?' Vicente suggested.

'*Finding Nemo?*' Rafi asked.

'Well, maybe something else...'

They got out and went up the steps to the garden, taking turns with the shower at the top.

'Wow, look at that agave log pile!' Ben said to Andie, looking along the path.

'I know. Trying to decide what to do with them.'

Then Rafi took Ben's arm, leading him inside to show him their painted *pitas*.

Andie turned to Vicente. 'I... should have thought of the hill from the start. And I'm so sorry, I should never have told him about going up there with Grandie.'

'Oh no, no, no, is *not* your fault! Andie!' Vicente said, shaking his head.

'But I don't understand, why did you think your

brother-in-law and Sebastián would take Rafi without telling you?'

He looked at the ground. 'It's difficult to explain.'

'It is. I don't know how you can bear to have Antonio here if—'

'It's not him, it's *Sebastián*.'

'No! What's the matter with that boy? I've heard of sibling rivalry, but kidnapping your own brother…!'

He looked up. 'Rafi is his *son*,' he whispered.

'What? But…' How could that possibly be? He'd have to have been…

'It's what can happen if a father is away all the time, not being a father. At fourteen he… went with older girl.'

'Oh… oh God. And you and Estefi…'

'We left Granada to live here, to have Rafi as our child. His mother is in Los Angeles now, never had interest, and Sebastián…'

'Let me guess, wants things his way, but no responsibility himself. Sorry, that's…'

He patted her arm. 'No, it's exactly this. Wants him to be normal boy playing football, doing well in expensive school, but also perform as flamenco dancer, lots of things, *everything*… that won't happen. Well, the expensive school happen, but he has to have special help there, and he isn't happy.'

'Oh… how difficult. I can't believe Sebastián can't…' Can't see how special and lovely Rafi already is, she wanted to say, but couldn't find the words.

Vicente was looking inside the door, where Ben was now admiring some of Rafi's birds, by the sound of it. 'Rafi does not know. Do not tell *anybody* this, Andie. I don't know why I told you…' He looked anxious, like he was regretting it.

'I won't. He's still yours as much as ever, for me. I'm already putting it from my mind.'

He looked at her with those rather serious, wild dark eyes she used to be afraid of. He opened his mouth to say something, but kept silent.

'I promise,' she said, thinking he needed more reassurance.

He put a towel round her and hugged her briefly, chastely keeping their bodies apart. *Friends*. Until they heard the patter of Rafi's flip-flops, and felt his little arms going round both of them and pushing them together for a moment before they broke apart. 'Thank you, Andie,' Vicente whispered.

Then he and Ben were chatting for a moment, Vicente apologising for interrupting their day, Ben saying he'd love to help with the garden when Andie was back in England. Everybody hugged goodbye, then Ben and Andie got into the car and drove off.

Once parked outside Valentina's, Ben turned to Andie, making no move to get out. 'I can see you're exhausted. You go up and chill out on your balcony, read your book, loll on the bed looking at YouTube dancing videos or whatever you need.'

'Ha! Yes, maybe. Thanks so much for—'

'And… I can now see what's happening at Casa Higuera.'

Oh no, she thought, she really didn't want to go into this now.

'An angel has arrived for that troubled man and boy,' he said. 'Not a guardian angel, but a *gardening* angel! Rafi can see it. Vicente is beginning to see it. And he's a very, *very* lucky man.'

'Oh, Ben, I don't know about that, but…' She put an arm round him and gave him a firm Spanish kiss on each cheek. 'You're not such a devil yourself.'

18

Andie was lying on the sofa, legs enjoying the early morning sun pouring through the balcony doors, a laptop full of Níjar pot photos, videos, invoices, shipping quotes, and Gerard's ecstatic email. She felt equally ecstatic about it; the pots were beautiful and perfect for English gardeners with Mediterranean dreams; the family – with backup translation from Kim – were friendly and grateful for the business; and... the project could be a part of her being able to afford to try living here.

She took another bite of the baker's wholemeal baguette covered in Vicente's fig jam. *Vicente*. It was important that any plan to try living here didn't depend on him – the income from looking after his garden, or the slim possibility that he might, despite any evidence so far, as Ben put it, *see* her... *Dios mío* this was delicious, no sugar apparently, just strongly flavoursome and naturally sweet – like its maker.

She put the laptop away and finished her breakfast; she needed to make a start on the mostly unshaded amphitheatre before the place turned into an inferno. Her hair went into bunches – a bit girly, but she'd gone off the somehow both silly and harsh topknot. Shorts and a pretty, pale-blue T-shirt, as today was going to be more about tiles than scratchy plants.

She drove in, unlocked the garage, and used the wheelbarrow for the boxes of broken tiles the Níjar workshop had given her when she managed to explain about the crazed paving she was going to repair. No sign of anyone in the kitchen, and all quiet except for the sound of María Ángeles singing upstairs as she worked.

Ángeles. He already had an angel – although of course that was not what Ben meant. According to him, Vicente was starting to see her as... a blessing in his life, but also a *woman*. Meanwhile – from what she'd overheard of the phone call at the zoo, and Rafi's insistence about her continuing to come here – it seemed Sebastián and Antonio viewed her as an *evil* in his life. Why? They thought her gardening had made him fall in love with the house and refuse to sell it to Antonio? Or they feared history would repeat itself, a family member falling for a *paya*, as Romani *'gitanos'* call non-*gitanas* – and an English one at that. *Paya*. Sounded like papaya. It was all so ridiculous. And she and Vicente had to cope with this disapproval without even enjoying... God, she really couldn't allow her mind to go down that track.

She pushed the wheelbarrow into the amphitheatre area. 'Oh!'

Vicente and Rafi were there, standing either side of a yellow, mini wheelbarrow. 'You're late!' Vicente said, Rafi nodding beside him.

'And you're late to start helping!' she said with a laugh, and once again marvelled at how any knots she tied herself in by thinking about him instantly untied themselves in his company.

Rafi pointed to his yellow wheelbarrow, held up his yellow-gloved hand, and flexed his fingers, then picked up a little matching trowel.

'Oh, they're *wonderful*! And what a colour. Were they for your birthday?' she asked in Spanish.

He nodded. 'Juanito *y* Iván.'

Vicente's uncle and his husband in Almería, who they'd visited for birthday lunch yesterday. She took an instant liking to them. 'What a great present!'

'It was a great visit,' Vicente said. 'And Iván played with Rafi while Juanito and I visited José Luis... Andie, he remembered you, and wants to see you!'

'Oh!' She felt tears prick her eyes.

'When can you come with me? If we leave too much time, maybe he won't—'

'Today?'

'Yes! If María Ángeles can stay a little longer.' He got out his phone, and was soon nodding at Andie and smiling. 'Perfect! We leave at five o'clock, *vale*? I can pick up you... *ay*... pick *you* up. My English! But...' He looked puzzled. 'Pick you up also means...?' He put his arms out as if carrying her.

Jesus. 'Yes.' They looked at each other, still smiling. Was he also remembering how they first met? 'Okay, let's get started, team!'

Vicente had agreed with her that Marcelo's concreting solution to the broken paving on the tiers and steps was practical but horrid, so Andie – and now the team – were going to painstakingly mend the crazed paving on each layer, regrouting and filling in the gaps. Rafi wheeled his barrow all over the place to pick up bits of tile or ceramic that had come loose and been washed or blown away; Vicente put Rafi's treasures, along with the tiles in the boxes, into the gaps – or in particularly bad places, created a new mosaic of a fish, a flower or a face; and Andie did Grandie's old job of grouting them in. When they'd finished about a third of one of the three levels and the steps down to the 'stage', they stood up and admired their work.

Rafi, despite having enjoyed himself, asked who the theatre was *for*.

'You and your family!' Andie answered in Spanish. 'When I was a child, my friends and I used to do little dance shows for my grandmother, your great-grandfather, and anybody else who could be persuaded to sit on a chair on one of the levels and watch! Luckily for them, the show didn't last long; the batteries in the old ghetto blaster usually gave up halfway through.'

'Maybe when Nico and Paulo next come over, he can bring his guitar and you and Paulo can do your *sevillanas* for us on it,' Vicente said to him.

'You dance *sevillanas*, Rafi?' Andie asked.

He nodded, went down on to the flat 'stage' and beckoned to Andie.

With Vicente clapping and humming a *sevillanas*, they danced the first *copla*.

'*Olé!*' Vicente congratulated them at the end, clapping.

'Now… music box!' Rafi was saying in Spanish.

'Oh, that was years ago. I don't know what happened to that,' Andie said.

Rafi was insistent, and seemed to be talking about a suitcase that played music.

'Oh yes! We found a... machine to play *discos*? Do you want to look? It's now too hot to do more here today.'

'Okay!' They made their way back along the path, Vicente having to carry Rafi's wheelbarrow because the little boy was flapping his arms and singing something about a bird that sounded familiar. It sounded like they'd been playing some of the vinyls.

Vicente insisted they had a quick drink in the kitchen first, and then they went through to the living room.

'It's Grandie's! I don't believe it!' Andie went over to the little brown case with its two built-in speakers that looked like eyes.

'I was clearing out a cupboard, thought it was a bit heavy for a suitcase, opened it and...' Vicente opened a leather box next to it. 'And these?'

Andie lifted out the old 45s in their little paper packets and flicked through them. 'Yes! Oh my God...' Bowie, The Three Degrees, ELO...

'All Seventies, but even still... your grandmother must be very young for age!' Vicente said.

'My father used to buy them, but at some point – maybe when he left home – they became Grandie's. Then she brought them out with her in 1980.'

Vicente picked up Ian Dury's 'Hit Me With Your Rhythm Stick'. 'Rafi went *loco* with this... I have the *moretones*,' he said quietly, showing little bruises on his forearm and putting the record at the bottom of the pile.

'Oh dear!'

Rafi pushed in and grabbed one. '*Esto!*' he said, holding up the Alessi Brothers' 'Seabird'.

Vicente took it out of its sleeve, put it on to the turntable and put the needle on. A little crackle, and then on came the bird-like flute opening, the gentle pop drums and the smooth, lispy voice of one of those sweetly handsome twins singing about how it was time for the seabird to come home. Rafi started flying round the room, but then responded to the beat and started moving with it, his arms turning graceful and fluid.

Andie and Vicente smiled and found themselves moving to the music as they watched him.

'Oh Rafi, that was lovely!' Andie said at the end. 'That's one for the amphitheatre already!'

'*Otro pájaro! El lori!*' Rafi demanded.

Vicente took the record off and found Alessi's 'Oh Lori'.

'Of course!' Andie had seen at the zoo that *lori* was Spanish for lorikeet.

On came the twins' falsettos to the irresistible jazzy pop, Rafi latching on to the bicycle-riding bit of the lyrics and putting it into his lilting little dance.

Vicente looked at his watch. 'Just one more, and then a chap's coming here to play on one of my tracks,' he said in Spanish. 'Let Andie choose one, Rafi; they're *her* records!'

Rafi folded his arms and bit his lip. Poor little chap, sharing and taking turns didn't seem to come easily to him. But he clapped his hands at her choice.

'*Love* this!' Vicente said.

'You know it?'

'Yes, an English musician friend sent it to me, years ago. Fantastic song.'

Andie put the record on, while Vicente translated the title for Rafi. '"Come Up and See Me... Make Me Smile!" It means—'

'I know, I know!' Rafi said, and anyway, the music had started. He bounced around to it, and Andie and Vicente joined in, trying to outdo each other with the zaniness of their movements to Steve Harley's quirky singing. Each time the music stopped dead, it was like a game of musical statues. Then came the Spanish guitar solo, and all three tried to put on intense faces and dance flamenco to it, Vicente throwing himself into some flashy – albeit barefoot – footwork, lightning-fast clapping and thigh slapping and whipping turns that made the other two stop and gawp for a moment and then whoop with appreciation. Then they all went into the last bit, singing along with the baba-baba and ooh-ooh la la-la backing vocals at the tops of their voices.

A smiling María Ángeles came in followed by a chap carrying what looked like a saxophone case. Andie didn't catch his name, but there was the usual two-kiss Spanish greeting even though she'd now be leaving.

'I'll be off then. See you later!' Andie said.

'Wait, there's a CD at the bottom of the box here and... yes, is album of your Take That boy you liked as teenage!'

He held it out to her. *Life Thru a Lens*. There was a song on there she really didn't want to hear.

'Andie?' He looked concerned, so she took it and thanked him.

*

She put on her new purchases from the boutique up the road: a thin, floaty, sleeveless dress of seahorses on tie-dye blues that reminded her of one Grandie had bought her; a cord necklace with a starfish like the kind of thing she used to wear as a teenager; and some low-heeled but prettily aqua-jewelled sandals. She smiled to herself; although she had a good collection of skirts, she should do dresses and all-out girlie more often.

She brushed her hair and, despite the heat, decided to leave it on her shoulders. Well, more than shoulders; it seemed to be growing an inch a week out here. For all she knew, having her fair hair more visible could make all the difference between José Luis recognising her or not. When he remembered her yesterday, what came to him? A general image of her, or the time they last saw each other? She felt butterflies in her stomach.

The CD looked at her accusingly from the bedside table. She put it in the drawer, at the back. Maybe it would get left behind – but then the cleaner would find it, and give it to Valentina, who'd probably want to post it to her in England. She couldn't seem to bin it, either. There was no escape. But what was the point of it? She could now listen to any of those tracks at the touch of a couple of buttons. No doubt Vicente thought it might have memories. It did, of course; but not all of them were ones she wanted back.

She went to the bathroom and put on mascara, even dug out the eyeliner pencil from the bottom of her washbag. Again, the more pronounced her eyes, the more likely he might remember her. Eyes were everything. Hers were blue-grey like Grandie's, with the same wide and open shape. José Luis' eyes she could only recall as crinkled up by a smile or the sun or both, but they'd be indoors now – and possibly not smiling. The long, black-and-grey hair would be white or gone. In fact, most of José Luis would be gone, but she wanted to connect with whatever was left of him. For Grandie.

She waited on the balcony, looking out for Vicente's car. So much for the free-spirited, unreliable flamenco stereotype; he was bang on time, just like when he picked her up for the zoo. Grandie would have approved; she was as free-spirited as they came, but was a staunch believer in lateness being a sign of arrogance. Actually, surely she would have approved of him totally – how could she not, when he was José Luis' grandson? – although for some reason she was keeping very quiet about it.

She glanced at herself in the mirror, reluctantly admitting to herself that her efforts were not completely all for José Luis, and went downstairs. Goodness, he'd brushed up well himself: smart, sand-coloured shorts, a crisp, white shirt with a tiny lizard on it, hair shiny and loose, those black-framed glasses she liked and he probably needed for driving, and a dark, rosemary-scented aftershave.

He looked her up and down. '*Dios mío*, what a delight *marino* for the eyes you… will be for José Luis! He loves the sea.'

'Oh good!' she said, getting into the car.

'Please don't be sad if today he doesn't remember you,' he said, driving off. 'Every day he is different. And even if he is well, he gets tired and then angry with himself quite soon. Always the best to leave while things are good, *vale*?'

'Of course.' They were coming out of the village, driving through the rounded orangey hills that hadn't changed since she was last here twenty years ago. 'How often did you and your parents visit him when he was here and you were in Granada?'

'Oh, about every month, but not August, too many people.'

'Ha – and I was one of them!'

'No! We should have met. I could have been one of the dancing friends on the amphitheatre!'

'Yes! Although you would have found me very silly, as I think you're a few years older than me.' If Sebastián was twenty-two, he had to be at least…

'I'm forty-two. And you?' he asked.

'Thirty-five.'

He glanced over. 'Oh? I thought you were, well, *much* less. Like… perfect for young Ben.'

'Oh, don't *you* start! My friend Kim keeps trying to make that happen. But I told you – enough with the gardeners! Actually, you might remember Kim; she used to teach Sebastián English at her school in Níjar.'

'Ah yes! Excellent teacher and a kind woman, Estefi used to say. Maybe I should go there for lessons.'

'Good idea! Although your English is already amazing.'

'My parents sent me to an international school in Granada. My father had a good estate agent business – with Estefi's father – and with only one child, he could pay for it. I had some English friends – and one I still talk to a lot on WhatsApp. And of course I need it for work, so some years ago I did a course in Almería.'

'Ah, that explains it! And where did the flamenco come from?'

'My mother danced flamenco, and my father played

guitar and *cajón*. Not professionals, but both half *gitano*, with the flamenco in the blood.'

'A-ha.'

'And you?' he asked. 'Where did your dancing come from?'

'I don't know – lots of swimming and diving on my father's side. But my parents did like their ballroom dancing.'

'And the gardening?'

'Probably from wanting to be outside to get out of my mother's way! She was very... pushy.'

'Push-y?' He looked confused, then smiled. 'Ha, I understand. Good word. I know about this – and is what I don't want for Rafi. But Sebastián...'

'Uh... but surely he's delighted with the improvement in Rafi's speech.'

Vicente shook his head. 'No. Because when Sebastián is there, Rafi is...' He raised his shoulders to demonstrate. 'Inside himself again. So he doesn't see it.'

'Oh *no*...'

They were driving alongside the sea, coming into Almería. 'We're here,' he said, turning off and parking outside a small modern building with verandas looking over a simple, shaded garden and the sea the other side of the road.

'Looks lovely.'

'It's not bad – but these days he is mostly in his room.' They got out of the car into a still-blazing-hot afternoon and went into the air-conditioned reception. Vicente spoke with a woman at the desk and then turned to Andie and took her arm as he led her down a corridor and stopped outside a door. 'I will go in first, okay?'

She waited outside the room, her heart tapping away, but he came out again within minutes and took her inside.

José Luis was in a high-backed armchair next to his hospital bed. On the other side of him, there was a table with several pot plants, and a pile of what looked like photograph albums and coffee-table hardbacks about nature... that she couldn't imagine formerly strong-armed José Luis lifting now, his arms thin and weak on the chair's supports. Just wisps of the black-and-grey remained, his face was dragged down into a multitude of folds, and those squinting, sparkly eyes were now sunken and vague. But he reached out a hand. 'Eleni?' he said in a thin, croaky voice.

Oh no, she thought. I can't be Grandie for him.

Vicente whispered that she needed to go nearer, and took her hand and put it in José Luis'.

The face crinkled into a smile. 'Eleni... *hija*?'

Grandie's daughter. Close enough. 'Yes! Hello, José Luis, it's lovely to see you,' she said in Spanish. 'I'm making the garden beautiful again!'

He nodded slowly and kept smiling, hopefully remembering the photos Vicente had shown him.

He looked her up and down and then muttered something like *strong girl, like Eleni*. Followed by a wheezy chuckle and something like *for my son*. It seemed Vicente had also jumped a generation.

She nodded. It was true; she was doing the garden for him – as well as Rafi, and herself.

Then, rallying strength, he looked over at Vicente and said something about these girls from the cold north being surprisingly hot, and chuckled even louder.

Oh.

He seemed to need confirmation, and when Vicente nodded and smiled a *yes*, looked obscenely delighted. This wasn't the gentlemanly José Luis she remembered. He was starting to ask something else, but before Vicente could agree with that too, she pulled out the photo Valentina had printed for her.

'Look. I found this of Gra... *Eleni*.'

Vicente helped José Luis put on some thick reading glasses. The old man peered at it in silence. It was a close-up of Andie and Grandie laughing as they untangled the swingball, almost certainly taken by him.

He stared at it some while. Sighed. It was quiet in the room. You could hear the lap of the waves – probably always could – like at Casa Higuera. It was such a happy picture, but it seemed to draw all energy from him, his lids lowering, a twitch at his mouth. His eyes closed, but when Vicente tried to take the piece of paper from him, the bony fingers gripped it hard. 'She... never leaves us.'

'And when she speaks, her voice is very clear,' Andie whispered, her heart in her mouth.

He gave a little nod. It looked like he might fall asleep. But then he opened his eyes, pulled Andie closer, and reached for Vicente's hand. 'And now... you together,' and nodded again, but this time his head too heavy for him, and going back on the rest.

Vicente asked him if he wanted help to get onto the bed, and he said yes.

Andie started to say goodbye, but the old man was too tired to respond. With a nod from Vicente, she left the room and went back to reception. She was glad to sit down, shed a few tears, but smiled to herself too.

Vicente came out and gave her a quick hug and held her shoulders. 'That was so much better than even I hoped. *Maravilloso.*'

They went back to the car and clicked their seat belts on. He looked over at her.

'That comment about girls from the north... is the disease, not him.'

'I know. But... should you have lied to him?'

He switched on the car and the air con, ran a hand through his hair. 'You *are* Grandie's daughter, in many ways, no? It's not so—'

'I think you know that's not what I mean.'

He breathed out heavily, although really it should be *her* doing that. 'Andie. We made him happy, more than for a long time, and this is the important thing.'

'But when you visit and I'm back in England and can't come with you, what will he—'

'He will forget, or I say you are visiting family, or... he won't still be with us. And whatever I said, he would make his own mind on this.'

He drove off along the seafront. Andie watched the waves – bigger now, or just bigger here – beating out time. In a few months, José Luis might not be here. Where would she be? Where would *they* be?

Vicente slowed down and pulled the car onto the gravel by the rocks and the sea.

She looked for warning signals on the dashboard and then at him. 'Something wrong?'

'No. Well, *yes.*' He turned to her. 'You are hurting, and I need to explain.' He took her hand in his. 'I wish I *could* have given you... romance for your time here. But Rafi needs...

stability. I have to think of him – I'm sure you understand. I'm sorry about what José Luis said. He is confused.'

She drew her hand away. '*I'm* confused. What on earth makes you think I want a holiday romance? I don't—'

'No, you don't. You are not this type of girl. So you would feel sad, and this the other reason.'

'I don't understa… Oh. You mean, I'm not this kind of girl, but would have given in to your charms.' She folded her arms and stared into her lap. 'You are *way* out of order, *señor*.' Although probably right.

'No, no… I don't mean… But you can understand, if you stay at house, Rafi would break his heart when you leave.'

But nobody had to break their heart, because she was probably going to try living here. She opened her mouth to say so… but he'd started the car again. Conversation over. If he were interested in a relationship, a real one, he would have asked about the possibility of her moving here – like absolutely everybody else had. Casually, maybe indirectly, but he would have asked. But he never had. He knew she'd be back from time to time; like the song, she'd *come up and see him, make him smile*. For him, that was clearly enough.

He patted her arm. 'Didn't you like the "Eleni daughter, strong!"?' he asked, smiling and trying to lighten the mood.

'Yes.' She was going to have to be.

19

Wednesday 22nd August

Andie put the top back on Vicente's *ciruela* jam and twirled the jar in her hand. Some kind of Spanish plum. Delicious. She looked over to the kitchen worktop; she now had more than enough jam for... let's see, the twenty-second to the fifteenth, three-and-a-half weeks. She'd probably be taking some back to England. Jarred Vicente, she thought with a wry smile.

Before dropping her back at the apartment, he'd taken her to the house because he'd forgotten about the six-pack jam gift box he'd picked up for her from his Uncle Juanito when he and Rafi had gone to lunch there on Monday. They'd gone into the kitchen, Vicente telling her about how Juanito was a teacher but had taken over the jam business now Vicente was so busy with music. Or at least, that's what she *thought* he'd said; she was finding it difficult to concentrate, after the José Luis visit and after what had been said in the car. She'd said thank you, but couldn't fend off the feeling that the jam pack in her hands was some kind of ludicrous consolation prize. Then Rafi had come in and asked if she was staying to dinner. It struck her that she and the little boy had already bonded. It was already too late to avoid them missing each other when she left, but she patted his soft, little, brown back and said she had things to do and had to get back to her apartment.

She took the rest of her breakfast tea out onto the balcony and went through their conversation yet again. *You are hurting, I have to explain*, he'd said. Did he not see how she'd now be hurting even more? How could it just be about Rafi, when Vicente had done nothing but encourage her friendship with the little boy? Was it not more to do with the *older* son, who clearly disapproved of her – and would no doubt much prefer him to be with La Soleá? Although she couldn't imagine Vicente letting Sebastián direct his life... She finished her tea, stretched, and tried to release the nervous tension in her body. She was going to have to face up to the almost certain truth behind what he said – which was that, despite his obvious affection for her, he just didn't see her as a romantic partner.

'Right. *Garden*,' she said out loud to herself, taking her cup back to the kitchen and getting her things together. That's what she was here for, after all.

Indeed. And yes, you do need to be strong, she could hear from Grandie.

Is that all you can say? You've been remarkably quiet about all this. I thought I could tell you anything, but you're—'

Come up and see me, make me smile, she heard in return.

That's just a song, Grandie.

No. It's time you came up and saw me. You know it is.

Andie stood still a moment and closed her eyes. She had a feeling Grandie was wanting to say something else too, but she went downstairs and set off in the car.

She drove in to find an open, empty garage and just the little white car belonging to María Ángeles in the drive. No Vicente. Maybe that was for the best, today.

'Hello, Andie! How are you? Cold lemon tea?' María Ángeles, in kindly slowed-down Spanish. How much friendlier she had become, compared to her first visits; the cool, near-wordless protective stance had almost completely gone.

'Please!'

'And they made some biscuits – come and try.'

Oaty again, this time with apricots and honey. 'Mm, lovely!'

'I know. He needs to start a biscuit business too,' María Ángeles said with a grin. She saw Andie looking over into the living room. 'After dancing on the amphitheatre and to the records, Rafi decided he would, after all, attend the children's flamenco dance summer school this week! Or what's left of it. So they've gone back to Almería for a few days, until the little show on Friday.'

'Ah, good for him.' So she wouldn't see Vicente again until at least Monday. Time to get herself together.

'They asked if you could leave the amphitheatre until they can help you again? Rafi's been asking if you could "mend the little hill" – if you know what that means?'

'Ah. Yes.'

Colinita. The little hill. But it didn't have to be... She collected her things from the shed and went along the path to the amphitheatre, listening to that bird with the sighing whistle call that she still hadn't managed to identify. Maybe Rafi would know.

She smiled at the work the three of them had done so far, and wondered when their next yellow-wheelbarrowed team effort would be. Over the other side, the steps, and a little further along, the path, went up the slope to the wide, flat area where Rafi wouldn't want to play football. But he might like to do something else up there.

You know very well this isn't the little hill Rafi wants mending, she heard Grandie say.

It wouldn't take long to tidy up the steps and the path. In April, going up among that stunning pink blanket of Hottentot-fig ground cover would be...

He doesn't want a pink blanket! Well actually, he probably would, as a nest for his flamingo... but come on, Andie, mend the little hill he wants you to mend.

She turned and looked back towards the Lookout Post, just visible through the branches of the giant fig tree. Maybe Rafi *needed* it, just like she used to. A place to survey the whole garden, the house, the bay. The *world*. Of course, she could leave it for Ben to do, once she'd gone back to England... but she could hear Grandie tut and growl at that idea.

'Okay, okay. I'm coming up,' she said out loud, and started slowly walking back towards it with her wheelbarrow.

She'd happily tramped past it hundreds of times in the last few weeks, but stopping at it was different. She folded her arms and looked up. It seemed to stare back at her, like they were in some kind of stand-off. The Walnut Whip, she'd called it. Or the Helter Skelter – although she'd never slid down it, and especially wouldn't now; rosemary and heaven knows what else was covering the narrow path going round and round through its russet rocks to the top. She swigged her water bottle. 'Okay.'

It turned out the overgrowth was superficial; she was soon halfway up, swigging her water again and pouring some over her head to soothe sweat-stinging eyes and a bit of vertigo. She'd have to suggest that Marcelo put in a wooden barrier or handrail at the least, before Rafi started coming up here. She pushed on. It had stopped bothering her; she just wanted to finish the job in one session. She didn't have to come up here again. Then she was there at the top... and her heart began to pound, The Ball digging into her insides.

Andie, Andie... come on now, you didn't think I'd still be...

She looked at the bench. Another job for Marcelo, but it was in remarkable condition, considering – as if the now-not-so-little olive tree had shielded it. Just like it had shielded...

Sit down, my dear.

She brushed away some eucalyptus leaves and slowly lowered herself onto the bench, as if it might not be real. 'I'm so sorry, Grandie...' she whispered, throat tightened, the bench and the view from it turning into a watery blur.

'You need to go through it again, see it as an adult. Think it through. You have nothing to be sorry for, my dear. *Nothing.*'

'Is that all you can say? You're being remarkably quiet about all this,' Grandie said, getting up to turn Robbie's

CD volume down. She came back and sat herself down on the sofa, next to where Andie was leaning against it but sprawling on the terracotta tiles trying to cool down. 'I was fifteen too once, you know. You don't forget these things, ever. Fifteen and besotted with—'

'I'm not *besotted*! That's an *awful* word!' Andie said, raising her eyes to the heavens. 'I just *like* Nando, that's all.' Although rather a lot. 'Anyway, he's not coming today; his family are going off on some rich friends' yacht or boat or whatever.'

'Ah well. When do they go back to Madrid? The first, isn't it? Twenty-second today, so that's—'

'I know, I can count.'

'Well!' Grandie said, with raised eyebrows. 'Come on, don't be a prickle fish about this. You know you can tell me anything; I'm not your mother.'

That was true. And there was no way Mum would have let a sixteen-year-old boy into her bedroom – even if only to chat and play backgammon when Grandie's rather loud Spanish friends took over the patio to drink a lot of sherry while they planned their campaign against some houses being built. Sometimes Grandie had even left her and Nando in the whole house alone together, which showed a *lot* of trust. At least, until this attempted inquisition. 'You're right,' Andie said, squeezing Grandie's rough gardening hand a moment. 'I'm sorry, I'm going into automatic; Mum spends her whole time lecturing me as if I'm about to become a complete tart – when all I've done is go to a few friends' birthday parties and watch boys puking up their sneaked-in beers!'

Grandie laughed. 'I know. She wants you to stay a little

girl forever. I admit a bit of me doesn't want to let go of little *Andita*, in a way. But I remember you said you wanted to wait until you were at least eighteen until you... had a proper boyfriend. Wanted to wait for somebody really special. I'm only asking how it's going because he's a beautiful Spanish boy in a beautiful setting with sultry weather and minimal clothing – it would be easy to get carried away.'

Andie shook her head. 'No. We haven't and won't. Just kissing and cuddles – that's it.' Grandie looked relieved. 'Although when he comes down again *next* summer...'

'But, Andie, you'd still only be sixteen! The best things are really worth waiting for, trust me.'

Andie got to her feet. 'Are there any of those watermelon lollies left?'

'No. Going to do a little shop later. You'll have to make do with one of those luminous Calippo things one of your friends brought round, or... *wait* for something better,' Grandie said with a grin.

Andie's eyes went heavenwards.

'I'll go after I've finished the Lookout Post tidy-up.'

''Kay.'

Grandie got up. 'You don't want to help me?'

'Too hot.' Also, she didn't want any more talk about 'waiting'; even with Grandie, this was *so* embarrassing. 'Don't overdo it,' she added, even though Grandie's energy and heat tolerance was that of a gecko.

Once she had the house to herself, she restarted Robbie's CD and whacked it up to the loudest you could get without distortion – a level conveniently marked by a tiny dot of pink that could actually be watermelon ice lolly. Nothing but the best for the best. *The best things are worth waiting for...*

She lay down on the floor and tried to starfish herself cool. Even though she'd been in the sea less than an hour ago. Trouble was – there was no denying it – the warmth was... *within* her too. Even just talking about how nothing was going to happen set off a crackling fire about... what wasn't going to happen. *Yet.* A fire but also a shiver, because wasn't it also a bit gross and yucky? Even the kissing was a bit that, although she was getting used to it and it came with cuddles and being able to look into those deep, black-brown eyes.

Wouldn't Mum be pleased to hear about her slight revulsion. Maybe she could take the credit for it; the cringey chats they'd had about 'sexual relations' never mentioned the idea of a woman enjoying it at all. No wonder Andie was an only child! Then there were the weird pregnancy warnings, in which Andie was apparently both 'just sure to get in trouble', that is, pregnant – but also sure, despite her regular and relatively painless 'monthlies', to have inherited her mum's and her mum's mum's severe problems with fertility! What? Bah, she'd show her. In ten years' time, after working as a botanical illustrator or garden designer in Madrid while Nando became an architect or something, his strong dark Mediterranean seed would do the trick. Oh no, the thought of that was making her even warmer...

Her Nokia played its tune. It couldn't be Nando; he'd be on the boat by now. Maybe Mum, with a sixth sense she was thinking about 'sexual relations', but she'd already called today, boring her to death about some church or something she and Dad were going to see in Seville – she could at least wait until she'd seen the damn thing.

Wait. What a word. Mum and Dad *waited* until they were married. Chatting after a glass of *fino*, Grandie once hinted that she and apparently then-gorgeous Gran-pa, *hadn't*. She and Nando would wait until next summer – by which time he might *not* have waited, having met a lovely local *madrileña*...

Uh, the phone, again. Just when Robbie's lovely 'Angels' was reassuring her with its soaring chorus about protection and affection. Like last time, the phone quickly stopped. She hauled herself upright and reached for it. *Grandie*. Aha. Probably the phone going off in her pocket again, like the other day.

She lay back down. This heat was exhausting. *Both* heats were exhausting. But perhaps lying here on her back wasn't helping. She would have been better off helping Grandie after all, taking her mind off it. She sat up again, sang along with the song. Picked up the phone again to call Grandie, but it rang in her hand... for actually the *fifth* time; previous calls must have hit loud bits on the CD. Maybe Grandie's battery was low – and she'd sprained that ankle again and needed help getting down the hill.

She quickly got up, grabbed a Coke from the fridge for Grandie, and went out into the oven-like afternoon. So much for only gardening in the mornings; there was just no stopping her these days, when she got excited about one of her little projects.

'Grandie?' She stood in front of the Lookout Post and looked up.

It's okay, Andie. Really, I'm fine.

'Your phone kept calling me. When we next go to Almería, we *are* going to buy a case for it, okay?' She took the path, round and round, stepping to the rhythm of Robbie's 'Angels' still playing in her head. 'Path's perfect now! Definitely time to go and get those lollies. God it's hot. Bought you a Coke.'

Grandie was sitting on the bench with her head in her hand, leaning against the olive tree, actually looking tired for once. Andie clonked the Coke down on the little wooden table in front of her... but her grandmother seemed to be asleep. She flumped down next to her on the bench, but this made Grandie lean further over to the tree, a lock of escaped hair falling further over her face.

'Grandie? You can't sleep out here, the ants'll get you – at least, that's what you always tell me.' She shook her shoulder gently and brushed the hair from her eyes... which were half open.

Her head reeled, heart punching her chest. 'Grandie?' No. No, no, *no*. '*Grandie?* Wake up! *Please!*' She shook her again, but Grandie just flopped right over to the side – and would have fallen from the bench, or even the hill, but the olive tree she'd planted and nurtured for years cradled her in its branch, as if it had grown this way for years just for this moment.

'Oh God...' Andie moved along the bench, leant against the olive tree branch, took out a tissue and blew her nose.

If there'd been anyway of saving me, I'd have tried to call an ambulance. But a heart attack, on top of a hillock in a big garden at the edge of a village half an hour from the hospital? No chance. I just wanted to say goodbye – as you saw on my phone, to you and José Luis – but my speech had gone, Andie thought she could hear Grandie say.

He missed you by minutes.

I knew he would, but I wanted him here for you, to deal with everything, and to look after you until your mother had you picked up by those inane English friends with the villa in Mojácar. And I didn't need to say goodbye to either of you; I didn't realise then that I would never leave you.

That's what José Luis said.

How perfect that you managed to see him. I think he's been holding on for that. Now he'll join me soon...

Oh God...

But, Andie, there really was nothing you could have done. You're too quick to blame yourself for everything – your mother's doing. It doesn't matter that you were lying there thinking of your love life while I was dying – actually, maybe it's rather how things should be.

Well...

And you're thinking that way again, rather appropriately, on the anniversary of my death.

What? No, nothing's going to happen.

The amphitheatre.

What?

That's the start. Possibly with a few bumps along the way, but the best things... I'm not saying any more – I mean, I'm not a witch with a bloody crystal ball.

Andie smiled through her tears. 'Okay!'

You've done a great job here – in every way – so you get back now.

Back at the flat, she showered and put a wash on, lay on her bed for a moment with the gentle whirring of the fan to plan the day still stretching before her. Feeling tired but peaceful, sensing a new start, a trust in fate. Even when she saw Johnny's name flash up on her phone screen, she felt she could deal with him kindly and gently, forgive him and try to make the first steps forward as friends.

'Johnny, how are you doing?'

'The better for hearing your voice! Listen, I was going to surprise you, but that would be crazy... I've managed to plan an escape for a couple of days! I'll be there on Friday morning, sadly got to fly back on Sunday.'

'*Here?*' What was he thinking of? There was no way he could stay *here*.

'Well no, your place sounds a bit basic... I've booked us a divine hotel.'

'*Us?* Johnny, we're friends. Friends don't share hotel rooms, I'm sorry,' she said, with her newfound patience.

He hesitated. 'Well... I'll be there anyway, it's just five minutes' walk from you. We can talk. I've missed you, baby.'

Baby. He was going to have to stop that. Somehow nobody treats her like 'little Andie' here; she's not used to it anymore. 'Obviously it will be nice to see you, but nothing's going to change, Johnny; it'll be a disaster if you don't understand that before you come out.'

'I don't want a disaster!' he said, which wasn't really answering the question. 'It's a short visit but we can have fun. And you won't believe it, I did some googling and even got us some tickets for a local concert on Saturday night!

Sort of flamenco-pop by the sound of it – not really my thing, but how bad can it be, in an amphitheatre next to a botanical garden?'

20

Friday 24th August

'At least he's not taking up mornings you could be seeing Vicente,' Shefali was saying on her phone screen.

'What? I wouldn't let him! That's my job – well, one of them. My *mission*.'

'Your *passion*.'

'Hm.'

'I meant for the *garden*,' Shefali said, with a twitch of a smile.

'Of course you did,' Andie said, even though Shefali had told her not to give up hope.

'And now we're all booked to come out at half-term. Are you going to have a word with Valentina?'

'Yes, and she's been talking about upgrading her patio, so maybe we can cut a deal. Look I've gotta go, need to send a fully emoji'd happy birthday message to Fabian before I go to the airport.'

'Ah, Fabian. Send him my love.'

'I will.'

They said their goodbyes, then Andie made another tea and settled down on the sofa to do her WhatsApp to ex-boyfriend Fabian. Everybody had loved solid, butter-gold, kind, hardworking, and modest Fabian. Even Mum, rubbing her hands at the idea of Andie marrying into the Van den Berg family, with their international seed nursery business. *She* had loved Fabian, although ultimately not enough to relocate back to his native Netherlands with him – especially after a confidence-sapping year of trying to grow a child. Since their civilised break-up nearly three years ago, they'd kept in touch with messages at Christmas and birthdays, reporting anything significant – such as Andie's TV show, and Fabian getting engaged and then married. She'd recently heard his wife was pregnant, but he hadn't shared that with her yet. She sent off a message with the usual birthday emojis along with tulips and his beloved cheese and a bicycle; the man was literally a Dutch caricature, bless him.

The phone rang almost immediately. 'Andie! Thank you for remembering! How are you?' he said in his soft Dutch accent.

'I'm fine! Having six weeks in Spain, and doing an hour a day on Grandie's garden!'

'*Fantastisch!* Look, have you a moment? I've been meaning to tell you something.'

'I heard about the baby, and I'm *delighted* for you! When is he or she due?'

'I don't know which type it is, but we still have nearly another six months. I also wanted to tell you… we needed help, they found I have a low sperm motility.'

'Oh…'

'So yes, this means… there may well be nothing wrong with *you*. It could have been all my problem.'

'God… well I'm so glad it worked out for you and Sanne! But thanks for letting me know. I was always convinced it was me.'

'I know, whatever I said! So, there you go.'

The alarm went off on her phone. 'Oh, I've got to go and pick a friend up from the airport. I'll text you again soon. Have a great day!'

'Thanks! You take care, sweetie.'

So maybe she *could* have a child. Or at least, produce one. She still wasn't sure she could look after one, keep it safe, bring it up to be a confident, happy human being. Maybe it was all those years of Mum telling her how useless she'd be at it – unless marrying Fabian and affording a full-time nanny, that was. Mum had died happily believing that was going to happen – and Dad not long after her. Also, being short and 'babied' by all four of her boyfriends didn't exactly make her feel like mother material.

Meanwhile, she had a tall Irishman to collect from the airport. Bloody hell. And she was going to be late and on the back foot from the off if she didn't get a move on.

Turning up outside the airport just as Johnny came out of the sliding doors, she gave the horn a little toot and they grinned at each other. It was the sort of unbelievable timing that you'd see as magical telepathy – if you weren't picking up an ex for an uninvited visit.

She got out of the car and was half squeezed to death; she'd forgotten how *big* he was. 'Can't really stop here,' she said, detaching herself. 'We need to move on.' Wasn't *that* the truth.

'Okay!' He flung his flight bag on to the back seat and got in next to her, beaming as if their relationship was on a new high, rather than on a rock-bottom like-to-stay-friends low.

She drove off, concentrating on the series of mini roundabouts to get back on the coast road.

A hand landed on her thigh. 'Can't tell you how much I've missed you.'

Ah. How she should she answer that? *Can't tell you I've missed you at all?* No, that wasn't true; she had at first. She gently moved his hand on to his own knee, patting it to soften the act.

'Oops, sorry,' he said. 'Difficult to get out of the habit.'

'How's Jazzy?'

'Doing very well. Looks like she'll only miss the first week of school now.'

'Oh, that's good.'

'And loves the turtle you gave her. Calls her Tandie, as in turtle-Andie.'

'Really? Ah.'

'I'm taking the girls to Longleat Safari Park for three days at half-term. They asked if you could come.'

Good God, the kind of situation she used to daydream about. Why *now*? 'That's lovely, but... we'll have to see.' She could have told him she was planning to be here at half-term, but that might have prompted questions she didn't want to answer.

'Wow, look at the colour of that sea!' he said.

She glanced over. Deep blue, with translucent turquoise in the frill-topped waves. A yellow flag flapped in the breeze, although really it looked like one of those stroppy but harmless seas.

'It'll be calmer in San José. How d'you fancy a wild beach with just sand, rocks, and dwarf palms?'

'Sounds *won*derful.'

She filled the rest of the journey with tour guide information and then drove in to the village looking forward to at least a half hour respite to get herself a bit more together after the Longleat suggestion. 'I'll drop you off at your hotel and let you settle in, and then—'

'What? No! Come in and see. Looked gorgeous in the photos.' He'd sent them to her, but she'd only really glanced to check where he was going to be. 'Quite a step up from your place.'

'Okay, but don't diss my little flat; I'm very happy there.'

It was indeed very marbled and spacious inside, with impressively large succulents in glitzy – rather than Níjar – pots, and oversize bulbous table lamps with shells stuck on them. Generic Mediterranean. Ah, but possibly saved by a beautiful mural of Genoveses beach.

'That's the one I had in mind,' she said, pointing to the mural, but Johnny was involved in some kind of confusion at the reception desk. They wanted to look at her passport too.

'Oh no, I'm not staying here,' she said in Spanish.

The boy and girl receptionists looked at each other, the girl then consulting a printout. 'Andrea Butt-s?'

'Yes, that's me, but—'

'I put her down because she's going to be coming and going. Can't she bring her passport later?' he asked, assuming they spoke English.

The man had to deal with a call, but the perplexed

girl was soon persuaded by Johnny's twinkly blue-eyed smile, nodded, and said they were still just in time for complimentary breakfast.

They went up to the room and opened the door. Was this the honeymoon suite or what? A wide balcony looking down over the pool garden, the village, and the entire sweep of the bay, and oh God, inside the coolly air-conditioned room... champagne, nibbles, fruit, and a vast acreage of bed. No wonder the receptionist looked confused.

'What d'you think?' Johnny asked, a hand on her back.

'Well, very nice of course. And why not, when you're only here for two days.'

He unzipped his bag, took out swimming trunks and a singlet, and started unbuttoning his shirt.

To avoid watching him change, she went out onto the balcony, closing the sliding door behind her. It would be easier once they were on the beach. Other people around. Gardening work talk. Sooner or later, hopefully a calm acknowledgement that they were moving on to a new phase as friends. The door slid open, and air-con-cooled arms were soon enveloping her and then turning her round and pulling her to him. Against the chest she used to love to lie against, and against the thin shorts that soon showed a more-than-just-friendly interest in her.

She hesitated a moment, her body remembering... then pulled back, her hands on his chest both keeping him at a distance but in gentle contact. 'Johnny... please don't make me spell things out.'

He put a cool hand to her face, searched her eyes. 'But what *changed*?' he said with a disarming gentleness. 'I don't understand. There was the accident. You felt terrible, but you know nobody blames you for that now. Certainly *I* don't, and never did. There's no reason why—'

'Have you forgotten how you lied to me about getting divorced? You took away all tr—'

'Of course I haven't. Look…' He let go and beckoned her to follow him inside, then pulled papers out of an envelope and held them out to her.

She took them and leafed through. Letters between him and a lawyer – an explanation, a checklist of things to do, an interim invoice… for divorce from Caroline O'Connor.

'Oh.'

'What I should have done before.' He was studying her face. 'Can't you forgive me?'

She looked up, handing the papers back and bracing herself for the full-on charm offensive – but he actually looked quite concerned.

'Give me time.' She smiled at him. 'How about we go down and try out their marbled breakfast? Come on.'

It was a buffet with an excellent spread of anything you could possibly want, and very obliging staff, considering they were turning up just ten minutes before it closed. Whatever concerns Johnny might have been having about the state of their relationship, it didn't seem to be spoiling his appetite – and Andie was surprised to find herself enthusiastically carbo-loading as if for a marathon. After she recounted how squirreling away lunch food from hotel breakfasts used to be essential for holiday budgeting, they exchanged a look and found themselves giggling as they stuffed tortilla slices, banana bread, pastries and apples into napkins and then – at the right moment – into Andie's voluminous cloth bag.

Half an hour later, having picked up towels, an umbrella, an ice box, drinks, and crisps from Andie's place, they arrived at the wild Genoveses beach.

'Shall we go up that end, near the pine trees?' she asked, knowing the barren landscape wasn't to everyone's taste.

Johnny was standing hand on hip, looking from one end of the beach to the other. 'This is spectacular,' he said. 'Do people in the UK even know this exists?'

'Seems not. They all shoot past on the A7 to Mojácar, where they can all be English together.'

'But Jaysus it's hot,' he said, his Irish accent sounding almost comical in the semi-desert. 'I say we just flop down straight ahead and get in that water as soon as possible.'

They were going to be where she was when she came here with Ben, Kim, and Carlito. But it was a Friday morning, so everyone she knew – except Kim, who went to the village beach on weekdays – was at work; nobody was going to see her here with him. In fact, if she could somehow keep him away from the village centre and the promenade, she might be able to get away without having to explain why on earth she'd let this visit happen at all.

They set up camp, swam in the waves – which were, as she'd predicted, just splashy ones. Hopefully like this weekend: some awkward moments, but fun in between. Sitting under the umbrella on their towels, she tried to avoid looking at his freckled, chunky, masculine physique. It was odd to be finding it both sweetly familiar and – after the hurt he'd caused, and the feelings she now had for Vicente and his dark, panther-like form – somewhat alien.

Then he reached over and took her hand. 'I love you, Andie. You do know that, don't you?'

Oh. Had he ever really said that before? Perhaps it was the first time it didn't just sound like pacifying words. Before she could think of an answer, a plastic football thwacked into her knees and bounced straight into Johnny's hands.

A fair-haired boy about Rafi's age approached, gave both of them a cheeky smile and said '*Merci!*' before scampering off.

'Could be ours,' Johnny said.

'Not really; he's French!' Andie said. Also, it was time he knew the truth. 'Anyway, both my mother and my mother's mother took at least ten years to conceive, and they started in their early twenties, not thirty-five. It's possible it wouldn't happen.'

'Oh?' His face was pinched with concern. 'Why didn't you tell me this before? Aren't there tests you could have?'

'Well, we weren't really at that stage, were we? I mean, I hadn't yet been allowed to meet the children you already have.' Oh no, it was all coming out now.

'It just had to be the right time, that's all. I told you I loved you, we talked about children… what more proof did you need that I was serious about you?'

'A divorce that you weren't lying about?'

'Which you will now have! What more can I do?'

What indeed; her more obvious reasons for rejecting him – other than her unrequited love for Vicente and her wanting to try living here – were being rapidly knocked down like skittles. She smoothed the soft, warm sand flat with her hand. There was nothing he could do, but *nothing* was an awful word. 'I don't know, Johnny. I'm a bit in limbo, to be honest…'

'Well, you won't be for long; Andie, the producers want

to do a spin-off show with just the two of us. Visiting gardens that first inspired various well-known gardeners, designers and horticulturalists... possibly including your grandmother's.'

'What?' Her heart began to tap.

'Starting in early spring, because some of the gardens are in warmer climates. We get to come here, St Lucia, Florida, Malta, Cornwall, Jersey, a boat on the Norfolk Broads, would you believe, and then Ireland of course... eight weeks. It'll overlap with *Challenging Gardens*, but they say they'll somehow make it work for me. And the money's ten per cent more! Plus all the magazine tie-ins et cetera. You're looking... shocked.'

'I am! I mean...' She shook her head, trying to process what it would mean: some wonderful experiences and a boost to her finances that could buy her the time to find her feet in Spain – but a prolonged awkward proximity to Johnny. He would also have to meet Vicente.

'Surely you can't be thinking of turning it *down*?'

She drank some water. 'Of course not!'

He took her hand. 'We work well together, you know we do. And the producers – and the whole country – can see that.'

'Yes, I know,' she said, smiling. 'It's fantastic news, Johnny.' But if they were going to work together, it had to be completely clear – to him, and 'the whole country' – that they were just friends.

'So tell me – it means so much to you, and it could also be one of the stars of the show... When can I see Grandie's paradise garden?'

'Ah. Well the owner's in Almería today and tomorrow.'

Well, he might be – although he and Rafi might well be coming back this morning after the boy's little flamenco show yesterday evening.

'Can't you call him and ask him to come back early?'

'I think he has family things on.' Not a complete lie; it was feasible they might be staying on in Almería to have lunch with Uncle Juanito and Iván.

'I'll just have to visit first thing on Sunday, before the airport.'

That sounded a better idea: a quick tour round, very little time for the two men to chat. 'I'll ask... God, I can't believe this, but I'm actually hungry again,' she said, opening the ice box and taking out some tortilla and, seeing him nodding, handing him a paper plate. She listened to a Spanish couple nearby laughing about their UK one o'clock lunchtime.

After lunch Johnny stood up and looked at the sea. 'Wow, look at those waves now. Shall we go in again?'

The sea now seemed to be intent on justifying its yellow flag, or even being offered an upgrade to red. 'I dunno...' People forget waves are more frightening when you're a small person.

'Come on, I'll look after you.'

He pulled her to her feet and they walked hand and hand into the sea, Johnny lifting her up and over some wobbly potentially washing-machine-like breakers. She screamed and laughed, but had soon had enough.

'Okay, let's get you out of this,' he shouted, although by this he meant carrying her into hilly but more peaceful deeper water – where she had no choice but to stay in his arms.

He held her close as the sea lifted them up and down.

Closer than a friend should be holding her... and kissed her cheek.

'Let's get out, brave these breakers before they get any bigger,' she said.

'Okay. And after that early start, I could do with a siesta.'

'Good idea.'

They packed up their things, walked back to the car, and drove back to the village.

Andie parked outside his hotel, looked at her watch, and yawned; the day seemed to be taking an enormous amount of nervous energy out of her.

'Okay, how about I come back here at about...'

He put a salty arm round her shoulders. 'You're tired too. How about you come in and have a siesta with me? I pro—'

'I don't think that's—'

'Just a friendly one, I promise.'

'No, I'll—'

'The bed's vast. It won't be difficult to be on top of each other... Jaysus! I meant, *not* on top of each other,' he said, laughing.

She laughed too, in spite of herself.

'I mean, we can build a pillow wall between us, if you're worried! Come on, it'll be nice.'

A companionable sleep, before or after which they could have a quiet talk about their friendship and how to manage it... 'Okay.'

They went past the smiling receptionists and up to the room, Andie giving Johnny the first shower, sure he'd be asleep by the time she was out of hers. She eventually crept out, wearing the sandy T-shirt and shorts she'd had over her bikini, wishing she had some underwear. He was turned towards the curtained window, his slow breathing suggesting he was indeed asleep. She was about to lie down next to him, when her phone pealed in her beach bag.

She quickly grabbed the bag and took it into the bathroom to silence it. It was a WhatsApp from Marcelo, inviting her to another barbecue Sunday lunch. There was also an early morning one from Vicente that she had missed. *'I will be CROSS if you have worked on anfiteatro without us! WAIT for me and Rafi. Come on Monday.'* He'd added the angry goblin's face, whose fiery eyes and pinched eyebrows looked laughably familiar.

She sent back a laughing face and a thumbs-up, turned the phone to silent, and went back into the bedroom. Crept on to the bed as gently as she could, so as not to wake him. Lying there next to him, despite everything, she felt a connection; she didn't *love* him, she knew that now, but there was an undeniable warmth and friendship between them that they might never lose. Like between her and Fabian – except she and Johnny would be working together, so they'd have to draw some boundaries. She'd talk about this when he woke up.

Then he turned over, his pale blue eyes looking into hers. 'Oh, Andie... you let me fall asleep. I nearly didn't get to feel you next to me again,' he said, pulling her into his arms.

Just for a moment, she thought, enjoying the closeness in the almost English climate of the room... but his hand had gone up under her T-shirt.

He groaned. 'Oh God... I've been waiting to do that all day...'

Waiting. *I remember you said you wanted to wait for somebody really special... The best things are really worth waiting for, trust me… WAIT for me and Rafi…* Of course, she could wait forever for Vicente. It was quite possibly hopeless, but it would be better to be on her own, waiting, than to mislead a friend like this.

She sat up and pulled her T-shirt down. 'I'm *really* sorry… but this can't happen.'

He looked down at the sheet for a moment, took a breath, then looked at her with a wry smile. 'Pillow wall?'

'Pillow wall.'

21

'*B*uenos días! Thought you might be coming for break-fast?' Johnny, sounding cheery in her ear.

'Had mine an hour ago!' she answered, finishing the sentence in her email with her other hand.

'A *second* breakfast again?'

'Ha! No. I've got some stuff I need to send to Gerard.'

'Have you told him about *Gardens that Inspired*?'

'I thought I'd wait until it's all…'

'It's definite, all right. You heard Hilary; you'll get the contract through in the next week.' Her agent had called when they were just off to celebrate the new programme in the swanky fish restaurant at the marina. Hilary had been delighted of course, and took credit for the idea of Johnny coming all the way out to tell Andie about it in person – although Johnny denied this.

'Gerard'll be worried about the Hampton Court Palace Garden Festival,' Andie said.

'Bah – he'll manage. Or maybe they can work it into the

schedule so you're free for that. Anyway, let's get in that sea! I'll be with you in half an hour.'

The village beach on a Saturday morning – much too high a chance of bumping into someone she knew. 'No, I'll pick you up. You're on the way... I've got a little outing planned – don't worry, involving lots of sea! We'll drive along the coast road to the old gold mining village of San Rafael in its own huge, beautiful valley, and—'

'But won't we see that when we go to the concert later?'

'Well, no wait... we'll then go to its lovely local beach, that has a *fortress* you can wander round.' That should do it; Johnny *adored* castles – probably from growing up on an island full of them.

'Ah. That sounds good.'

'We can stop off at a little bakery in San Rafael that does amazing *empanadillas* for some lunch bits – but don't forget to pinch some banana bread.'

'Okay!'

She put the phone back on the table, checked and sent off her email, and then put her laptop away. Sprawled out on the sofa for a moment. Now that it had sunk in, she was really excited about the new programme; she'd meet some interesting people talking about their gardening passion, and travel to some beautiful places – which was more than could be said about *Challenging Gardens*. Best of all, she'd have enough money coming that she wouldn't have to worry about spending her savings while she looked for the right opportunity in Almería.

The only niggling worry was Johnny. That new insistence that she should give him another chance, after his being quiet for a while, seemed to have coincided with news of the programme; as she'd always suspected, their romantic relationship seemed to depend on working together. She just had to completely clarify that working together didn't depend on them having a romantic relationship.

So far, so good, she thought, waving back to Johnny over on the flat, white rocks surrounding the fortress and then lying back on her towel. Even if he'd annoyed her by going on about the lush rainforest-clad mountains of St Lucia rather than appreciating the starkly beautiful, stubbly, red-earthed ones here.

She sat up again and helped herself to another spinach-and-cheese *empanadilla*. God, if coping with Johnny was going to keep needing such constant refuelling, they'd have to roll her on and off set by the end of the series.

'Well, well!' She turned to find Ben behind her, accompanied by a Spanish girl with a closed smile who she might have met before.

'Oh hello! Finished work already?'

'Once a month I get the whole Saturday off.' He pointed to the size eleven Crocs by the other towel. 'So who have you brought here then? No way can those belong to Vicente's powerful but fine-tuned feet.'

'Oh, Ben, will you *stop* about him! Actually, I'm having a bit of a mare – my ex has come over to discuss a new TV programme we've been offered. Staying in the Atalaya two nights. It's great news and all that, and won't stop me coming here, but…'

'Christ, congratulations but… *awk-ward*! Can we rescue you in some way?'

'No, I'm being mean; it's fine.'

'An English voice!' Johnny was back.

'Yes, Ben's a gardener at the botanical garden, and this is...' She pointed to the girl and Ben introduced Rosi, a biology student at the university.

Johnny and Ben chatted about the botanical garden for a bit, Rosi joining in with a bit of English.

'Shame I didn't get to see it,' Johnny said. 'But the garden I really want to visit is Andie's grandmother's old place.'

'But Vicente's in Almería this weekend, so all we've managed is a drive-by and my photos,' Andie said.

'Ah. I'm afraid he's a bit of a recluse. Practically chased one of the local builders from the property!' Ben said, rather overdoing his support.

'We wanted to include his garden in the programme, if it lives up to the photos,' Johnny said, scratching his chin. 'How's that going to work?'

'Programme?' Ben asked, and then listened with interest to Johnny telling him about it, no doubt for later relaying to the expat group.

'He just needs some notice,' Andie said. 'He's a private person, that's all.'

Ben's girl was saying something to him in Spanish.

'Rosi needs to swim. See you later.'

Once they'd gone, Johnny sat down on his towel, shuffled through the ice box, and took out a couple of Cokes. 'Nice chap. So he lives here? All year round?'

'Yes. Loves it. Wouldn't go back to soggy Sussex for the world.'

'No doubt the local girls love *him*.'

'So I've been told.'

Johnny looked puzzled. '*He* told you that?'

'No, my friend Kim did.'

'What does *he* do here?'

'Kim's a girl. Teaches English. She's become quite a chum.'

'So you're an honorary member of the expat set?'

'Well, all of about six of them, yes. There's a bar they meet at once a week.'

'Aha. And you go to the beach with them, go to their places?'

'Sometimes. There's also a Spanish builder in their friendship group who so reminds me of Steve. Even has a nurse wife, too.'

'Aha,' he said again.

'And Shefali came over, of course. That was great. It's been lovely, and I'll probably be coming over quite often to manage the importing of the pots for Gerard.' This was good, gradually introducing the idea of her living here; if she told him outright, he'd laugh his head off.

'Oh yes. Well, if you have time. That's going to feel like chicken feed. I don't think you realise how you're going to be on a whole new level of demand once this programme starts.'

'That sounds… frightening.' But surely it would be up to her how much she wanted to do with that demand.

He reached over and squeezed her hand. 'Don't worry; I'll be there.'

'Yes, but as a *friend*, right? Please don't expect more.'

'I know, you need time.'

'I need time to… get used to us being friends, Johnny. To be completely relaxed with you… in this new phase.'

He was still holding her hand. As far as she knew, no

woman had even turned Johnny down; it was *him* who needed time to process.

She squeezed his hand and let go. 'Come on, let's get in that sea.'

They jumped and body-surfed on the waves, shouting, screaming, and laughing.

Then it was back for their siestas, Andie gently turning down another pillow-walled one.

The plan – unfortunately one she couldn't wriggle out of – was to meet at Andie's and go for a stroll and an early dinner in the little village square that Johnny had discovered on his own, and then drive over to San Rafael for the concert.

'Sunflower Andie – suits you!' he said, when she came down to him on the pavement in front of Valentina's.

'Thanks!' He was dressed in linen trousers and a crisp designer shirt that were more than he needed for any of the *plaza* eating places or the old mine ruin amphitheatre.

They walked to the *plaza* and he stood right in the middle and surveyed it: the brightly painted cafes and ice cream parlour; a tatty-looking doctor's surgery and Third Age meeting place; a gecko logoed, incense-smelling shop of thin, drapey clothing; a mobile book stall; and numerous and mostly occupied stone benches under the clipped, wide crowns of Southern magnolias. There were sandy holidaymakers still in beachwear; elderly locals greeting each other; and shouty, happy children on the swings and playframes under the Washingtonias.

'Where's the church?' he asked.

'Up on the hill going up to Grandie's. Just a small one, but very pretty.'

He looked around again. 'Pretty basic, but has a charm.' It sounded like he was appraising it for the programme. 'Heavens, why don't they paint the surgery?'

'I don't know. The *ayuntamiento* seem to spend all their money on the roundabouts.'

'Of course, that could be done for the programme. Little bit of smartening up here and there without changing the vibe or pissing anyone off.'

'Sounds good. Where did you want to eat?'

'I don't mind, babe. You choose.'

'Maybe the one with the flamenco chill music then, to get us in the… oh!' A child had barrelled into her and now had slim arms round her waist. 'Rafi! Hello!'

Lucía beamed beside him, and Andie now spotted Marcelo and Beatriz standing by the climbing frame and waved. Rafi must be on a play date – and Vicente must be back from Almería too.

'How was your flamenco show?' she asked Rafi in Spanish.

'Good! I was good! And everybody else!'

She could sense but didn't look to see Johnny's amazement at this little friendship.

Beatriz had come over. 'Andie! How are you doing?' she asked in Spanish. 'I heard all about the little hill in the garden, so cute. Marcelo has already put up the railing.'

'Oh great, that was quick!'

'Now they're talking about a little shelter from the sun up there.' She looked at Johnny. 'Oh, I'm sorry… we have to speak in Engl-eesh! We speak of something in the garden of Andie's grandmother.'

'Ah yes! I'm Johnny, by the way,' he said, pointing to himself.

'Beatriz,' she said, surprising him with a kiss on each cheek. 'My husband Marcelo is builder. He works in the garden too.'

'Ah yes, Andie told me.'

'Johnny's over to talk about a new TV programme we've been asked to do,' Andie said.

'Yes!' Beatriz replied, unsurprised; clearly word had already got around. 'Then you must meet two stars for the show – Marcelo and Vicente!' She pointed back to the climbing frame, where... good God, Vicente was talking to Marcelo and some parents whose children were playing with Rafi and Lucía. Andie's head reeled; Vicente had picked a truly terrible day to come out of his unsociable shell.

Beatriz took Johnny by the arm, and Andie followed on wobbly legs. There were introductions and double kisses, and then a distinct moment when Vicente and Johnny looked each other up and down with barely concealed suspicion.

Seeing Andie had gone speechless, Beatriz leapt in with an English explanation of why Johnny was here, and Johnny suddenly snapped into affable celebrity mode and described in slow English what the programme was about and how he hoped they could include the Casa Higuera garden.

Rafi came up again with Lucía and a quiet little girl, and grabbed Andie's arm for attention. 'I'm going to the village school, with Lucía and Doina!'

The other parents smiled and looked over at Vicente.

Vicente said they were going to talk about it, but that was enough to make the children jump up and down.

Vicente turned to Johnny. 'Of course you must see the garden, but today I am busy. Tomorrow morning?'

'I'm afraid it would have to be eight o'clock; I'm off to the airport.'

'It's okay, Rafi gets me up early,' Vicente said, with a nod and a polite smile.

'Great. We're about to have something to eat before the concert in San Rafael…' Andie said, keen to bring the conversation to a close, and after saying their goodbyes, she and Johnny went over and sat down at a table and ordered some drinks.

'A *bottle* of wine?' Andie asked after the waitress had left. 'I won't have a drop, with a cliff-top drive ahead of me. Shall we change that?'

'No,' Johnny said. 'I'm *not* driving. In fact, I'm not sure I want to go at all. Here's your ticket,' he said, pulling a folded printout from his pocket and slapping it on the table.

'Why?' she said, bracing herself for the inevitable.

'You said he was in Almería all weekend and, with Ben in cahoots, painted him as some kind of sociopath. You've done everything you can to keep me hidden from your friends – particularly *him*. Are you going to tell me what's going on?'

'There's nothing "going on". He *was* in Almería; I didn't know he'd be back today.'

'Oh come on, this is more than a bit of gardening for him now and then. The boy clearly sees you as a future stepmother.'

She took a deep breath. 'The garden is important to Rafi, so obviously he's become attached.'

'As has his father. Not quite the little bespectacled nerd you had me believe, is he? What is he, an actor?'

'He used to be a flamenco dancer, but now works on music at home so he can look after his little boy. He's a widower.'

'Ha! Perfect!' he said, with a sneer. 'So now he's—'

'A *friend*.'

The wine had arrived, and Johnny nearly spat out his first mouthful in amusement. 'A *friend*! Dear Mary Mother of God. Andie. A dark flamenco animal like that does *not* have women as *friends*. He's just waiting for his chance to—'

'Well this one does. And he's not an *animal*. I can't believe you're coming out with this racist stereotypical crap.'

'Whoa, keep your voice down; the locals will string me up.'

'He *is* a friend, and he's never once treated me with anything but respect, never stepped over the boundary... unlike *you*!'

He put down his glass. 'What? A month ago we were—'

'And now we're *not*, and it's time you accepted that. It's highly unlikely that I would have started something with someone else, but if I had, I would have told you.'

He fixed her with those pale blue eyes for a moment. 'Yes. I think you would,' he said quietly. 'But...'

She looked down at her juice, heart beating. He'd rumbled her.

'You're in love with him, aren't you.'

She took a sip of her drink. She couldn't lie about that. She checked to see that Vicente had gone. 'I'm in love with Vicente, Rafi, my new friends, the blue skies, the cacti, warm sea, fuzzy orange mountains, ceramics, flamenco, the lot. I'm going to try and live here.'

'Ha!' he said, throwing back his head. 'So you can move in with Señor Sex-on-Legs *and* have your grandmother's garden! Fecking *brilliant*!' He put some notes down on the table. 'I'll see you tomorrow morning at the garden. Some guys in the hotel invited me to join them for a drink tonight; I'm sure they'll be much better company than a deluded, throw-your-life-away little cat on heat.'

He got up abruptly, making their drinks slop over the table, and strode off over the plaza.

The waitress came up and wiped the table, asked if she was okay.

'I *will* be, thanks,' Andie said, her heart still pounding.

Back in the apartment, she flopped on the bed and unfolded the wine-splattered printout of the ticket. It was actually two tickets, on the same page. Was she up to going? She still had an hour to calm down before she had to drive. She messaged Kim and flopped back down.

Had she scuppered the TV programme? She reckoned probably not. She'd never seen Johnny like that before; he was usually such an easy-going chap – with a business head firmly screwed on. Maybe this thunderstorm blow-up was what they'd needed, before settling into an understanding. She was more worried about Vicente; if there was the slightest chance that he could see her as a girlfriend, seeing her still tied up with the ex she'd said she'd finished with might put him off for good.

Her phone buzzed a message. Kim. '*Andie! God, I'm sorry. What a mess. But I can't make the concert. We're having a little do for Mum's birthday. How about asking another friend who likes flamenco?*' she asked, with a winking emoji.

Hm. But actually, they were friends weren't they, so why not? Or was she going to buy into Johnny's stereotype of a man who wouldn't expect a woman to ask him out? She went over to Vicente's WhatsApp – and saw she'd missed a message. '*All okay?*' he'd asked, followed by a worried-face emoji. He'd somehow picked up on the tension between her and Johnny.

'No. *He now doesn't want to come to the concert – having a drink with some guys in his hotel instead! I've got two tickets here. Would you like to come?*' She sent it off, pleased she'd mentioned Johnny wasn't staying with her – but then realised how thoughtless she'd been, and started typing: '*if you can find someone to look after Ra—*'

'*I'm already going!*' he answered. '*I'm meeting a friend there who is playing at the end. I can pick up you at 21:00.*'

'*Okay!*'

They were quiet in the car, Vicente looking over and smiling a couple of times, as if encouraging her to explain if she wanted to.

'He just came over, uninvited. To tell me about this programme they want us to present,' she said.

He nodded.

'But also to try and repair things between us and start again. Which is *not* what I want at all.'

He nodded again and smiled; for a probably deluded moment, she thought he looked relieved to hear that.

'You need to make that clear before the television show,' he said.

'I've spent two days trying to do that. I think we needed that argument to clear the air.'

'Argument?'

'In the restaurant.'

'About the *show*?'

She looked over at him. He glanced back sheepishly out of the side of his glasses.

'*No*, Vicente. About *you*, obviously. You and everyone else. My life here.'

His lips parted for a moment in surprise.

My life here. Oops. Well, she was going to start telling him sooner or later. They'd come to the part of the coastal road with a steep drop to the dark blue sea below, and then there was the turn inland to the blind summit and the revelation of the San Rafael valley in all its full deeply shadowed and sunset glory.

'*So* beautiful,' she said.

'Nowhere more beautiful! But not many see that.'

'Which is good – keeps it nice and uncrowded for those who do!'

'Yes. Although maybe if I allow this garden programme here, all the English will come! *Qué fatal.*'

'Fatal indeed! You *can* say no; there'll be other gardens they—'

'Andie, is joke! Of course I want to do it; people will be happy when they see the wonderful Grandie-Andie garden on their television. And with the money we can make it even better.' He patted her shoulder and they exchanged a smile.

He drove down into the village and then up to the car park opposite the amphitheatre. Just as they parked, a van pulled in next to them and Vicente and the man in the other car raised a thumb at each other.

He turned to her. 'Poor Josemi. He's very sad at the moment, because he recently broke with an Englishwoman, a designer from London who treated him like toy. I'm telling you this because it's possible he will look at you with... *horror*.'

'Oh dear, okay.'

They got out, and there were the usual warm Spanish greetings. Josemi had Vicente's naturally intense look, but was tall and bear-like with a mop of mad hair. He did indeed look bothered by Andie, until Vicente introduced her as his 'super gardener and friend'.

Vicente said something in Spanish, and Josemi nodded and pulled a harmonica out of his shirt pocket.

'Josemi goes up at the end. He is fantastic painter, you should see, but also a *monstruo* with this thing!'

'Vicente could be guest also. They have asked, but he says no,' Josemi told her in heavily accented English.

'Maybe next year,' Vicente said.

'Ha! Well, is more than you say last year!' Josemi thumped Vicente's back.

They were allowed in early, with other special '*invitados*', and took their seats in the front row. During the day, the amphitheatre wasn't much more than a rectangle of concrete with a single tier round the edge, but at night it was transformed, overlooked by the silhouetted mountain behind it, lit round the edge as well as on the wooden stage. There was a lively drinks van with people queuing, greeting friends, and women laughing as they pulled out fans to cope with the evening heat.

Half an hour later than scheduled, as seemed to be the flamenco way, the band – all six of them – came on. The music was a chilled flamenco-pop-Latin fusion, with some well-known songs that some of the audience were singing along to. Andie recognised a couple of Chambao tracks she had on an album. She found herself smiling, as if the harmonies and pulsing rhythms were throwing a soothing shawl over her.

Eventually Vicente nudged Josemi, and his friend got up to join in with a version of the plaintive *Contigo en La Distancia*, which can't have been easy, thinking of his London ex-girlfriend, now very distant in every way. Then he joined in with an upbeat final number and the concert finished with thundering applause, whistles, and exclamations.

A man got up to give thanks to various people. She couldn't understand everything he was saying, but there was something about a concert being cancelled.

When Josemi came back and they'd both congratulated him on his performance, he explained that their second concert in a couple of weeks' time had been cancelled because the council had to dig up the road for some drain works.

'What a shame!' Andie said, making an effort to speak in Spanish. 'Isn't there another place they could play, near here?'

'Another *amphitheatre*, perhaps,' Vicente said, exchanging a lip-biting grin with Andie.

'What?' Andie exclaimed with a laugh. Could they get it ready in time?

'But where?' Josemi asked.

'In our garden!' Vicente said. 'It's the same size as this. People could park…'

'Fantastic!' Josemi said. 'Let's go and talk to the manager.'

22

Sunday 26th August

Johnny put down his coffee and took her hand over the breakfast table. 'I really didn't think you'd come.'

Andie squeezed and let go. 'I really didn't think you'd ask. Thought you'd boil for a few weeks before speaking to me again.'

He shook his head. 'Not my style.'

'No,' she said with a smile.

'*Please* forget those awful things I said. It's your life, you've made friends here, and have obviously thought it through. It was just a bit of a shock, that's all. Honestly, babe, I wish you luck with it.'

'Thanks. And please, you don't have to keep apologising.'

'Obviously I'd prefer you to live in England, and I still doubt Vicente would be good for you... but then I'd probably think that about any guy at the moment, to be fair.'

'I might not like actually living here, who knows what'll happen with the pot importing and finding enough work – and as for Vicente, we really are just friends. But, Johnny, I *would* still like to do the programme.'

He nodded. 'And you don't have to keep saying that – I'm not going to boot you out of it! We're going to make a fantastic show, and have a great time together.'

She looked up from her tea.

'As *friends*,' he added.

She smiled at him. 'Absolutely we are.' She looked at her watch. 'Aha! Time for your tour of the garden. Now come on, wrap up that slice of banana bread for the plane, and let's go.'

They were a bit early, but the gates were open and Vicente came out to greet them. '*Buenos días!* I won't go over the garden with you, it's better you concentrate and see point of view of the programme.'

'Oh, okay,' Johnny said, looking pleased.

They thanked him and set off round the garden – the paths, the little 'rooms' for games, play or resting, the enormous fig specimens, even the Lookout – with Grandie nodding approval, rather chuffed at the thought of having her creation on the telly. They stood on the cliff path, admiring the monstrous agaves and the view of the bay.

Johnny had been a bit quiet but finally turned to her. 'Andie, I completely get it. But there's a lot to do... not that you haven't already done a lot, by the sound of it, but... you know, it's a garden not a holiday programme, so you're going to have to get it up to scratch. Get a tree surgeon in for a serious bit of tidying up.'

'Gawd. I think Vicente likes it natural and wild. As do I.'

'The money he'll get will more than pay for it – and you can always let it grow mad again afterwards! I'll trust you to reach some kind of a compromise. Like the plaza, we want to pretty things up a bit without pissing anyone off. Good karma. Everyone happy.'

'Okay, that sounds good.'

'Now, just the amphitheatre, isn't it? Can't wait to see that.'

She'd hoped he'd forget it; after last night, it felt more intimately linked with Vicente and Rafi than ever. When they arrived, she gasped.

'What?' Johnny asked.

'Vicente and Rafi have been working on it in my absence!' They must have come back on Friday evening after Rafi's show, and worked on it on Saturday morning. As if they'd sensed it would soon be needed, even before last night's enthusiastic response from the band's manager. There was a whole new section of crazy paving waiting to be grouted. She'd have to tick him off for not waiting for *her*.

'Wow. This has potential. I thought he never helped you?'

'This was an exception. Rafi's idea.'

'Ah. Maybe there could be a little scene at the end of the show with them dancing.' He looked at his watch. 'Oh, better get going, I suppose.'

'Is it safe to come out?' Vicente said with a cheeky grin at the front door when she came back from the airport.

She laughed. 'He calmed down and apologised. It's all fine now. And he loved the garden. We just need to have some tree maintenance done, which the programme will pay for.'

His eyebrows pinched together.

'But nothing too drastic or cruel, I promise.'

He looked relieved, and motioned her to come inside. 'Come and have something to celebrate our amphitheatre!'

'Oh? They came *already*?'

He handed her an orange lolly. 'They have just left, the manager and technical guy. There is a list of things to do, but... *yes*!'

'Oh my God – we better get on with it then!'

'It's too hot for you to work now. Tomorrow, Andie.'

'I'll just put the hose over myself once in a while.'

'What?' asked Rafi with a grin, as he came into the room.

'Do you want to be in charge of keeping us cool, Rafi?' Vicente asked him in Spanish.

Rafi nodded vigorously.

Andie went back to her apartment to change, putting a modest bikini on under her loose gardening clothes – she didn't want any embarrassing wet T-shirt moments. Then she went back to find that Vicente had managed to get Marcelo, Beatriz and Lucía to come and help them for a bit on their way to the beach.

'Ha! We'll soon get the paving done now!' Andie said.

'Yes,' Marcelo said, 'and then we need to do the path and the steps, so people can go down to here from the car park – which will need a gate in the wall...'

Vicente looked up at the flat area Marcelo was talking about. It was one bit of the garden he never seemed to be interested in, for some reason.

'It's yours right up to the *rambla*, isn't it?' Marcelo asked Vicente.

He nodded.

At that point, Rafi and Lucía decided it was time to cool

Andie and Marcelo down with the hose, and shrieked with laughter at the shocked reactions.

'Hey!' Vicente said. 'You're meant to ask first!' He grabbed the hose and doused the two of them down, causing more screams of laughter. 'Now come on, back to work, you two!'

After an hour or so, they were halfway along the second of the three tiers, and Rafi and Lucía had had enough and wanted to swim. Vicente and Beatriz went down to the beach with the children, while Marcelo and Andie assessed the path for wheelchair access, went up the steps – counting how many wooden slats they'd have to replace – and then walked along the edge of the car park to see where they could suggest the gate should go.

'Oh look, the next house is for sale,' Andie said, seeing a board up the other side of the *rambla*.

'Probably they hear about the concerts!'

'Well, surely not too loud from here – and there's only *one*.'

'What? Of course not only *one*! Every summer some concerts here now. First place for concerts in San José, will be *fantástico*! Already he ask me to put in earth *cable eléctrico* from house to *anfiteatro*. He is thinking in the future.'

'Oh!' As she was doing. She hadn't really had the chance to ask him if he felt the same.

'Also, I must ask him if he want gates into the garden, that the people don't go in there.'

'Yes…' She rubbed her temples; it was wonderful but a bit overwhelming, especially after her late night and early morning.

'You must rest today and start again tomorrow, no?'

'I think you're right,' she said. 'What would you like me to bring for the barbecue? Four o'clock, isn't it?'

'Yes. Something *dulce*? We are going to need energy this week! Now you go home. I will explain to Vicente and talk with him about plans.'

'Perfect with our ice cream and fruit!' Marcelo said, taking the box of a variety of *bizcocho* cake squares from her as she came in through the gate to his swimming-pool-and-succulents garden. 'Nice sleep?'

'Yes, it was.' She looked around. 'Your garden is so pretty. Last time I was here, I was too spaced out to really notice.' It was just three weeks ago, but so much had happened – not least in her heart – that it felt like three months ago.

'Thank you, we try! I think that only person you don't know is Doina.'

On hearing her name, the quiet little girl in the park – now floating in a little rubber boat with Lucía – looked up and gave a shy smile when Andie said hello and waved.

Marcelo lowered his voice. 'Romanian. Mama and Papa work with the kayak company, very good people. They are here two years now, and finally Doina starts to talk – with help from Lucía!'

'My God, and with Rafi too... your daughter is going to be a speech therapist.'

'Ha, yes – maybe!'

'And *abuelo*!' Lucía called out, pointing to an older man exhausting himself pumping air into an inflatable dolphin for them.

'Oh yes, sorry – my father. Also Marcelo, but called Chelo.' On hearing his name, Chelo turned and said hello.

Andie thanked Beatriz for the non-alcoholic sangria put in her hand, and followed her to a rattan sofa to start chatting about how Vicente was considering moving Rafi from his private international school in Almería to the village one. She said hello and how-are-you to Jaime and Ana, but was glad to have the pool and the chattering Lucía between her and them; she didn't want to hear any more of their negative ideas about Vicente. But while Jaime helped Marcelo with the barbecue, Ana surprised Andie by asking when they could see the garden.

'Oh – well…'

'Easy. Come and help prepare the amphitheatre for the concert!' Beatriz said in Spanish.

'Yes,' Lucía said. 'He's very kind when you help; you can swim on his beach and he gives you lollies!'

'Oh! Well, what d'you think, Jaime?' Ana said.

Jaime turned round. 'He's really becoming part of the village now, isn't he. Yes, let's give him a hand, if Marcelo asks him – in exchange for visiting this wonderful garden!'

Andie was amazed to find that – unlike last time she was here – she could follow nearly all the Spanish. 'That would be great! I'm sure it'll be fine with him.'

'We'll have to ask Mónica too, when she comes. And Ben, of course, if we can tear him away from the girlfriend – although Rosi will be going back to university in Granada soon.'

They heard the gate opening. 'Can I hear my name?' Mónica said with a laugh.

'Yes.' Beatriz got up and kissed her, and explained Ana's plan.

'The amphitheatre... where's that then?' Mónica asked.

'Further down the hill after the flat bit that'll be used for cars – once we've made a gate. There's a steep slope down to it; you can't see it from the road,' Andie said in Spanish.

'Well... I'd certainly love to see it. I'll have to check when I've got time in the week.'

The barbecue was ready, grandfather 'Chelo' persuaded the girls to get out of the pool, and there was lots of enthusiastic passing of plates and salads. Andie learnt that Ana and Jaime were buying the tiny place next to them, so they could expand their plant shop. Beatriz told them about some improvements at the village health centre, and wanted to know about Andie's new TV programme and whether she felt she could work with her ex.

Through all this, Mónica, sitting next to her on a bean bag, had been very quiet. Andie turned to her. 'How are things with you, Mónica?'

'Oh, busy. If I keep doing more photography, I could be less at the estate agent's, or even stop... which would be good.'

'You're not enjoying it?'

'Not much. Ignacio is more and more difficult – I think he turn *loco*! And also... it angers me what people do.' She took a sip of her beer, and then lowered her voice. 'Like Vicente's place. I know is just empty piece of the land, but is a shame, no?'

Andie's heart started to race. 'Sorry?'

Mónica looked up in surprise. 'He not told you?'

'What?' she asked, her voice hoarse. That For Sale board

just the other side of the *rambla*... She and Marcelo hadn't bothered looking the other side to see what it said, assuming it was to do with the next house. There was a wait while Jaime asked Mónica about some family photographs some friends of his wanted. She started to feel faint.

Mónica turned back to her. 'They want to build six apartments on the flat bit.' Andie must have been looking shocked, because Mónica put a hand on her arm. 'Is new... we got the instruction yesterday. I'm sure he will give his reasons – which will be about that brother-in-law who develop houses, I'm sure. But anyway, maybe it not happen; the usual thing is to advertise, put a poster, and see if there is enough interest before build anything.'

'Why *wouldn't* people be interested?' Andie said sadly, but also with a flame of anger that was soon going to be difficult to control.

Mónica shrugged resignedly, got up, and offered to get Andie a drink. 'Maybe something stronger than that. Or English cup of tea, whatever you need.'

She went for the tea. She needed a clear head. As soon as she could politely leave, she was going to go straight up there and find out what the hell was going on.

She crawled past the old rounders' pitch that was going to be a car park – well, until the builders arrived – and stopped the car. How small could a block of six apartments be? They'd need parking. A bloody swimming pool. She tried to envisage. Then got out of the car and walked over to the board... and swore. There was a facile illustration of a Lego-design block, with rectangular, all-seeing windows and soulless box planting that seemed specifically designed to mock the wild and wonderful garden just metres away.

She got back into the car and sped down the road – almost crashing into Vicente's closed gate. It hadn't been closed to her for so long… but of course, he didn't know she was coming. Although surely he'd guess it wouldn't be long before she did. She prodded his name on her phone.

'Andie.'

'I need to talk to you. *Now*. Open the gates.'

She drove in, parked and got out, her head spinning, heart pumping with anger. He was waiting for her by the olive tree bench with a couple of lemon teas. Television cartoon sounds were coming from inside the house, so hopefully Rafi wouldn't hear any of this. Vicente was looking sad. Or maybe ashamed, as he damned ought to be.

'Why are you selling the land? And why didn't you *tell* me? We need it, for the amphitheatre's car park!'

He put up two surrendering hands. 'Please,' he said, indicating the bench. 'I can explain.'

She sat down to steady herself, but ignored the can pushed towards her. '*How* can you explain? You're *ruining* everything!' she said, her voice wobbling and her vision starting to blur with tears.

'The house was too much money. I could only buy it with some help from Antonio, and for this, I agreed he build one little house at the end. But the land will be his, and already he has permission to do more. It's not what I wanted, I am calling him all the time to change his mind, it *can't* happen. I—'

'Wait, the land *will* be his? It isn't yet?'

'The house became mine on Friday. So now I have to

make that part of the land his, for the money he gave me. Andie, if I didn't do this, I couldn't buy the house – and one day he would persuade the owner and buy all of it himself and…' He shook his head.

'How much.'

His eyes widened. 'What?'

'How much did he give you… towards the house? For the land?'

He hesitated. 'Twenty thousand. If I could have found it another—'

'Sell *me* the land, and give the money back to him.'

He clapped his hands down on the table, looking cross but also slightly amused. '*What?* Andie! What are you going to do with it? You would give yourself trouble paying this. It's madness.'

'I've got some savings from *Challenging Gardens*. I have money coming from the next programme, so can raise the rest from credit cards in the meantime. A loan. Whatever. I *want* it. I can't have a horrid building put on it – and we need it for the car park.'

He put his elbow on the table, his head in his hand. 'It is okay for the car park in two weeks! What are you *saying*?'

Maybe Marcelo was wrong; the concert *was* just a one-off. As usual, she was being completely deluded about her and Vicente being partners – even, in this case, just business ones. 'I thought… maybe you would want to do concerts *every* summer, maybe not many, just a few each August, I don't know…'

He nodded slowly. '*Claro* I have been thinking of this… but Andie, not myself, only if you are here.'

He needed her here – for concerts, anyway. 'I *will* be here.

In August and... most of the time. I'm going to try *living* here for a year or so.'

He looked up from examining his drink can, mouth open in surprise. 'Why you not say this before?' he asked quietly.

'I sort of told you on Friday, didn't I?'

'No! You *never* say this. *Why* you not tell me?'

'Because I didn't want to say until I was sure. I needed to sort out my work, but now I have this new programme, it buys me time. Let me buy the land, Vicente.'

He laughed and shook his head again. 'But you are crazy woman! What good is it for you?'

'It's very good for me – and for the concerts.'

'You would be owner of the car park... half of the business. We would be business pair.'

'Yes. So stop paying me to do the amphitheatre, if it's our business.'

'No, no, we have to argue more about this,' he said, shaking his head.

'No, we don't. Please say you will let me buy the land.'

'I suppose... you could buy and put a little house on it. Would make worth it.'

'Oh all right, if that convinces you, maybe one day, a tiny one, but please just say yes, will you?'

She stood up and held out her hand, like they were doing business. He stood up too, but just gave her the kiss on each cheek thing as if they were saying goodbye. 'Is that a *yes*?' she asked. Maybe shaking on things was an English thing.

He put his hands on her shoulders and looked into her eyes. Rather seriously, strangely taking her back to when she first met him – the dark-haired Jesus man she struggled to understand. 'I want you to think for a few days, talk with people for advice, maybe. Then if you still want to buy it, you can.'

'Oh!' She could feel her throat constrict.

He wasn't letting go. 'And...' He looked down. A fun argument about paying her or not would help her get back to her senses – but he let go and picked up a crimson-red bougainvillea petal and put it in her T-shirt pocket. His fingers so close to her breast, she could hardly breathe. 'And... I'm *so* happy you will try to live here. We were going to miss you,' he said, smiling broadly.

Rafi came running out, and wanted to know why they were going to miss Andie. Was she going away?

'No, Rafi, she's *not* going away,' he said, hugging the boy to him. 'Ah...' He looked at his watch. 'We need to get ready to go to your uncle's,' he said to him in Spanish. He turned to Andie. 'The *residencia* wants me to visit José Luis.'

'Ah... send him my love.'

'I will, and I will tell him about the concert and... no, already in some way he knew you were living here!'

23

Andie sat on the bench on top of the Lookout Post, leaning against the olive tree exactly where she last saw Grandie – which always felt a bit like sitting on her lap when she was a little girl.

I told Vicente I didn't need to go to the funeral; for me, José Luis would be here in the garden, with you.

Of course he is. And don't be sad; I told you it wouldn't be long. He saw you, he had a wonderful send-off with Vicente and Juanito being there when he left – and he's now in a much better place.

Andie looked around, almost expecting José Luis to join in the conversation – but that was going to be difficult; as far as she could remember, he didn't speak a word of English.

I'm surprised Vicente even invited me; I can't imagine it would go down well with Sebastián, Antonio and some of José Luis' wife's relatives...

Oh good God no. It was better to stay here with us, get on with the garden.

Andie stood up and went over to the edge for a view of what would soon be her land. *Just 'cause it's going to be a car park, doesn't mean I can't do a bit of planting in there. A big roundabout-type island in the middle, maybe. What d'you think? Although there won't be that much room, if I'm going to build a tiny house one day.*

You're not going to need a tiny house, Andie.

Now come on, just because Vicente looked so pleased I was going to live here, it doesn't mean—

She heard someone driving in and parking and went over to the other side to check who it was. Marcelo. Vicente and Rafi would be back from Almería a bit later, along with María Ángeles. She couldn't wait to show them how much she and Marcelo had done in the last two days, with a bit of drop-in help from Ben, Jaime and Ana. She also couldn't wait to be relieved of the temptation to snoop around the house while she had the key.

'Marcelo!' she called out, and laughed as he looked around, not being able to work out where she was. 'Up here!'

He looked up, grinned and waved.

'I'll be down in a minute,' she yelled in Spanish, and checked her phone to see if there were any updates from Vicente. There was a message.

'*Hello Andie, we are leaving now. I have been talking with Soleá about the concert, and she is coming back with us, so we have a par of days to work on some music so she can be a surprise guest. Lots of family, but also I have made progress with the list... we WILL have chairs!*'

How had she missed that? Three-quarters of an hour ago. Must have been when she was making a noise sanding down the pita poles and hammering them together to make temporary barriers stopping entry to the garden from the amphitheatre. It sounded like Soleá had been to the funeral. How long had she known Vicente and his family? Perhaps they went back a long way, and it was likely Antonio – and particularly Sebastián – approved of Vicente's relationship with a flamenco diva, which could only help Sebastián in his career. But Vicente wasn't having a relationship with her or anyone else; at the zoo he'd said there was 'nothing to tell' on that score. Maybe it was so casual it wasn't worth talking about. Or maybe it just wasn't any of her business. Anyway, it looked like she was going to meet Soleá, unless she could somehow escape before they arrived – but that would be stupid, there was work to be done... and oh God, Vicente's car, followed by Soleá's red sporty number, were now coming into the drive.

She watched Vicente get out and greet Marcelo, followed by Rafi, who was probably asking about Lucía. Then La Soleá made an appearance, and she saw Marcelo step back and almost bow to the woman, for heaven's sake. Was she so special? Ponytailed and flowingly clad, she drifted over to the olive tree bench and looked down the path, then floated back to Marcelo to say something. Vicente had his hand on Rafi's shoulder and seemed to be encouraging him to answer Soleá – who'd done a bit of flamenco clapping and asked the poor little boy a question he didn't seem to know what to do with.

Then Vicente went to Soleá's car and chivalrously lifted out an overnight bag that would have done for five rather than a '*par*' of days. He took Soleá by the arm, as if they were walking down an aisle – the beautiful, black-haired flamenco couple, his ponytail so sleek, hers a long waterfall of waves – and led the three of them inside. Of course she was special; she was a successful, talented and exquisite one of his own kind – and how the hell Andie could have thought she'd ever stood *any* chance of interesting him romantically suddenly felt delusional in the extreme.

'Come on then, it's safe to come down now!' Marcelo was saying from just below her.

She made herself laugh – what else could she do? – and started winding down the little hill.

'What's she like?' Andie couldn't help asking when she joined him and they started walking towards the amphitheatre.

'Like you'd think. All big, fiery eyes and a bit of a queen,' he said in Spanish. 'But she did say she'd like to be shown *all* the garden, not just the amphitheatre where she's going to sing, so she can't be *that* bad.'

Andie stopped and put her hands up in mock indignation. 'Did I say she was bad?' she replied in Spanish.

'Well... *no*, but...' He chuckled and started walking on. Then he patted her arm. 'I don't see her as "The One".'

'What? You spent five minutes with her!'

He shrugged. 'So anyway, what's the plan? The path coming down from the car park to the amphitheatre is fine – I'll check it again nearer the time, after we've had the rain – just in case there are any wheelchair users. Let's see if we can finish the steps. We'll leave that last bit of amphitheatre paving for them to do when they come out later. Sorry, all in Spanish, d'you understand?'

'Yes! But... *them*?'

'I shall personally hand La Soleá a bucket.'

Andie laughed.

They'd arrived at the amphitheatre, crossed over and admired the path, then went over to the steps and started going at it with their spades between fitting the new wooden risers in place, thanking God for the overnight drenching making their work so much easier.

Andie sighed. 'Why do they need *two* days to rehearse a song, anyway? Do one she knows already, for heaven's sake.'

'I think his guitarist friend can't make it until this evening. He said something about him and his boy coming over then.'

So how much could they rehearse without the guitarist she was going to be performing with? There was an *hola* from the other side of the amphitheatre. María Ángeles was calling out, Rafi beside her. So now Vicente and Soleá had the house to themselves – for whatever they had planned for the day. She started to hurt all over with that thought, then snapped out of it because Rafi was advancing with his wheelbarrow and asking what to do.

'As you did before, Rafi, picking up any little pieces of stone or ceramic "treasures" and putting them in your wheelbarrow so I can stick them all,' she called out in Spanish from halfway up the steps. 'You were *so* helpful.'

'We specially left it for you and your dad and Soleá to do,' Marcelo added.

'*Soleá?*' Rafi said, looking puzzled. Then walked along the unfinished tier, eyebrows raised, glancing from side to side disapprovingly, and finally picking up a little piece of ceramic between two fingers and staring at it in pretend disgust.

Andie couldn't help laughing, Marcelo put a hand to his mouth, and María Ángeles starting defending the singer, saying how she was giving up her time to help the amphitheatre by singing at it for free.

'And I'm looking forward to hearing it,' Andie said.

'But we need to hurry up and get things done before the rain comes down in jugs for a couple of days,' Marcelo said.

Rafi did a double thumbs-up and got to work with María Ángeles.

'In *jugs*? I take it that means the same as raining cats and dogs in English?'

Marcelo laughed. 'What an expression! In Almería there is very, very little rain, but when it comes... you would have to say "raining elephants and rhinos"!'

Andie looked down anxiously over all the tiling work and sweeping they'd done in the amphitheatre area.

'But don't worry, this is why we have the *ramblas*. Dry rivers – all except a couple of times a year, sometimes less – that take all the rain safely to a drain or the sea. Come, I'll show you.'

They clambered up to the top.

'The *rambla* will be your kindly next door neighbour; you need to get acquainted,' he said, taking her hand to pull her up the last step.

Andie stopped at the top and surveyed the old rounders' pitch that could, according to the solicitors, be transferred from Vicente to her as early as the end of next week – just before it became a beautiful, sea-view car park for the concert. How this was going down with Vicente's property developer brother-in-law Antonio, she didn't know – but someone had removed the hideous For Sale board for the Lego apartments, thank heavens.

They'd already smoothed the area down a bit and cordoned off a tyre-wrecking rock-fall area that Andie wanted to plant up as a wild rockery. At the far end, near the *rambla*, they'd dismantled the dry-stone wall to put in a wooden gate that they would replace with something more substantial at a later date.

They picked their way through some scrub to get to the edge of the *rambla*, which, some ten feet below, currently had an oasis-like band of green next to a meandering swirl of dry sand.

'I think I remember my grandmother telling me about it, but I never saw it in action.'

Marcelo pointed up to the top of the hill. 'Water from up there collects in the *rambla* the other side of the road, see? And then goes into the drain under the road that pours water into here and then eventually over the cliff rocks and into the sea.'

'Ah. I know the solicitor was checking for any history of floods, but was apparently satisfied.'

'It is part of the work of the *ayuntamiento* to check the *ramblas*. There's nothing to worry about, and it makes a good boundary to your land.'

Just as he was saying this, the middle-aged neighbours in the house a little further along waved. Apparently, they'd been delighted when Vicente visited to tell them the land was *not* now going to be sold for development, and they were looking forward to coming to the concert.

They heard voices behind them and turned: Rafi had

come up the steps and was running towards them, María Ángeles a little out of breath at the top of them.

'Will you put an English house on your car park?' Rafi asked.

'Not at the moment! But if I do it will be very small, very Spanish, and keen to welcome neighbours bringing jam, singing birds, or gardening skills.'

Rafi laughed. 'Come and see what we've done.'

They went back to the steps, Marcelo going back to working on them, Andie following María Ángeles and Rafi down to the amphitheatre. The tiling was in place, just waiting to be grouted, almost up to the end.

'Wow! You've nearly finished it! I'll get sticking it all in.'

'I think we *can* finish it!' María Ángeles said. 'Come on, Rafi!'

Andie came back with some grout and found them working on the last bit, making a little, bird-shaped mosaic. 'Oh, that's *brilliant*! I'll get all that stuck in and we can finish before the rain comes.' María Ángeles, turning out to be a fast and skilled worker, offered to lend her a hand, while Rafi swept the 'stage' – or rather, the paved area over which the wooden stage was going to be erected next week. So Andie was on hands and padded knees when Vicente and a flushed-looking Soleá came out to see how they were getting on.

'And here is the lady who has made all this possible!' Vicente was saying in Spanish.

It took Andie a moment to realise he meant *her*. She looked up. Then stood up – too quickly; she'd rather overdone the sun, even if it was alternating with ponderous dark grey clouds. She hung on to the post at the end of the tier while the twinkling stars and blackness subsided. 'I'd shake hands, but that might not be too good a—'

Soleá had grabbed her by the shoulders and kissed each sweaty cheek. 'You and your grandmother have created a paradise. How lucky Vicente is to have you,' she said in Spanish, looking Andie up and down with interest.

Soleá watched Rafi pull Vicente away to look at the mosaic bird. 'And you have got Rafi outside more, instead of always playing with those stuffed birds! And dancing too, I hear,' she said.

'Well, he's his own little person. I...' By the look on Soleá's perfectly made-up face, this wasn't translating well.

'Rafi. Rafi?' Soleá called, trying to get his attention. 'Rafi?' He finally looked up. 'Are you going to show me your *sevillanas*?' She clapped her hands and then held out one to him.

He frowned.

'Could you just do the first bit for Soleá, on our lovely stage?' Vicente asked him.

Rafi got up from his tiles, came over to Andie and dragged her down the steps to the stage. An 'oh...' from Soleá could be heard, but it looked like it was going to be *sevillanas* with equally basic-stepped Andie, or not at all. They did the clapping thing at the beginning, both not sure how many, and then went into the steps with rather too much giggling, a couple of accidental bumps but a triumphant *ta-da* ending with each striking a pose.

There was applause all round, and as Andie felt a few dollops of rain, she hoped that was the end of it and she could get on. She came back to the tiling and bent down. Tried to ignore the fact that Vicente was saying something to Soleá that for some reason, even in this unusually stifling and humid heat, necessitated linking arms and a squeeze.

Then Vicente's sandalled feet were in front of her.

'Nico and the band's percussionist are coming over in a couple of hours. Why don't you come back later to the rehearsal? Tell us what you think?'

Soleá looked over to see what Andie was going to say, but with no encouragement. Why would she be interested in whether the gardener was there or not? And why would Andie want to sit and watch them, like some grateful fan? She'd seen enough already.

'No, I... I've got things to do. I'll enjoy the surprise at the concert.'

24

She put the phone down after talking to Gerard. All was well. The Hampton Court garden was finished, and its planting all planned; there was a further order for Níjar urns; he and the clients were delighted with the gardens she'd designed from Gerard's videos and information, and he was sending her details for a further one. At this rate, she'd only need to find a bit of part-time work locally before the programme started in early spring. She'd also just signed the TV contract, much to Hilary's delight. This was good, because it made her feel better about taking out her savings and doing the transfer from her credit card in preparation for completing on her square of San José next Friday. Everything was going to plan, other than yesterday's migraine after overdoing it and getting dehydrated on Wednesday. But spending a day in bed, and now probably a morning on the sofa, was quite cosy, when it was still raining elephants and rhinos outside. The only negative was that, yesterday and right now, Vicente and Soleá were probably doing much the same thing.

Sweet Jesus, when was she going to get over this? She and Vicente were probably going to be partners in a little summer business, and occasional partners in swingball, silly dancing and bird trips… but that was it.

A WhatsApp. Vicente asking how she was. As he had done on Wednesday evening – when Marcelo had, by the sound of it, over-dramatised her going home earlier than planned – and yesterday.

'*I'm fine now, thanks,*' she typed back – which she was, in all but mood.

He sent a smiley face, a thumbs-up and the crimson-red bougainvillea-type flower. Like the petal he'd put in her T-shirt pocket on Sunday.

His profile photo was now Soleá's one of him and Rafi crouching by the bird mosaic when, just before he and Soleá had disappeared again, they had laid the final stones. Without thinking about it, she sent him a kiss-blowing emoji.

How ridiculous that even just a warm little exchange with him seemed to energise her. She got up, put some reggae on, and started dancing between living room and bedroom as she picked clothes off a heap of clean washing to be hung up in the wardrobe. Then the phone rang.

A Spanish child's voice talking about snakes. What? Ah, Rafi – on the telephone! – talking about snakes and *escaleras*. Snakes and Ladders. Then about pizza, and rather bossily telling her to come *now*.

'Oh! Well…'

She could hear Vicente saying something to him. 'Andie?'

Rafi said. 'Please...' More voices off. 'Woo-joo-like to come?' he said in English. 'Lunch?'

'Okay! *Sí!* Yes!'

He laughed and squealed.

'Is that okay?' Vicente now. 'We will make pizza. After the game, you will need it. When can you come?'

'Oh... a few minutes?'

'*Perfecto*. Be very careful on the road.' He put down the phone.

She looked down herself. She was in a floaty, cactus-design thing from the market that wasn't clearly either a shirt or a dress, so she tended to pair it with her old, soft, green, cotton shorts. Super comfortable flop-about wear for a Snakes-and-Ladders-cooking invitation; if Soleá was still there to look her up and down, it was just too bad. She brushed her hair, put on a little mascara, pulled on the yellow mac-in-a-pack she'd used to go to Gatwick, and set off.

Outside in the dark grey day, the rain roared down on the car, windscreen wipers barely coping. The little hill road going up towards Grandie's house had a stream pelting down it, people in cafés and locals at their doorsteps staring at it in wonder.

At Vicente's, lights on in the house were a welcoming sight – as was the absence of Soleá's sports car in the drive. María Ángeles' car was also not there – and she now remembered her saying something about going away for another long weekend with her sons in Tabernas. It was going to be just the three of them.

Vicente opened the door as she jumped over the puddles. 'Come in!' he said with for some reason a slightly anxious smile, taking her jacket. 'Rafi was doing the same, but jumping *in* them. Already we have two showers for the...' He pointed at the ground.

'Mud? I suppose you don't get to see it very often here! Will the amphitheatre be all right in all this?'

He nodded. 'The *rambla* will take care of the water – and earlier I saw men from the *ayuntamiento* checking it. Better to have this now than at the weekend!'

'Heavens, yes. And where's the Snakes and Ladders boy?'

'In the bedroom choosing more clothes. Come.'

She followed him into the kitchen, trying not to think how huggable he looked in his soft, blue, tie-dye shirt. She thought he was going to offer her a drink, but he turned and looked at her, still with that concern in his face. 'I'm glad you are better. But, Andie, maybe you have *migraña* because you were angry.'

'*Angry?*'

'About Soleá.'

Good God, he could at least have had the grace to pretend he hadn't noticed. 'What? Why would I be—'

'It's true, what I said before; I don't have... *relaciones* with Soleá.'

She bit her lip. They might not be in a relationship as such, but twice in the month she'd come to stay for a few days, and the physical affection between them suggested... and why was he telling her this? So she could feel better, hearing that another woman was also being excluded from a relationship, to protect Rafi's stability? But what did Rafi make of Soleá staying the night? It didn't make sense.

Vicente had put a hand to his face, and was glancing into the hall, listening out for Rafi. '*Uf...* I don't know the words for these things in English... perhaps you don't understand... I want to say, we don't go in the bed together – well, or any other flat place!'

Now Andie put a hand to *her* face.

He chuckled. 'We broke two months ago, although already it was finished.'

He listened out again for Rafi, who could now be heard da-da-da singing the song from *Aladdin* upstairs with one of his birds. 'The thing is,' he said, lowering his voice, 'Soleá and I are... tied together forever, because her daughter Cecilia... she is Rafi's mother.'

'Oh!' That would be quite a bond, dealing with difficult teenagers, making that decision, the shock of becoming thirty-something grandparents together.

'She sees her Cecilia very little, because she went to live with her father in *Estados Unidos*... Rafi is *everything* to her. He doesn't realise, of course; just knows she is his *madrina*.'

'Godmother?'

'*Sí.*'

'Oh dear, I can imagine...'

'But she is a very good person, and you will be friends too, after a time. Because...' He took her hand in his. It sent a warm current through her that made her smile, even in her puzzled state. Because what?

Rafi's little feet could be heard pattering across the tiled floor next door, and he was calling out about why Andie wasn't there.

'She *is* here!' Vicente called back in Spanish, squeezing Andie's hand and letting go.

Rafi came in – and seemed to have used up all his blue

and yellow clothes, because he was wearing a bright green shorts and T-shirt set covered in chubby T-Rexes.

'Hello!' Andie said in Spanish. 'I like your dinosaurs!'

'*Papi* says blue and yellow make green,' he said to the cactus on her shirt-dress. 'We have to play Snakes and Ladders now – it's ready!'

Vicente told him it was kind to offer visitors a drink when they arrived, but Andie said she was happy to start playing. Rafi hopped and jumped towards the living room in a peculiar way – but when they went through she understood why. He was practising for the game – which was a huge mat of squares, snakes and ladders on the floor, a giant inflatable die, and… no pieces. Because *they* were going to be the pieces.

'Oh *wow*!' she said, laughing.

After they'd each rolled the die to see who was to start, it was Vicente who was the first to move along the squares. Rafi threw the same number, and insisted on sharing the number 4 square, standing on his father's feet. Then Andie threw a five, and had to edge round the two of them and stand immediately in front, her elbow touching Vicente's warm, T-shirted side. Rafi pointed to her feet and started complaining; it turned out he was a stickler for rules. Pushing her back into place with his hand, Rafi would have overbalanced her out of the square, had Vicente not pulled her back. So the game went on, a very bumpy and touchy one, with a lot of laughing and healthy competition, and Vicente for some reason having to go up more ladders and down more snakes than the other two put together. When they got to the top row, Andie and Vicente in adjacent squares and Rafi having just slid down an enormous snake, the little boy said he needed the bathroom.

Just as he was leaving the room, he turned and looked at the two of them – in the eyes for once, if only briefly. 'You can kiss when I'm not here,' he said, and scampered off with a giggle.

'Rafi!' Vicente called after him. Then he turned to Andie, who was still staring in disbelief at the doorway through which Rafi had disappeared.

'I'm sorry, he's been watching *Aladdin*,' he said, looking embarrassed.

'Ah.' She looked down at their bare feet. 'I suppose we *are* standing on a sort of... *carpet*.' She took a step back; it was ridiculous to be stood so close to him when the game had stopped.

Out of the window, the rain had turned the dusty cliff path dark orange. 'Is Rafi happy I'm buying the square next to your garden?' she said, to change the subject.

'You know he is. We both are. We both want you... in the next square,' he said, taking her arm and pulling her back into hers, catching her as she buffeted against him.

She turned and looked at him, her heart tapping as the steadying arm stayed round her. He stared back uneasily, so she went back to looking out of the window. 'I was thinking I could make a shortcut to the amphitheatre. A whole new path further along the top that—'

'A whole new *path*!' Vicente sang to the *Aladdin* tune.

'Don't you dare close your *gate*!' she sang back, laughing.

'A hundred da-di da...' he sang, then put his other arm round her, and looked at her, his eyes darker than ever. She looked back, in a daze. 'Andie... I'm sorry. I have been idiot.

Rafi understands how I feel before I do. I just hope he is also right about...' He pulled her closer, but looked adorably worried she might not feel the same.

'Me?' she whispered, and couldn't seem to get anything else out, so just nodded.

A relieved smile spread over his face, and as they heard Rafi coming down the stairs, he quickly pressed his lips against hers.

'I'm back!' Rafi announced, looking from one to the other.

'Ah... good... come on then, it's your turn,' Vicente managed.

Andie stood stunned, glad he still had an arm round her, or she could have completely toppled over. Vicente didn't seem to be quite himself either, because he allowed Rafi to get away with shaking the die several times until he got the 6 he needed to whizz up a ladder, followed by a dubious counting of the exact number to arrive at the final square.

'*Yes!* I am the winner!' Rafi shouted out, grinning from ear to ear and looking at the two of them still standing there. He went to Vicente, who'd finally let go of Andie, and pulled his arm as he begged for pizza. After Vicente whispered in his ear, he came out with an English 'Do-you-like pizza, Andie?'

'Of course, *claro*, I like pizza!' she replied.

'Even healthy pizza with cauliflower in the flat bit?' Rafi asked in Spanish.

'Even better.'

Rafi lead the way into the kitchen, and it was just as well Vicente had already made the base because he started dithering around pulling things out of the fridge onto a work surface and then, only after words from Rafi, wiping the table and transferring everything there.

'We have to wash our hands!' Rafi instructed, and pushed a little plastic step in front of the sink to do his. After exchanging a few looks of amused shock with Andie, Vicente finally snapped to and displayed chef-like chopping skills, soon filling little Níjar ceramic bowls with grated cheese, serrano ham, onion, green peppers, tomato, pine nuts, spinach, asparagus, and pineapple.

'Okay, we start,' Vicente said.

Rafi said something about halves and quarters and asked why he wasn't getting the usual maths lesson.

'Ah... well... I think you know all that now.'

'Yes, and I can do Maths in English too, look...' He started putting toppings onto his pizza, counting in English. Then Vicente's phone rang.

Andie tried to concentrate on joining Rafi with the pizza toppings, rather than listening to the phone conversation, but Vicente seemed to be speaking in slower Spanish than usual, as if he wanted her to hear it.

'But driving in this weather? See how it is tomorrow... Oh... Yes about an hour from there... Are you on hands-free? What...? That's Rafi, counting pizza toppings in English... Look, I *really* don't like you driving in this. You should turn back... No of *course* we want to have you for the weekend, but there's a storm forecast. It will get even worse... Are you okay, Sebas? Has something happened?' There was a longer gap, in which Vicente glanced at Andie and did an eyes-to-heaven look and shook his head. 'We *have* talked about that... Sebas, concentrate on your driving, we'll see you later. Shall I make you a pizza? Okay. Take care.'

Vicente turned to Rafi. 'That's a *lot* of things you have on there! I thought you didn't like green peppers?'

'I do now. Where did the blue and yellow come from, to make the peppers green?'

'Er... you can ask Andie that one! But come on, now, leave some peppers for your brother, he'll be here in hour.'

'Oh...' Rafi said, sticking out his lower lip. 'Does that mean Andie has to go?'

'No, it doesn't.' Vicente put their pizzas in the oven.

She smiled; it was nice that he didn't want to hide her away. 'It sounds like you need to talk; after lunch I'll leave you to it.'

'It'll be about the school again,' Vicente said quietly in English.

'Uh... poor you.'

By the time they'd put away the game and laid the table, the pizzas were ready.

'Mm! Don't think I've ever had a pizza this good,' Andie said. 'How are you enjoying your mountain one, Rafi?' she asked him in Spanish.

'Mm!' he said, nodding. He patted Vicente's arm. 'Can Andie come to play and have lunch again soon, *Papi*?'

'Of course!'

Afterwards, the rain still thundering down, Vicente put *Aladdin* on again for Rafi and came with Andie to the door. The moment they could, they put their arms round each other and kissed again – only to hear Rafi calling out to Vicente about a problem with the television.

'I better go,' she said. 'I'll see you on Monday. Thank you for...'

'Thank *you*... for the *best* rainy day ever, my Andie!'

He helped her on with her jacket, zipped it up, and pulled the hood over her hair. Then he put a hand to her cheek, shook his head, and grinned. 'Still I can't believe this.'

'Nor me!'

25

Saturday 1st September

Andie opened the balcony doors just enough to let in the sharp scent of damp, orange earth without letting the rain make too much of a puddle on the floor tiles. Rain: for a lifetime an essential but too frequent irritation, spoiling her outdoor plans, covering the radiators with wet washing. Now it would be forever linked to the cosy indoors time that led to her first kiss with Vicente.

She went back to the sofa with her tea and reread some of the river of WhatsApp messages between her and Vicente since yesterday. Trying to track when they first fell for each other, she'd had to confess to having found him alien at first – until she found out he made jam, could make her laugh, and cope with The Ball making her vomit on his toes. For him it had been seeing her dancing with Shefali, that perfect dark-light synchronising, the passion she had for dance and music, as well as her plants and colours. But having seen his friend Josemi twice have his heart broken by London girls enchanted with the area, apparently in love, but then getting on a plane back to their 'real life', he hadn't wanted to make the same mistake – for Rafi or himself.

He didn't seem to want to talk much about Sebastián's continued disapproval of Rafi's switch to the San José village school, or Antonio's fury at not being able to buy the land and develop it. She imagined that there was still a disapproval of *her* too – which was probably about to get stronger, once he told them they *were* now together – but maybe he felt he could sort that out with time, and didn't want to hurt her hearing about it.

She scrolled down to where he'd listed some of the funny comments Rafi had been coming out with about her: she needed a man to do cooking for her; she would soon learn, he hoped, to 'join up' her Spanish; she had smiley eyes; and – Andie's favourite – she was 'speckled but nice'.

Then there was Vicente's promise that, much as he enjoyed sharing her with Rafi, they *would* have time alone together – especially once school started on the tenth. What butterflies she had about that. At least he'd mentioned, in case she came across it, that he wasn't the super stud that magazine had made him out to be after twisting the interview with Soleá…

She looked at the pile of laminated posters on the table, and then outside again – where the rain was already lighter, the sky brightening out over the sea.

They'd been told the concert was already half sold online – and apparently the Spanish didn't tend to buy tickets until the last minute, so this was really good – but there were still a few more places in the village where she could put a poster, and after another tea she'd—

Her phone rang. Vicente.

'*Hola!*'

'Andie... I'm sorry *cariño*, I have bad news. There is a flood. *Very* bad. I have—'

Her heart thudded. 'Where? The amphitheatre?'

'And the car park, some of the garden... The neighbour called me, then I saw a river coming from the path and went to see... Marcelo and a friend are coming now to see if they can make repairs before Friday when come the stage and chairs...'

'Oh my God...' Her head reeled; she couldn't think straight. An image of Rafi's bird mosaic came to her. 'How's Rafi?'

'He's with Sebas upstairs. He doesn't know but he's asking things... Look, we will learn why this happen, and make it not happen again. We *will* have concerts there. Hopefully even next weekend, because tomorrow the sun returns, and maybe with hard work and many people... but we will see what they say.'

'I'll come right now.'

'Please.'

She put her mac over some gardening clothes, slipped on Crocs, and drove over there. How could this happen? The *ayuntamiento* men had checked the *rambla*, and there was no history of flooding there.

She parked next to Marcelo's van – and a stream that came down the path and hurtled both across the drive and towards the steps going down to the beach. Vicente, Marcelo, and his builder friend Jorge were waiting for her, and after a consoling hug from each, they picked their way along the side of the flooded path. Grandie seemed to be watching from the Lookout Post and telling her all would be well – although goodness knows what she meant by that.

'I took the swingball to the shed. It had fallen and the bats gone away in the water... but I found them!' Vicente said, trying to be cheerful. But then they reached the amphitheatre.

The stage was now a lake. Marcelo was saying something about making a channel to drain it. The tiers... were unrecognisable. Hardly a lovingly placed tile in sight, among the mud and streams of water.

Andie put a hand to her face, her throat tight with effort not to cry... but then, through watery vision, she saw the steps going up to the car park. Or rather... where the steps *used to be*. Marcelo noticed at the same time and gasped. Jorge let out an expletive. The steps were now a waterfall that had gouged a huge crevice into the Hottentot-fig-covered hill, with half of the timber they'd used for the risers gone, presumably buried under the piles of mud and rock at the bottom.

'And the *path* up to the car park?' Andie splashed through the stage-lake to go further along for a better look. It had suffered a similar and even deeper cut. 'Oh God!'

Marcelo and Jorge – who sounded like he had some kind of digger – started earnestly discussing how to fix one or the other. It sounded like there was more hope for the steps than the path in the time available, and any wheelchairs or buggies would just have to be brought through the garden – which might be feasible if they fixed the gravelled path. Of course, *everybody* could come through the garden, but even before Vicente could say anything about that, Marcelo pointed out that up to a hundred and fifty people being allowed to wander through your private property was not on – even without the parking problems of that, as they all tried to park on the road instead of the car park so they didn't have to walk back as far in the dark afterwards.

It was time to find out what state the car park was in. They trudged back through the stream to the driveway, and drove up to it in Marcelo's van, parking by the wooden gate. Further would have been difficult; a torrent of water was coming over the road and channelling through the car park to pour over into the amphitheatre, as if with a deliberate vengeance.

'What the *hell*?' Andie found herself saying in English, as she and Vicente stood staring at the stream then went over to the *rambla* with its comparative trickle.

'Something very wrong here,' Vicente said.

Marcelo and Jorge had crossed the road to look at the *rambla* coming down the hillside to the drain supposed to take the water under the road into the *rambla* on the other side. They came back over, both looking furious, Jorge talking into his phone and then putting it away and saying something to Marcelo.

'Nobody from the *ayuntamiento* was checking the *rambla* yesterday. I know a guy on this team, and he will check and get back to me if he's wrong,' Jorge said.

'*What?*' Vicente said, eyes wild. 'So these guys I saw were…'

'Deliberately changing the direction of the flow, to come over your land – in what they must have known was one of the worst rains for many years.'

The three of them started talking about redirecting the water as quickly as possible, but there was also mention of the police.

'I could talk to my brother,' Marcelo said.

'No,' Vicente said. 'There is only one person who would do this – or *arrange* to have it done – and I need to deal with him myself.'

The other two tried to persuade him to get the police round so that they would at least have the evidence. Jorge, seeing how this was going, started taking pictures from all angles with his phone.

'Let me go back to the house and… make a call. I'll walk back with Andie,' Vicente said.

'Okay,' Jorge said. 'We'll get the digger – call us if you change your mind about the police.'

Vicente linked arms with Andie and they set off down the road.

'You think it's Antonio?' Andie asked. 'He'd really want to stop us having our concert just to get back at you about the land?'

'I *know* it's Antonio.'

'Then what's wrong with letting the police deal with him? He's committed a crime!'

'Because it wouldn't end this madness.'

'What *would*? God, what will he do next? He's dangerous!'

'There will be a way, you'll see.'

When they came into the drive they could hear Sebastián trying to reason with a shouting Rafi. As they went in, Rafi came bursting through from the living room, Sebastián following in time to see the little boy fling his arms round Andie's waist before she'd even had time to take off her rain jacket.

'Andie! I can see from the window upstairs… water

*every*where... the garden drowning!' he shouted, gasping with tears, his eyes wild with fury.

'No, no Rafi,' she said, sitting on a hall chair to be at his level and putting an arm round him. 'Listen...' Vicente took the remaining arm out of her jacket. 'The plants will like the drink. Stones, ceramics, paths, steps... they look sad and muddy – but they can be mended.'

'I want to see! I want to help! Sebas trapped me in the house. It's not *fair*!'

Sebastián was looking on, mouth open in amazement.

'Because there are bits that aren't safe at the moment,' she said. 'But we will make it safe and beautiful again, you'll see.'

'Yes Rafi, you see?' Sebastián said. 'If the gardener tells you it's not safe, you have to listen. Fast water and landslides are dangerous for small boys.'

'And that's why you insisted on coming this weekend, Sebastián?' Vicente asked steadily.

Sebastián looked over to his father.

'You were worried for Rafi's safety?' Vicente continued. 'Well, at least that's something.'

'*What?*'

'You knew what Antonio was planning, and you've come down to report back.'

'What are you *talking* about?' Sebastián retorted.

'Oh come on, boy, please don't make me describe it...' Vicente glanced at Rafi to make his point.

'The... *rambla*?'

'Yes, the *rambla*, of course the *rambla*!'

Rafi was looking from one to the other, but didn't like their angry voices and buried his head in Andie's arms, covering his ears.

Sebastián put a hand on Rafi's shoulder, but the little boy shook it off. 'See? Why are you making him hate me? He talks to the *gardener* more than—'

'He doesn't hate *anyone*,' Andie said. 'Come on, Rafi, while *Papi* and your brother sort this out, I think we should go up and talk to your birds.'

Rafi nodded, and rather slowly, with his arms clamped round her, they made their way out of the hall.

'Okay,' Sebastián could be heard saying, breathing out heavily. 'He told me what he wanted to do, but I didn't think he'd actually...'

She couldn't make out Vicente's angry reply.

'So yes, I came down just in case. To make sure Rafi was okay.'

'My God, when are you going to see your uncle for what he is?' Vicente shouted.

'He's been good to me.'

'Well he's not good for you or any of us now! You need to get away from him. Move back to Almería.'

Sebastián seemed to say something about that killing Antonio.

'Then he has to change. Either we report him to the police, like the builders want to do, or you've got to make him come to his senses.'

Their voices were getting calmer, as Andie and Rafi reached the top of the stairs. The first bedroom was his, as she'd guessed.

'This was my bedroom when I used to come to stay with my grandmother,' she said in Spanish.

'It's the best!' he said. 'I can see the garden. Papi's can see the sea and has a balcony. Sebastián's and Soleá's and Uncle

Juanito and Iván's, it can only see the cars. But we can put a plant *in* the room if you stay. Or some *pitas*. Are you going to stay in it?'

'Oh… yes I'd love to.' She sat on the bed next to him and stroked the birds and made them sing – but saw he also had a very new-looking giraffe. 'And he's rather cute!'

'I'll look after him, but he's a bit silly, as there aren't any giraffes around here.' He put him behind the birds. 'My brother brought him.'

'Ah. Well give him a chance.' Andie picked up a small penguin. 'There aren't any of these chaps around here either.'

'Yes but there is.' Rafi took a book with a penguin on the front out of a box by the bedside table. 'Can you speak Spanish reading words?'

'I think so.'

It was cosy and quiet up there, with not a sound now down below. With the two of them sprawling on the bed surrounded by soft animals while she read, she could have almost nodded off, after the exhausting drama downstairs and outside. After a third book with the same penguin, Andie got up and went to the window. 'The river has stopped coming out of the garden! Marcelo and his friend must have sorted out the *rambla*.'

'So everything will get better now?' Rafi asked.

'Yes. It might take a while, but yes.'

They went downstairs to report this, and found Vicente and Sebastián in the kitchen making coffee.

Vicente smiled at her. 'We were just about to call you.'

Rafi told them what he saw, and went to the front door

and looked out. 'And I think the sun is trying to come back!'

'Come and have a snack, Rafi,' Vicente said. 'Then the four of us will all go out and start putting things right.'

26

Thursday 6th September

Andie squeezed her car into a corner of the drive, leaving room for Kim, Ben, Vicente's harmonica friend Josemi, and other wonderful volunteers who'd said they'd try and put some time in today. It was the final push to get the amphitheatre ready for tomorrow's arrival of the stage and chairs as well as the evening's rehearsal. It was extraordinary what could be done in six days if the will and the man-and-woman power was there. She just wished they didn't have to worry about whether Antonio would try anything else to stop the concert going ahead.

Sebastián greeted her at the door. 'Well, good morning *jardinerita*, the first here as usual!'

Jardinerita meant little gardening girl – but could also be a small window box or planter. Either way, it raised her sizeist hackles – especially coming from a chap so little in age.

'Good morning, Sebastián. I think it's time you started using my name now, don't you?'

He shrugged.

'Have you heard from your uncle again?'

'Yes. He didn't do it. And if he says that—'

'You're going to believe him.'

He stared at her, eyebrows pinched with a mixture of hurt and anger that made him look like his father in his darker moments. 'I'll come and help as soon as María Ángeles gets here for Rafi,' he said.

'Great,' she said, smiling at him; although he'd been hidden away in Vicente's studio practising his dancing for an upcoming show in Almería for much of each day, he'd also proved himself to be an energetic digger and sweeper.

'My father is on the telephone, he...'

'Not now, all done!' Vicente emerged from behind him, all smiles. '*Buenos días, cariño*.' He hugged Andie tightly, causing Sebastián to fold his arms and scowl like a teenager. Vicente let go of her and patted her shoulders. 'Good news – you *are* doing it! With the Chambao "Voces" song that you know and like. The band think it will be fun to have two backing dancers when they play it at the end of the first set.'

'*What?* I thought you were joking!' She put a hand to her mouth. The dances she and Shefali created together were usually a living room thing.

'He is sending you a recording. We can manage without you and Shefali later, so you will have time to *coreografiar* before you rehearse with the band tomorrow.'

'Shefali is coming?' Sebastián asked.

'Yes, she'll be here later this morning.' Andie turned to Vicente. 'God... she's going to kill me. You sure about this?'

'*Totalmente*. And if you don't dance, I don't dance,' he

said with a grin. He took Sebastián's arm. 'Next year, we *all* dance!'

Sebastián nodded but couldn't bring himself to smile.

'Now come on, you have to *see* what did Marcelo and Jorge last night, using football lights!' Vicente said.

'Okay!'

Marcelo had worked so hard, and insisted on working for a low rate to help them out. Although even that, with Jorge's time and the materials, must have been adding up horribly – and Vicente wouldn't let her contribute.

'Uh, we could do with another layer of gravel on this,' she said, as they walked down the path arm in arm.

'Nothing will be perfect, but at the least the concert *can* happen,' he said. 'And we won't need the path for the wheelchairs now – as you will see.'

'Oh?'

They'd reached the beginning of the path going off to the cliff, and after a quick glance at each other, went down it to the lovers' bench that now had V + A in a heart scratched on it, not far from E + JL. Then in one movement, Vicente grabbed her and sat down with her on his lap for a kiss, their hands soon slipping under T-shirts to stroke each other's warm bodies.

He drew back for a moment and put a hand to her face. '*Ay, mi Andita...* do you think of your Grandie and José Luis here?'

'Of course! And they are watching us and cheering and laughing!'

'I think this!' He kissed her again. 'But that is all their *diversión* for now. You have to see what Marcelo and Jorge have done.'

They got up and walked back down the path.

'Apparently Antonio's still telling Sebastián that he didn't do it,' Andie said. 'Has he not answered *any* of your—'

'No.'

'Oh God. So how do we know he won't try something else? Or turn up and make a scene on the day?'

'Because he's talking to Sebastián. We don't know exactly what he says, but they're talking. Sebas is everything to him, and although he is a difficult and angry boy, he is beginning to grow and hates what Antonio did. While we have him here, nothing more will happen. Well, that is what I believe.'

They came out into the amphitheatre and Andie gasped. Marcelo and Jorge, having parked above in the car park, were putting some finishing touches to the new red-brick steps, but alongside it, in the gorge created by the flood, they'd created a smooth path of concrete. Access to the concert was now not only possible, but set in stone.

She dashed over and called up to Marcelo. 'That's amazing! Suddenly there's a path! Brilliant!'

He stood up and grinned. 'I know you and Vicente hate *hormigón*, but after the concert we can use paint for it same colour as the red earth, very nice.'

'Sounds *great*.'

'Wonderful, isn't it?' Vicente said. 'So now we must finish down here. One more day. We can do it.' They looked over the amphitheatre. There was still a large heap of landslide earth encroaching the stage area and blocking the entrance to a tier – and it had to be moved by spade, because neither Vicente or Andie could face damaging the garden by bringing the digger down the path. Underneath, there would be tiling to do, or at least a smoothing of the surface. The two other tiers had almost been cleared of mud now, but the damaged tiling was a trip hazard and had to be redone in many places, since even Marcelo hadn't had the heart to take the easy option and concrete it.

'Okay, I continue with that,' Vicente said, tipping his head towards the mound and going over to where they'd left spades and wheelbarrows. 'Even if it never seems to get any smaller!'

'Hopefully you'll have some help soon. And once Marcelo and Jorge have finished—'

'Helloo!' A workmanly dressed Kim came over to Andie, followed by Mónica in less hardy attire. 'I can do the whole morning, and then this afternoon you'll hopefully have Jen as well as Mónica, and Ben later on.'

'Brilliant,' Andie said. 'Mónica! I thought you were at the estate agent's on Thursdays?'

'Not now, I stop! Ignacio will have to find other stupid person to work with him. Or maybe soon he stop too, and put his self into development of property; I don't know and not my problem,' she said, with that wonderfully dismissive flick of the hand over the head that she'd also seen Vicente and Marcelo use.

'Good for you!' Andie said. 'Much better to put all your energies into your fabulous photography.'

'I hope,' Mónica said, making a crossed-fingers sign.

'I'll leave you two arty types to the tiling, while I get back to digging,' Kim said, and went over to join Vicente and her old pupil Sebastián.

★

'Wait,' Shefali said, before Andie put the track back on. 'Much as we hate air con, I think we…'

Andie joined her at the box on the wall in the corner of the living room. 'As far as I can fathom it, we're already on refrigeration level.'

'Dear God,' Shefali said, wiping her face with a wet tea towel again. 'How do people dance in this climate? This is madness,' she said, shaking her head but laughing. 'If your new *novio* wants to watch you dance, can't you do that for him in his *dormitorio*?'

'Shefali. You always said we should do more dance shows! And I told you, Vicente and I might be *novios*, but we aren't at the *dormitorio* stage yet.'

'I suppose not, with Sebastián staying there the week.'

'Yes. But anyway, we're both rather enjoying taking things slowly. Neither of us can quite believe it's happening.'

'Ah… that's lovely! I'm *so* happy for you,' she said, giving Andie a quick hug.

'Well, you always thought there was hope! Come on, back to work. I think we could do more with the intro.'

'And we need more flamenco arms in the—'

Andie's phone went. 'Is it going okay?' Vicente asked.

'Well…'

'D'you want me to send Sebastián?'

'Hang on.' Andie repeated this to Shefali and got a horrified face and a mouthed *no*.

'No, you keep him digging. We'll keep going, have some lunch, and be with you in a couple of hours.'

'Andita, look. Ben is coming, and Marcelo is down here now. Mónica, your English group, Jen, Josemi, and his artist friend Kiko are doing miracles with the tiles. You have worked so hard every day this week. It's okay to rest and relax now with your friend before tomorrow.'

'I don't know, somehow I've just got to be there.'

He laughed. 'I understand. But take your time, *cariño*.'

They rehearsed until they felt the dance just needed a final polish that evening, went for a quick dip in the sea, came back for lollies and cold showers, and then went down to the boutiques to look for something to wear for the dance.

Shefali shrugged. 'Everything's either too beachy or…'

'Trying too hard. I know.'

'I think we already have our outfits,' Shefali said.

'You brought your little turquoise floaty skirt?'

'Of course!'

'Well why didn't you *say*, you daft mare!'

'I don't know!' Shefali said, laughing. 'But anyway, that's saved us a bit. I say we splash out and carbo-load with a paella at that smart place near the marina.'

'Well… why not? We deserve it!'

By the time they arrived at the amphitheatre, the workforce consisted of Vicente, Ben, and the two builders finally looking like they were flattening the landslide lump, while Sebastián and María Ángeles – aided and distracted by Rafi alternately using and riding a broom – were putting the finishing touches to the tiers.

'You see? I told you there's no need to worry,' Vicente said. 'Hello, Shefali, how are you? I'm sorry to put you suddenly in show!'

'Ha – I think it'll be fine, thank you!'

Sebastián came forward. 'It is true wonderful that you

come to Spain to support your friend, and will dance for us,' he said to Shefali, smiling at her.

Andie muttered, '*Jes*us give it a rest, boy,' under her breath, making Shefali laugh, then introduced her to the others. She was about to try and persuade Rafi to hand over the broom so she could help, when Vicente asked her to come with him to fetch an ice box of drinks for everyone.

'Uh, wait, I have so many *bichos* walking on me!' He took off his T-shirt and, in his swim trunks, used the shower at the top of the beach path – while Andie stood there watching him with a confusing mix of admiration and hand-to-face coyness that made him laugh.

'Oh, that's better,' he said when he'd finished. 'And now I can touch you!' he said, putting a cool arm round her and squeezing. They went into the kitchen and put the ice box on the table, but then stopped still, too distracted by the realisation they were alone, looking at each other with the crazy unstoppable smiles that being together brought about these days.

'Uh... I can't stop thinking about you,' he said, pulling her towards him.

She nodded, ran her fingers through his wet, black hair, then pressed herself against him rather more than she'd done before.

He groaned, and put his arms round her tightly until their bodies felt like one.

'Cokes, lemon teas, water bottles,' he said into her hair, 'put yourselves in the ice box, *por Dios*, can't you see I can't move?'

She laughed... but then screamed and jumped back. 'Who's that!'

A heavy-featured, angry face was peering in the window.

Vicente swore. 'Antonio.' He squeezed her arm, told her not to be frightened, and went to the door. 'Next time, try knocking. And calling on your damn phone first,' Vicente said, in Spanish.

'From what I saw, you wouldn't have noticed,' Antonio said, coming through into the kitchen. He was a bulldog of a man, but smartly dressed, gold glinting on his neck, hands, and – when he spread a sickening smile on his thick lips – teeth.

'So this is the hot little gardener,' he said in Spanish, looking Andie up and down.

'So this is the big bad uncle,' Andie replied.

Antonio threw back his head and guffawed.

'Why have you done this?' Vicente shouted. 'You think it'll change my mind about the land? You've gone completely *mad*!'

'What makes you so sure I—'

'You haven't answered my calls all week!' Vicente shouted.

'Like you didn't answer me, when I was calling you about—'

'About the deal you went back on – I said one small house, not a block of ugly apartments! But no, you had to get carried away with your usual *greed*!'

'Business, Vicente. Something you wouldn't understand – unless it's bloody *jam*. And *you're* the one getting carried away. One minute you're having a little seaside holiday – fixed by *me*, remember – and the next thing we know, you're pulling the boy out of the best school in the province and shagging the gardener.'

'How *dare* you!' Andie burst out with in English, at the same time that Vicente was objecting. 'That is *not* what's been happening – not that it's anything to do with you anyway!'

'Well, it *is*, because I want the best for my dear sister's son and grandson,' Antonio continued in Spanish.

'You think I don't?' Vicente said.

'Not since you've lost your head here, no. Sebastián should be able to decide on the best school for Rafael. If you don't want to pay for it, *I* will.'

'Rafi will do best where he is happiest.'

Just at that moment, Sebastián came in with a limping and tearful Rafi. 'He tripped over the broom, needs a patch.' He exchanged a greeting with Antonio, not looking the least surprised to see him, so maybe he'd known he was coming. He was intent on grabbing the box from Vicente and being the one to deal with the graze on Rafi's knee, but the little boy, looking from his father to his brother and picking up on the tension, asked Andie to do it. Once it was done, he disappeared off to the bathroom.

'Why *did* you pull him out of that school without asking Sebastián?' Antonio asked.

'He was getting more and more behind, he was miserable, had no friends other than the reluctant Paulo in the year above. Once he started making friends here, he wanted to be with them. I've told Sebastián all this.'

'But, *Papá*, look at him now, he's *talking*,' Sebastián said. 'Next term he'd do *much* better. Give him a chance.'

'He's talking *because* he's happier back here, facing what happened, enjoying the garden, making new friends – including Andie.'

Antonio shook his head. 'This isn't right. His father should be the one to decide where he goes to school.'

'He *is* my father.' A little voice among them.

They all turned to see Rafi standing at the kitchen door, looking from one stunned face to the other, and then coming over to Vicente, putting his arms round his waist and looking up at him. 'How can my brother be my father, *Papi*?'

Vicente bent down to him. 'Sebas is... *like* a father to you, in some ways, that's all.'

'But in all the important ways, *Papi* is your *Papi*, of course,' Sebastián said, drawing a relieved look from Vicente.

'I'm going to the school up on the hill, with Lucía and Doina,' Rafi asserted, glaring at Antonio and Sebastián, even if just at chest level.

'Yes, you are,' Sebastián said. 'Well, at least until you are a little older. D'you want to go to the swing?'

'You don't know where the swing is. Andie mended it.'

'You can show me,' Sebastián said, taking his hand and going outside with him.

'You and your loud mouth!' Vicente directed at Antonio, once he could see that Sebastián and Rafi were far enough into the garden not to hear. 'He's not ready to understand, that could have been...' Vicente looked shaken, and put a hand over Andie's when she took his arm.

'But Sebastián came to the rescue – and also seems to have been talked round, I see,' Antonio said.

'Yes, it suddenly seems so. Anyway, just as well Rafi isn't going back there; even with all our volunteers, repairing the amphitheatre has cost a lot more than a term's fees at that school. The builders wanted to call the police, but I—'

Antonio took an envelope out of his pocket and whacked it on the table. 'That should more than cover it.'

'Well... that's something.'

'But I didn't do it.'

'Of course not, you paid some poor—'

'No, *I didn't do it*. I thought about it. Joked about it to Sebastián. Unfortunately, I also joked about it with a guy who has very little sense of humour and a lot of ambition and willingness to please.'

'Ignacio Méndez, the estate agent,' Andie said.

Antonio opened his mouth in surprise, then tilted his head at Andie. 'She's smart, Vicente, I'll give you that.'

'Just putting pieces together,' Andie said.

'She's smart, talented, kind, and Rafi adores her. As would Estefi. I know it's hard for you, Antonio, but I'm moving on. And you need to as well; you're going to lose Sebastián's inexplicable devotion to you if you keep pulling him away from me. He's finally growing up a bit and starting to thinking about more than just himself.'

'You underestimate him. Always did.'

'Well, being a father is incredibly difficult – unless you just come along and take on someone else's eighteen-year-old, like you did. Now, if you don't mind, we need to take drinks out to the people helping us repair the damage you've caused.'

'I'd like to come and see this amphitheatre. In fact, if Soleá is involving herself, this show must be pretty good. Think I'll come along on Saturday; I'm staying in Almería for the weekend.'

'Okay. Anyone can buy a ticket. Just don't go making any jokes to anyone about setting fire to the stage.'

'Oh, don't worry, jokes are the very opposite of what Ignacio Méndez has been getting from me this week.'

They stared at each other a moment, then reluctantly smiled and patted each other's shoulders.

Then Antonio turned to Andie. 'Andrea, was it?'

'Andie.'

27

Shefali got up from the sofa and stretched noisily. 'Uh… I've woken up so nervous. What the hell?'

'I know, me too,' Andie said, flexing her legs on the other sofa.

'I think we should go through it now.'

Andie put down her tea. 'What? We haven't even had breakfast.'

'Yes, but we might feel like *eating* breakfast if we know it's okay.'

'True.'

They each grabbed a hair elastic, got into position, and then started the music, its slow introduction taking them into the rock-flamenco groove.

'*Olé*, not bad!' Andie said at the end.

'Just a tiny bit out of sync on that first chorus.'

'But it's going to be all right!'

They high-fived and made toast with Vicente's spiced fig and pear jam.

'So was it our dance that changed David's mind?' Andie asked.

'Seems so. I told him Zara having sleepovers on two school nights wouldn't be the end of the world – but you know how he is about the *school*. Then I asked him, what's more important, seeing your wife in a show or one dodgy spelling test and a PE lesson with a dirty polo shirt? He finally saw sense.'

'And changed your flight home so you two can have a three-day mini-break! Brilliant.'

'He's even got a few properties he wants us to check out.'

'Really? Let's see.'

They rinsed their jammy fingers and sat down with Shefali's iPad.

Andie flicked through the marked properties. 'On no, that one's right by a bar... That's nice, but a sea view there means dealing with hundred-step stairs to the beach... This one with the shared pool is more of a holiday complex; Mónica tells me they're noisy in the summer and ghostly in the winter.'

'You've been looking too?'

'Not really, I'll rent at first, of course... Ah, now *this* one, I know this road – really pretty, pedestrianised, and a flat three minutes' walk to the beach.'

'God, I don't want to keep you from your gorgeous new *novio*, but can you come with us to look? As well as help me drive around and show him the area?'

'Of course. Actually, Vicente's already sent me a message telling me to just relax with you two today. Apparently Soleá has already come over from her hotel, and she and

Sebastián are competing for Rafi's attention. Neither of them are going to be able to see him for a while.'

'And if you go over, they wouldn't either of them stand a chance.'

'Well, that's pretty much what he said, yes! And with his guitarist friend Nico turning up later, he says he can manage the few things to be done. We should just come along for the sound check at half seven.'

'Perfect.' Shefali went into the EasyJet app on her phone. 'Ah, the plane's going to arrive half an hour *early*. It must know it's got Mr Punctual on board. We better get going.'

A grinning David came out of Arrivals already in beach shorts, singlet and sandals, sunglasses in hand. Andie remembered how, although he was often a perfectionist, cantankerous sod, he tended to be more engaging company in the summer; if anyone needed a sunny bolthole, he did – for everyone's sakes. Apparently, the winter temperatures and sunshine hours in Almería – along with the stunning beaches and hill walking he'd gleaned from Shefali's photos – were a major draw for him.

After hugs all round, and the observation they'd all made, on arriving, that the airport was more like a station, Andie took them off down the seaside route. An hour later, with a stop-off for ice creams by the sea, they came over the hill where you first see the village, marina, and pale, sandy beach between the russet-rock, stubbled mountains.

'San José,' Andie said proudly, having already had a calm-it-down hand gesture from Shefali during her full-on tour guide spiel.

David gasped. She took them up round the perimeter road of hillside villas to get views over the village beaches and marina; past Grandie's garden; down through the village, pointing out restaurants overlooking the water; and parked briefly so he could take in the village square before going back up the hill a little to Valentina's.

'Even without all those wild beaches a few minutes away, this is incredible. I never knew there was anything like this hidden away in Southern Spain,' he said, going up to the apartment. 'Right. I need to get in that sea.'

They spent a couple of hours at the beach, had lunch there, and did a detour on the way back to look at the little pedestrianised road with the three-bedroom flat for sale.

He shook his head in amazement. 'Just think, school holidays, half-terms – the occasional child-free weekend...' He put his arm around Shefali. 'And we could rent it out when we're not here. Hey, we could rent it to *you*, Andie, until such a time as you're ready to buy your own place.'

'Probably a bit big for me. But there's a lovely English couple who've had a property services business here for years – they'd look after rentals for you. I think they also have some places for sale. They'll be at the concert.'

'Well, we'll see how it works out. Obviously we wouldn't charge you much, as it would save us agency fees and we'd have peace of mind. Uh, I'm getting carried away here!'

'Don't we all!' Andie said.

Vicente came over and greeted Andie and Shefali as they came into the amphitheatre from the garden.

'Wow. Beautiful,' Andie said, looking over the tiers with

their solar-lit lamps in the shadows of the early evening, and the succession of different colours being tried out over the stage against a background of pink-blue sky and calm sea. 'And you even managed to re-gravel the path!'

'That was Uncle Juanito and Iván. They remembered me saying you were unhappy about your Grandie's path, and arrived early with bags of little stones! They are in the house changing clothes, you will meet them soon.'

'Oh, great!'

A guy at the sound desk at the back was calling Vicente.

'Ah, they will want my feet.' He went off to the stage, where Nico, Josemi and the band were checking their microphones.

Shefali's phone buzzed. 'Oh… it's Zara ringing me back, wanting to say goodnight.' She put the phone to her ear, but couldn't hear anything, with the band playing bits of the songs. 'Wait, darling, I'll just go somewhere quieter.' She went off into the garden.

Andie decided to sit down in the front row to watch what was going on – which would hopefully include a little preview of Vicente's dancing that she'd somehow managed to miss at yesterday's rehearsal with a badly timed trip to the loo. Unfortunately, she was going to have to sit next to Soleá, unless she rudely put herself down in a chair much further along.

They smiled and said hello to each other, Soleá doing her usual look-up-and-down thing, as if wondering what Vicente could possibly see in her.

'This is such a beautiful setting for a concert; you're going to do *very* well next summer, you'll see,' Soleá said in Spanish, gazing straight ahead at either the sea-sky background, or maybe at the other half of the plural 'you' – her ex-lover Vicente.

'I hope so. It'll be fun.'

'You could of course open the garden before the concerts, and charge more.'

'We have wondered about that – but for a charity donation on entry.'

'Ah yes.'

Well, that wasn't so bad. They listened to Nico playing something loud and guttural, then gentle and sensitive, on his guitar. Presumably they'd need to check Soleá's voice on her microphone – hopefully sooner rather than later.

'In just a few weeks, you've turned that jungle back into a garden.' Soleá squeezed Andie's right bicep and patted her leg. 'You must be very fit and strong.'

'Well I had—'

'Which is perfect; with your youth and energy, you'll have no problem giving Rafi a sibling – *two* perhaps! Vicente would *love* that.'

Even in the heat, Andie suddenly felt cold all over.

'Early days, I understand – but he must have told you how much he—'

'Yes, *very* early days.' Vicente already basically had two sons; this couldn't possibly be true.

'He'd like a daughter. Although with so many sons in the family tree, I'd say that's unlikely.'

With Andie's maternal family tree of only-children arriving after some years, she might not be able to produce one of either type. The Ball, banished for some weeks here, started to make his presence known. She stared at the stage, willing them to ask for the grand La Soleá to join them absolutely now. But no, Vicente had put his flamenco shoes on and was waiting on the special sound board part of the stage.

Soleá leant over to her. 'You probably haven't seen him dance *live* yet,' she said, through the haze of her dark floral perfume.

Andie had seen that tantalising bit of flamenco among the crazy dancing they'd done to 'Make Me Smile', but she didn't want to share that. 'No.'

Soleá looked at her with raised eyebrows and a knowing smile – as if saying, *If you think you're already in love, brace yourself, my dear.*

Andie didn't stick around to see if she was right; this time, her trip to the loo to miss the dance – or rather, the scrutiny of her face *watching* the dance – was deliberately timed.

She'd hoped to find Shefali still in the garden, but just as she was leaving the amphitheatre, she saw her friend at the back of the amphitheatre – with David, who had arrived ridiculously early, even by his standards. She'd told Soleá she was going to the *baño*, so she couldn't very well walk past her to go over to Shefali – who was neither in the direction of the house or the car park's mobile loos.

She made her way down the path, but turned off towards the cliff, past the fairy statue, and on to the Lover's Bench – invisible in its kink in the path, unless you knew where it was. She just needed five minutes to get a grip on herself – but good God, even from here she could hear the rhythmic rattling of Vicente's dancing, so strong, so potent. Virile. *Fertile.*

Deep breaths. She was not going to let La bloody Soleá

ruin her enjoyment of the evening they'd worked so hard for. Grandie was telling her not to worry, and just visible from here, Eve the Cactus was reminding her of her solo pink flower…

'Andie.' Vicente suddenly there in front of her – while Soleá could finally be heard expressing a florid bit of flamenco. 'What did she say?'

'You saw? Oh, the usual patronising gardener stuff I seem to get! Never mind.'

'No, another thing. I saw your face.' He sat down next to her, looking concerned.

'She said you wanted a sister for Rafi.'

'What?'

'But my mother and grandmother took *years* to conceive, so I might never have a child.' There, it was out, with surprising simplicity.

'Oh… I will have to talk with her, if she is like this.' He put his arm round her and drew her close. 'Listen. Maybe we will have a child, maybe we can't. Anyway, already we have Rafi, who loves you. Yes, he wants a sister, but would also like a nice little dog! Please, don't worry about this.'

She smiled at him with relief. 'But Soleá seems so… bitter. I feel sorry for her, but she—'

'Don't feel *too* sorry. It was never… *exclusivo* between us. Well, for me, yes, because I don't have time for more than one woman! What happened with Soleá and me is that we became good friends when our children had produced Rafi, and then…' He shook his head. 'One time things went too far. We have never been a real couple, and she thinks this too – but she doesn't like it that it was I who decided to stop. Very proud woman. But I will talk more with her, and soon she will be okay.'

'Oh...'

'Now come and have something to eat... and if everything is with ham, that you don't like, I have some jam san'wich in box behind stage.'

She opened her bag and grinned as she produced a large, film-wrapped, jam roll.

'Aha! We can share now?' He laughed and took it from her, and they walked back to the amphitheatre, taking alternate bites.

'Ah! This has to be Andita, Superwoman garden dance girl, and *aficionada* of jam!' a voice in accented English said behind them.

They turned to find a smiling couple – one greying but prettily handsome and with José Luis's wide smile, the other older and balding but also good-looking – who had to be Uncle Juanito and Iván.

They introduced themselves and double-kissed Andie enthusiastically.

'Thank you for my path!' Andie said.

'Thank you for making the garden beautiful again!' Juanito said.

'Oh, there's so much more to do...'

Juanito lowered his voice. 'But how happy was my father in his last week, looking at photos, thinking of your grandmother...' He hugged her. 'Thank you, Andie.' He stood back. 'And you must come to have lunch with us soon! I know you have only little time now with Vicente before you go to England, but when you are here again, no?'

'I'd love that.'

Iván leant forward. 'But... warning. You will be asked too much about our garden on the roof, which we want to change!'

'What?' Vicente said. 'Already it is so beautiful. You will love it, Andie.'

Andie couldn't answer, as she'd been given the last mouthful of jam roll.

'*Higo y pera* that I sent?' Juanito asked.

Andie nodded.

When they arrived back at the amphitheatre, they found that the band's helpers at the barrier in the car park had started letting people in. Among them were Kim and Carlito, chatting with Shefali, David and Sebastián; Marcelo, Beatriz, and Marcelo's dad, Chelo; and next to them, María Ángeles keeping an eye on Rafi and Lucía, who were running along the tiers. Nico's son Paulo – who'd just turned up with a young woman who had to be Nico's new girlfriend – was now being introduced to Lucía.

'I can't see Soleá,' Andie said.

Vicente pointed her out, chatting with Nico and an enthralled double bass player. He chuckled. 'She's okay. And if Antonio comes...'

Andie looked at him. 'Surely she doesn't like *him*?'

'They are sort of friends. She has promised to make sure he behaves well.'

More and more people were coming down from the car park now, getting something from the refreshment stall and hanging around there, or taking their seats. Andie spotted Ben with a group of boys and girls, Ana and Jaime, Valentina and family along with several other guests in her apartments, little Doina's parents, a doctor and one of the nurses from the surgery, and the chap in the lilo kiosk. Ah, and Shefali and David were now chatting earnestly with Jen and Phil, hopefully about apartments.

Vicente had started getting approached by people who remembered his dancing and wanted to know about any plans to return.

'Uf, enough,' he said to Andie. 'I'm going over to the band behind stage. Come with me if you want. Anyway, it's soon time to start!'

After saying hello to everybody and showing Shefali where their reserved seats were, she joined Vicente for jam sandwiches, lemon teas, and a ribbing from the band guys.

'Rock 'n' roll!' said the band guitarist, and '*Qué vida flamenca!*' said the double bass player, both hitting the rioja – while both the girl keyboard player and Josemi laughed but cadged a sandwich. Soleá had wandered off, and Vicente nudged Andie and tilted his head towards the back of the amphitheatre to show her why: Antonio had arrived – and was waving to them with a smile.

They looked out at the audience in amazement; it didn't look like there was going to be a seat free. It was night time now, and behind them the dark sea below glinted with the light from the full moon and flashes from the marina's little green and red lights.

'Look at María Ángeles and Lucía's grandfather, his hand on her arm...' Vicente said. 'There is something there, I tell you! And it is time; it's five years since her husband died.'

Andie turned to look at them. 'Oh yes!' So when Vicente took her on to help with Rafi, María Ángeles was also recently bereaved. 'Chelo is a sweetheart, and does a lot of childcare himself; that could work beautifully! And what about Mónica and Josemi's friend Kiko? Over there... walking round the edge to be on their own?'

'I tell you, it's this place. It's the Garden of Love,' Vicente said.

Andie thought how Grandie would agree.

The manager had arrived behind the stage, ready to go up and introduce the show, the stage lights brightening.

It was time for those not on until later to take their seats in the front row. Andie sat down with Vicente, Nico and his son and girlfriend, and Josemi; Shefali and David were the other side of her. Rafi and María Ángeles were on the tier above, at the end of the row; Rafi had insisted on being by the bird mosaic he'd help make, and wanted to be with Lucía and her family. Soleá was with Sebastián and Antonio just behind Rafi; the little chap ignored them, but they seemed to be enjoying watching him chat with Lucía.

The manager and the local mayor said they were delighted to introduce such a beautiful new music venue to the area, and thanked Vicente and all the gardeners, builders and volunteers who had made it possible. The mayor seemed to address something to the *rambla* that made the audience laugh, and then asked everyone to be extra generous with their contributions to the children's charity collection box.

As soon as they'd left the stage, the band came on – and Andie and Shefali exchanged a gritted-teeth grin as they realised they were now on a countdown to their dancing number at the end of the set. Andie enjoyed the contrast between the sweet voice of the crop-haired girl singer and the gravelly one of the chunky, male vocalist. She was nervous, but soothed by the flamenco-pop-Latin rhythms of the band and their delicious harmonies.

Then it was time: following Josemi's plaintive harmonica on 'Contigo en la Distancia', the female singer invited 'the girl whose grandmother created the garden, with her best friend from childhood' to help them with their last number before the break.

They took their place on the stage, to some encouraging cheers from friends, and then it started, with the fluid flamenco arms and hands in the slow introduction and then... off they went along with the chugging groove of the lovely 'Voces' song about making a better world for children, each aware of the other in the corner of their eye, perfectly in sync, both finding that extra energy for the accelerating last chorus in which the band and many of the audience sang or clapped along – including Rafi who'd come forward to share the moment with his father.

There was huge applause and whistling. The manager thanked everyone and announced a forty-five-minute refreshment interval before the band would be back with their surprise guests. Andie and Shefali came off in a daze to hugs from Vicente, Rafi, David, and all Andie's friends. Sebastián was the most surprising, with his insistence that she and Shefali could be an Instagram and TikTok sensation, and even Soleá nodded and said 'adorable'. The girls downed Cokes that Kim had put into their hands, wiping sweat from their faces and talking about cold showers.

'You can have showers if you like, girls,' Vicente said. 'I have to go back to the house to get changed – you can come with me.'

'Oh...' Shefali said, 'it's okay, I'll survive. And I know David's keen to talk more to Jen and Phil.'

When Rafi was back playing with Lucía under the watchful eyes of María Ángeles and Chelo, Vicente and Andie managed to escape into the garden.

'Oh... lovely and quiet,' she said, running her hand along some fig leaves as they walked along. 'If one more person had hugged me, I'd have fainted – except you, of course,' she said, linking arms so tightly with him that she steered them into the mass of bougainvillea. 'Oops!'

He laughed and grabbed a handful of crimson-red petals.

They reached the house. 'Come up and cool yourself in my bathroom; you can talk with me while I change.'

She followed him through the living room and up the stairs.

He turned at the top of the stairs and put his arms round her. 'Alone!' he said, 'as we will be on Monday, at last.'

'Yes.' When Rafi started school. They'd already agreed that tomorrow she'd spend time with Shefali and David, giving Vicente more mending time with Sebastián before he left for Granada. Monday was the day. The day they would probably... He was so gorgeous in every way, but *Dios mío* it also gave her such butterflies in the tummy thinking about it.

They were in his room now, where light from the moon out over the sea was throwing an almost comical spotlight through the balcony doors and over the white bed.

His arms came round her. 'Andie, we will have Monday together but we don't have to... hurry things.'

She turned in his arms and smiled. Was he going to keep reading her mind? 'Maybe just... rehearse?'

'*Ensayo*, exactly,' he said, then shook his head, smiling back. '*Madre mía*, we are like teenagers again with these things.' He looked at his watch. 'Okay, here is the bathroom.' He pointed to a room at the side that she remembered as a walk-in wardrobe in Grandie's days.

'Right.' She let go of him and went in, ran the cold water until it was cold as it was going to get, splashed her face with it, wiped off smudgy make-up with a tissue. Oh, it felt good. She could hear a cupboard opening next door.

'You could still have a shower,' he called out.

Take off all her clothes. 'No, I'll just have a wash.' When she came back through, pulling her top back on, he was putting a white shirt on the chair – but his neat, dark-haired body was in nothing but a pair of boxers. 'Oh…' Distracted, she found herself half in and out of her top with her arm stuck.

They looked at each other a moment, wide-eyed.

He came forward, with an amused smile on his lips. 'Can I help with that?'

'Please.'

He caught hold of the fabric, his fingers brushing against her tummy and sending a tingle through her body.

'On, or off?' he asked quietly.

'Um… I think it'll have to come off first.'

She helped him pull it over her head, and then he drew her to him, his warm chest against hers, except for her bra… which, between them, they soon made drop to the floor.

He held her tighter, and whispered '*ay… que te quiero*,' meaning he wanted her, or he loved her, maybe both. Then he chuckled and asked how on earth he was now going to get into his flamenco trousers. He seemed to have lost his English, and she seemed to have lost speech altogether.

She answered by taking off her skirt, as if being equally undressed was only fair.

'*Que haces?*' he whispered.

What indeed was she doing? 'A little *ensayo*,' she managed. Rehearsal.

He looked at his watch again. She was grateful that one of them still had connection to time. Then he picked her up in his arms, like he'd done that first time they'd met, but this time with a little laugh, and put her on the moonlit bed. Lay on top of her and started kissing her neck and breasts, pushing himself against her.

'Oh...' She ran her fingers through his soft black hair, down over his smooth back... 'Maybe... *not ensayo*.'

He stopped kissing her, his dark eyes looking down into hers. Said something like *no*, there would be no time to hold her afterwards, so maybe she would feel...

'But we'll go back through the garden, holding each other...' she managed.

'The garden, yes...' he said in Spanish, 'the first time should have been there, but... ah, wait, I know.' He let go and reached over to the chair, took out bougainvillea petals from his shorts' pocket and let them float onto the patch of moonlight on the bed, and onto her. He said something about being quick.

'Good,' she surprised herself by answering, and then after a kiss and more wanting-loving words, everything did happen very quickly, with an intensity that soon had her gasping with an almost painful ecstasy, followed by his shuddering in her arms as he said her name.

★

Taking her seat next to Shefali as the stage lights came on, she shared a smile with Vicente, now by the side of the stage and getting a slap on the back from Nico, who'd probably wondered if his friend had decided not to dance after all. They'd reckoned they'd get away without anyone realising what they'd been up to; Andie's wet hair was expected after the shower she'd mentioned, and Vicente's just looked like he'd wetted his down, as many flamenco dancers do before a performance.

Shefali looked at her with raised eyebrows.

'What?' Andie asked.

'Was it okay?' Shefali whispered.

Andie put a hand over her mouth. When had she ever been able to fool her old friend? Even when she'd acted so impulsively, compared to her usual slowly-slowly with boyfriends, Shefali had been able to tell. She raised her own eyebrows and nodded in reply.

Shefali chuckled and gave her a squeeze.

After an introduction by the manager, Nico came on to a spotlit stage to enthusiastic applause – especially from his girlfriend and son Paulo. They'd been joined by Rafi and Lucía, along with María Ángeles and Lucía's grandfather Chelo, who had moved down to take the seats of this set's performers. Nico introduced his song, saying something about it being dedicated to lovers everywhere. It was one of those slow numbers with rippling chords, somehow reminding Andie of the feel of the delicious shower she'd just had with Vicente. Nico was then joined by the band's guitarist for an upbeat duet.

After that, the rest of the band came on and started a song Andie recognised, the beautifully resigned 'Lo Bueno y

Lo Malo', about life moving on. After the girl singer's first verse and chorus, La Soleá joined her – with much applause – to sing the second verse, in her more floridly flamenco emotional style. The two women couldn't have been more contrasted, in hair, height, clothing or voice, but they were soon singing in harmony, responding to each other's ad libs, and warmly embracing at the end. Andie loved it, and it also made her hope that she and Soleá, also so different, could one day be friends.

Another song for Soleá was introduced as 'La Estrella' – The Star. Well, how appropriate, Andie thought, as she enjoyed the irresistible one-two-three-*four* flamenco tango rhythm... but after a gentle verse from Soleá, on came Vicente. Of course; he said he'd refused to have his 'own' number but... it was hard to be aware of anybody else on the stage, and it wasn't just Andie, the whole audience seemed to be holding their breath as he marked out the rhythm, that broad-shouldered but cat-like body taut with intensity, arms and hands flowing with expression... building up into a crescendo of rattling footwork. Next came a quiet interlude with just Nico and the percussionist, in which, rapt in the music, Vicente seemed to dance for himself, his serious face giving way to a smile as his hands circled each other in front of him like he was giving an embrace. He'd said he'd think of her when he danced... Then the song came to a loud climax of singing, *palmas* and playing, Vicente finishing with a series of ecstatic whipping turns at the end.

It had been made out to be the last song, they bowed and came off the stage... but of course they had an encore prepared for the clamouring audience: the song from the Penélope

Cruz film, *Volver*. To Return. The audience loved it, and sang along with the words. The mother of Penélope's character in the film – a ghost at that point, Andie seemed to remember – had also loved it, because hearing her daughter sing it meant that the girl remembered her. As the song finished to more tumultuous clapping and cheering, Andie glanced over towards the top of the Lookout Post, where she was sure Grandie and José Luis had enjoyed it too...

Rafi was pulling her arm and trying to drag her up on the stage. The manager and the mayor had come up and thanked everyone again, and it looked like they'd been thanking Vicente, but he wasn't having any of it. He was beckoning her up on stage, and with Rafi's insistence, she had to go.

Vicente put his arm round her and a hand on Rafi's shoulder. '*This* is who you have to thank,' he was saying in Spanish slow enough that she would understand. 'She returned to her grandmother's garden with a vision, and – despite having to deal with an attacking wild boar, a grumpy, unsociable, ex flamenco dancer, and then a freak flooding, she has created a place of music, dance, fun and... love.' He drew her close and gave her a kiss on the lips, then turned back to the audience, now making 'Aw' and 'Ooh' noises – including Rafi, burying himself between them. 'And we look forward to you returning next summer to share it with us!'

Epilogue

'Ah, so you *did* build yourself a little house on your car park land, Andie!' Johnny said, pointing over to the far end of what they called the rounders' pitch most of the year.

They were standing there with the director of *Return to... Gardens that Inspired* and Johnny's pretty, twenty-something assistant – and now girlfriend – Daisy.

'Yes, most of the ground floor is storage for chairs and lighting and so on, and loos for the summer concert audience, but upstairs there's an apartment for visitors.'

As if to illustrate this, Gerard and Hughie came out onto the little balcony overlooking both the sea and the amphitheatre, called out a hello to Johnny, and got a wave back.

'They've come out to visit the pottery workshop you import from?'

'That's the excuse, yes!'

'And it's good for your friend Shefali, so she can come over and do those Instagram dances with you!' Johnny said.

'No, they've got a place just down the road. They come over whenever they can.'

'Oh yes, Johnny showed me you two dancing. That's *amazing*!' Daisy said. 'How d'you have time to be an internet sensation, do the garden, the summer concerts, import pottery, this mini-series and—'

'I wouldn't say we're a *sensation*! Vicente's older son does most of the technical stuff for us, so that's not a big deal. As for the rest, María Ángeles still helps out part time, and although Vicente dances quite a bit locally in the summer, he mainly works at home and is amazing.'

The director cleared his throat. 'Right, let's get on. Much prettier up here, with all these shrubs round the edge, but the amphi and the garden – tell me again about the main changes since last time?'

'Well, let's see...' Andie still couldn't believe that the garden was one of the three chosen to be revisited for the new mini-series – even though, what with one thing and another, she hadn't had time to develop it as much as she'd like.

She heard feet pattering behind her. 'One thing: we had to put a fence for Candi to be safe!' Rafi said, coming up to them with Candi on her lead. He smiled, but was still unable to look people he didn't know in the eye. 'I speak English very well.'

'You do indeed!' Andie put an arm round him and squeezed.

'Also, we have a path from the *anfiteatro* to the beach,' Rafi continued, 'which has small rock garden with crassula. Ah yes, and splendid lantana by the house – near our little swimming pool with fence, that *finally* my parents allow.'

'Oh! You sound like you'll be a gardener too when you grow up!' Daisy said.

Rafi looked at her as if she was stupid. 'No. I will be zookeeper.'

'Ha – wonderful! And what a lovely dog, Rafi,' Johnny said in slow English, patting calf-like, little, brown and white Candi. 'Looks like a whippet crossed with something smaller,' he said to Andie.

'No idea,' Andie said. 'She came from the dog rescue place.'

Having checked out the visitors, rather like a little dog himself, Rafi scampered off down the slope with Candi to go back to his friends.

'Oh my God, that boy is so cute!' Daisy said, taking Johnny's arm.

'So, any changes to the amphitheatre?' the director asked, walking over to the slope. 'Wow, lots of colour!'

At least coming at this earlier time of the year, the garden would *show* itself differently: there was the pink sea of Hottentot-fig covering the slope down to the amphitheatre, and on the other side, all the acacias with their mass of deep-yellow blob flowers.

'I'm afraid it's mainly just the practical one of having access to get a van in there to transport stuff,' Andie said.

The director looked over the edge. 'Ah, I was wondering where the crew had got to.'

'Well done, you've managed to get quite a little rent-a-crowd on for the concert bit,' Johnny said. 'They'll definitely fill the first tier.'

'Yes! Although the performers are all complaining about it being a very un-flamenco hour of the day. They've only just had breakfast.'

At that point, however, the complaining was coming from the babies and toddlers who'd been brought along: Lucía's little brother was having a tantrum about his buggy; Kim's one-year-old was fractious and sounding like he needed his morning nap; and Josemi's tiny boy was crying for a feed from his mama. There were also the excited screams of the nine-to-ten-year-olds – Rafi, Lucía, Paulo and Shefali's Zara – running around the place. 'I'm sorry, I know it's resembling a crèche, but we've got María Ángeles and Chelo here to take small people off to the house, as needed.'

Johnny looked like he was about to ask something, but Andie wanted to get back down to the amphitheatre and led the way.

'The kids'll look good, now we're going for more of a party vibe than pretending we're doing one of the concerts,' the director said. 'But yes, as long as they don't squawk too much. Who are these two, taking photos?'

'Mónica and Kiko. Mónica's taking photos of the shoot for the local paper. She's a friend; don't worry, she'll keep out of the way.'

They stopped off at the coffee, drinks, and biscuit stall, where Ben and his long-awaited and newly returned first love Florrie were chatting with Uncle Juanito and Iván about the botanical garden.

The director looked over at the stage, where Sebastián was introducing Soleá's ridiculously handsome duet singer Lorenzo to Josemi, while Nico and the cajón player sat running their fingers over their instruments. 'Good God, I'm sorry Andie, but which of those three insanely gorgeous chaps is your husband again?'

'*What?*' Andie said with a laugh.

'That would be *me*, I think,' Vicente said, with a puzzled smile, coming up and putting a hand round her waist before exchanging a very English handshake with the director and Johnny, followed by the customary two-kiss thing for a startled Daisy. 'If you want to begin with the little show, I think we're nearly ready. We're just waiting for Soleá.'

'Yes, she's being a *long* time...' Andie said.

Just as all eyes turned to look for her at the entrance to the garden, Soleá appeared – complete with matching baby in spotted pink flamenco dress.

Lorenzo projected his beautiful speaking voice over to her. '*There* you are, *cariño*.'

'Sorry, she needed changing,' Soleá said in Spanish.

María Ángeles started protesting that she could have done that.

'No, no, you enjoy the party!' she said to her, then turned to the gummily grinning baby. 'And we don't mind, do we, Josefina?'

'She's called *Sefi*,' Rafi corrected her.

'Yes, of course,' she said to him. 'Anyway, I thought I'd give Sefi a costume change while I was at it. All part of my godmother duties! Now she just needs Mama for a feed.'

'Oh *no*,' Rafi said, raising his eyes to the heavens.

Andie came forward and put a hand on Rafi's shoulder. 'Can you look after Soli for me?' she asked in Spanish, using Rafi's name for Soleá these days. 'She probably needs a nice drink *and* a bottle of water, for her singing, and then you need to introduce the television people to her, okay?'

Rafi nodded.

Andie took Sefi in her arms. 'Well look at you, lucky girl – you've got more flamenco clothes than your mama! Thank you so much – she looks lovely in it.' A bit over the top, but then so was Sebastián's teaching of an eight-month-old how to do flamenco hands, and even Vicente – full of she-can-be-zookeeper-gardener-or-whatever – had managed to source a flamenco-spotted pram, car seat, and changing mat.

'I'm sorry,' she called over to the director and Johnny, 'I shouldn't be too long.'

Johnny came over and stroked Sefi's cheek. 'So *here* she is! And goodness me, she's *gorgeous*. I'm so happy for you.'

'Thanks, Johnny.'

Shefali was stroking Sefi's little feet, a rapt Zara beside her. 'Look at this instep, I tell you—'

'Oh don't you start!'

'Mummy, if you have a baby now, they could be best friends too,' Zara said.

'Uh-oh!' Andie said, and shared a lip-biting smile with Shefali.

'Off you go, see you later,' Shefali said.

Vicente took Sefi from her. 'Come to *Papi*. Mami's shoulder needs a rest.'

'It's not that bad.'

'Yes, but it's a good excuse to escape with you two for a moment,' he whispered in Spanish. He kissed the soft dark hair on the top of Sefi's little head and came out with that Spanish expression about the baby being eatable.

'She really is… and so are you and Rafi, which is why I'm so glad I've decided that after this and the trips to present the other two gardens we're revisiting, there's no more TV for me. We don't need it.'

'No, we don't. But I wouldn't try to stop you.'

'I know.' They were going past the Lookout Post. 'Actually, the bench will be in the shade now... I think I'll feed her up there.'

'Shall I get you some water?'

'Oh... yes please.'

Andie took Sefi, went up the winding path, and sat on the bench under the olive tree. 'Say hello to Yayo and Yaya,' she whispered in Spanish to Sefi. *Great*-grandparents really, but there didn't seem to be easy words for that.

Now her Spanish was so much better, she could hear José Luis as well as Grandie. They were both happy to see her, but telling her to get a move on – as was Sefi.

She helped Sefi latch on and closed her eyes in bliss. How could she have spent so many years telling herself she couldn't and wouldn't want to be a mother?

I did try to tell you, Grandie was saying.

Vicente came up and sat down next to her with the water, putting an arm round the two of them. 'Well? Are they happy?'

In the distance, she could here Soleá and Lorenzo singing that soft and beautiful 'De Alguna Manera' song about not forgetting.

'Who?'

'Grandie and José Luis, of course. I assume you've had a word,' he said gently in Spanish.

She smiled and looked at him. He knew she still often thought about Grandie, but she'd never quite let on that they sort of... *spoke*. 'Might have done.'

'It's okay, I do it too. And now my English is better, and with all the things you've told me... ha! This is going to sound crazy... but sometimes I can hear Grandie too.'

Acknowledgements

The idea for *The Spanish Garden* came to me over many a stroll round the perimeter hills of my village, San José in Almería – often with my wonderful next-door neighbours María José Martín and Paulino Espigares. It's amazing how many gardens you can peek into, and stories you can make up about the possible inhabitants, while trying to do your 10K Fitbit steps.

A huge thank you as ever to my husband Phil for his encouragement and critiquing, and, for this book, tolerance of my endless 'what's-this-one-called-again?' as I point at the local flora.

As an obsessed but talentless fan of dance, I've really enjoyed 'being' dancing gardener Andie. I'm really grateful for the inspiration from my flamenco and sevillanas teacher Alvaro Guarnido (Instagram: @alvaroguarnido), and my nephew's girlfriend's Instagram dance group with her sisters (@gregoriansisters).

As usual, it was great to be able to check my own observations of the region with the engaging and uniquely informative *Flamingos in the Desert*: Exploring Almeria and *Where Hoopoes Fly*: Exploring Almeria 2 by Kevin Borman.

A big thank you to my wonderful editors Hannah Todd and Martina Arzu, cover designer Leah Jacobs-Gordon, copyeditor Helena Newton and all the team at Aria Fiction (Head of Zeus) for turning my story into a beautiful book.

Many, many thanks as always to my super awesome literary agent / guardian angel Kiran Kataria (Keane Kataria Literary Agency), for her input, patient guidance and calming of my angsty author moments.

Thank you to the fellow writers who have so generously supported me, and the friends and family who've cheered and generally put up with it all – including my sons Jack and Robin, who have finally started reading my novels!

Last but not least, I can't forget my half-Spanish (and eccentric gardener) mother's part in the inspiration for this story. She would have loved it.

LOCATIONS IN *THE SPANISH GARDEN*

The house and garden in *The Spanish Garden* are fictional, but the village of San José is very much real – I live here!

San Rafael, as anyone who's been to the Cabo de Gata-Níjar Natural Park in Almería will quickly realise, is basically the old gold mining village of Rodalquilar. I changed the name for this series so that I could add a few amenities for Juliana's convenience in *The Spanish House*, and also because I couldn't bear the thought of the name, so beautiful in Spanish, being read as 'Roddle-quiller'!

All the other villages and towns exist – including the wonderful Níjar, famous for its ceramics and pottery. Come and see for yourself!

Book Club Discussion Questions –

The Spanish Garden

1. Accident Andie

'She was short, accident-prone, given to laughing things off, liked a cuddle, and often taken for younger than her thirty-five years, with her childish features and silly, fly-away, fair hair – but she wasn't a baby. Surely there must be a man out there who could one day… take her seriously.'

Did you feel Andie eventually managed to 'grow' and be taken seriously?

2. The Garden

At the beginning, Andie is a TV programme's garden 'clown', but by the end she has, according to Vicente, *'returned to her grandmother's garden with a vision, and – despite having to deal with an attacking wild boar, a grumpy, unsociable, ex flamenco dancer, and then a freak flooding – created a place of music, dance, fun and… love.'*

Do you know of anyone else, real or fictional, who has been changed by the therapeutic power of repairing or designing a garden?

3. Andie and Grandie

'Right. Garden,' Andie said to herself. That's what she was here for, after all. Indeed. And yes, you do need to be strong, she could hear from Grandie. Is that all you can say? You've been remarkably quiet about all this. I thought I could tell you anything, but you're – come up and see me, make me smile, she heard in return. That's just a song, Grandie. No. It's time you came up and saw me. You know it is.'

Did you feel Andie's growing closeness with the memory of her grandmother helped her? I've read that Spaniards tend to believe that their deceased loved ones continue to live on in spirit and are still very much a part of the family. Certainly, some of my Spanish friends in the village feel this way. Should the English have an annual 'All Saints Day' to visit family graves, like the Spanish do?

4. Vicente

'Dark. Darker than she remembered, even though they were now in daylight. Black, serious eyes, no glasses today, and the black Jesus hair tied back. A face all cheekbones and seriousness. A panther-like stroll as he came towards her. Rather unnerving. He said something she couldn't follow – in Spanish, and as if to himself. With absolutely no smile. A cold fish. Fish? She thought fish because… unbelievably, there was a small fish on his white T-shirt. A blue cartoon fish. How bad or grim could a man be, if he wore a cartoon fish?'

It takes a while for Andie (and us) to get to know Vicente. Would you have liked to have heard his side of the story?

5. Almería

'San José. She gasped and pulled over to where it looked like many a car had stopped to admire the view of the village – or perhaps take a walk over to the rounded, tawny hills with their mountainous backdrop. Hills of fuzzy scrub and the odd stubby fan palm. The semi-desert landscape that didn't appeal to everyone – and certainly not to her horticultural friends.'

I worried that my adored but stark semi-desert Cabo de Gata Natural Park area of Almería wouldn't go down well with readers, so I've been delighted to see how often reviewers have said how much they enjoyed 'being here'. Did you feel the unusual setting contributed to the story?

6. More or less?

Who – or what – would you like to have seen more (or less) of in the novel?

7. The Ending

Were you happy with the ending? If not, what would you have liked to have happened?

8. Spotify Music Playlist

'The song came to a loud climax of singing, palmas and playing, Vicente finishing with a series of ecstatic whipping turns at the end.'

Music is so important in my stories. I enjoy putting a Spotify list together so that readers can listen to the tracks during the chapters in which they occur. Do you think all novels should have one?

9. Who would play the film roles?

If *The Spanish Garden* became a film, who could you imagine playing the roles? If he could learn some flamenco (I think he used to be a dancer?), and do a good Spanish accent, I'd suggest the brooding Aiden Turner for Vicente!

10. Return for more!

Which minor characters in *The Spanish Garden* would you like to see appearing in future novels set in this unspoilt corner of Almería?

About the Author

CHERRY RADFORD has been a keyboard player in a band, a piano teacher at the Royal Ballet School and a post-doctoral scientist at London's Moorfields Eye Hospital. She began her first novel in a coffee break at a scientific conference.

She writes uplifting novels about identity, renewal and finding soulmate romance when you least expect it. Having inherited a love of Spain and its culture from her half-Spanish mother, all her novels have a Spanish connection or setting.

The Spanish Garden is the second in her series of stories set in the starkly beautiful and unspoilt Cabo de Gata region of coastal Andalusia where she now lives. She is married to a musician and has two sons.

Website and blog:	www.cherryradford.com
Twitter:	@CherryRad
Instagram:	@cherry_radford
Facebook:	www.facebook.com/cherry.radford